ISBN-13: 978-1-63177-250-4
CPSIA Code: PBANG0417A
Library of Congress Control Number: 2017902534

Printed in the United States

www.TripleCrownDreams.com
www.mascotbooks.com

BOOK TWO
TRIPLE CROWN TRILOGY

THE EYE OF
THE STORM

KIMBERLY CAMPBELL

*In honor of Lilly Bear,
my trusted Thoroughbred mare.*

Acknowledgments

The Preakness Stakes has always held a special place in my heart. On May 20, 1995, I met the man who would become my husband. Kelly continues to support me on this journey into the world of Thoroughbred racing. Little did I know on that third Saturday in May over twenty years ago that I would be writing a trilogy about these glorious races.

The story of Lilly Garrett within The Eye of the Storm *was garnered through reading as many books as I could about jockeys (there aren't many), watching numerous YouTube videos, and conducting a few very important interviews. Both interviews took place because a friend knew someone who knew someone, for which I am extremely thankful.*

I had the privilege of talking to Victor Espinoza for over an hour on the phone a week before he won the Kentucky Derby aboard American Pharoah. And Erin Walker, an up and coming female jockey, provided valuable insight into the world of racing from a female perspective. Their words are weaved throughout the dialogue of The Eye of the Storm *and I have tried my best to do them and the world of racing justice within these pages.*

Once again, Hannah Wagner has been a critical component in editing, providing valuable feedback, and fleshing out the story. Thank you to Susan Roberts and Naren Ayral for putting the finishing touches on the book.

My hope while you read The Eye of the Storm *is that you will learn more about who I consider the unsung heroes of Thoroughbred racing: the jockeys. Often the jockey is overlooked during the road to the Triple Crown, horseracing's greatest achievement. The horse is considered the athlete, the jockey the passenger along the way. But the work these men and women put into their trade is many times that of the most famous athletes in other sports. Jockey athletes are up at 5am or earlier to exercise horses, then they do the meet and greet with owners and agents to book rides, and all of this is followed by riding in several races in the afternoon's race meet. The most sought after jockeys ride as many as eight or nine races per day, five or six days per week, year round.*

In no other sport is the athlete expected to get on an unfamiliar horse, listen to instructions for the upcoming race, and execute those instructions in a field of 8, 10, or more other horses and jockeys with different instructions. In no other sport does the athlete suspend himself over a 1,200 pound animal traveling 35 miles an hour for almost two full minutes, while making split second decisions with only a hands width between competitors.

Jockeys are not signed to multimillion-dollar contracts. They are paid on a per mount (race) basis. If they don't ride, they don't get paid. There is no sick leave or vacation pay.

A jockey is entrusted with the well-being of the horse they are riding. The horses are worth thousands, or even millions, of dollars, as is the case with those running in the Triple Crown races. And the owners and trainers of these horses rely on the jockey's expertise for their own livelihood.

A jockey is an athlete, an entrepreneur, and a caretaker rolled into one. The pressure on these petite men and women of muscle is overwhelming.

I hope you enjoy the ride in The Eye of the Storm.

"This is not about going back. This is about life being ahead of you and you run at it! Because you never know how far you can run unless you run."

- Penny Chenery, Secretariat

Prologue
The Preakness

The middle child.

That is the role that the Preakness plays: sandwiched between the royalty of the Kentucky Derby and the test of champions, The Belmont. The winner of the Derby must pass through this race in Maryland in order to get to the bright lights of New York and the crown that may await them there: The Triple Crown. Awarded to the horse that can win all three races within the five week time span, The Triple Crown is coveted by owners, breeders, and jockeys alike. The prestige that comes with winning even one of these historic races is immense; the fame and recognition that comes with winning all three is beyond most people's wildest dreams.

The Preakness is the second leg of the Triple Crown Series. It is run two weeks after the Kentucky Derby, the third Saturday in May, at a distance of one mile and 3/16th. Slightly shorter than the Derby, it is no less challenging.

While the Derby caters to the who's who, Millionaire's Row, and fancy hats, the Preakness attracts the working class of Baltimore: the everyday men and women, as well as the younger party crowd, all eager to attend the biggest party of the year, the InfieldFest. The festival, which takes place in the center of the track, boasts all-day entertainment with top-caliber musicians, large sponsor tents, and open areas for groups to lay their claim on for the day. On the morning of the Preakness, over 120,000 people stream into the grandstand and infield in hopes of seeing history made, watching a potential winner of the Triple Crown: a feat which has only been accomplished by a dozen horses in the last hundred years, the entire history of the series.

On October 25, 1870, Pimlico Race Course opened and a horse by the name of Preakness won a stakes race. The horse was from a farm called Preakness Stables, in a town called Preakness, New Jersey. The race held today is a tribute to that horse and its origins.

The first Preakness was held on May 27, 1873, two years before the first Kentucky Derby. In 1890, the race was moved to New York where, for the next three years, the Preakness was not run at all. When the race did come back, it continued in New York until 1909, when it finally returned home to Pimlico. From 1890 to 1916, the Preakness had no restriction on the age of the horses that ran it, but eventually the race returned to being restricted to three-year-olds. Interestingly, there were eleven times up until 1931 that the Preakness was held prior to the Kentucky Derby.

As in the Derby, the fastest time in the Preakness is held by Secretariat at 1:53 during the running of the race in 1973. Different from the Derby, in which 20 horses can run, the Preakness is limited to 14 horses. The limit is due to the number of horses that the starting gate at Pimlico can accommodate.

The excitement of the Preakness lies in the fact that it is the next step in a potential Triple Crown winner. Since the Triple Crown became prestigious, only one winner of the Derby has elected not to run in the Preakness. In 1985, the Derby winner, Spend A Buck, was lured to race in the Jersey Derby with a $2 million bonus. The race was a week after the Preakness, so Spend A Buck's team decided to skip Baltimore. Since then, incentive bonuses have been added to the Triple Crown to help heighten the appeal for the Derby winner to run in all three races.

Not many trainers follow the Derby winner to the Preakness, given that there are only two weeks between the two races. Most horses are rested four to five weeks, or more, before they are asked to race again. Not only does the short turnaround between races put strain on the horses, but the stress can permeate through the entire team, causing mistakes and injuries. There is a reason there have been so few horses that have been able to pull off the incredible feat of athleticism required to even come close to winning the coveted Crown.

In the Preakness, the Derby winner comes up against new challengers, including some that didn't even run in the Derby. There are those that possibly sustained an injury or failed to gain enough points to qualify to race in the Derby; others whose trainers thought the Preakness' shorter distance would be a better fit for their horse. These horses are generally better rested, which makes them just as fierce, if not more so, to compete with as the horses that did run in the Derby. Derby runners that follow the winner to Baltimore do so for many reasons. It could be that the trainers and owners believe that their horse just had an off day or got stuck in racing traffic. Many trainers are willing to challenge the Derby winner in the Preakness in order to prove their horse's ability, and that he or she is indeed among the best three-year-olds of the generation.

While the Crown is the goal of many, a win in just one of the three races is still enough to put a team or trainer on the map. With a purse of $1,500,000 available to the top four finishers, the competition is no less challenging, and the reward is enough to make most equine enthusiasts push the limits for a taste of the glory.

PART ONE

First Light

Lilly ran the length of the barn, turned right, and continued down the road between the barns and the track. As she ran, she waved to all the grooms and trainers.

"Hurry up, Lilly. Don't want your mom to get on your case," someone called.

She smiled her big white smile, jumped on her bike, and pedaled out of the backstretch of the barns of Pimlico Race Course.

It was 7am. She had a full day ahead of her.

Lilly biked down Northern Parkway, avoiding most of the usual traffic, turned right onto Winner Avenue, and dropped her bike outside of number 5606.

She quietly opened the old back door and cursed the squeaky hinges while looking out for her mom. Their deal had been that she could work, so long as she was never late for school. On days like this one, Lilly knew she was cutting it close, and an argument would only put her even further behind. She raced past the kitchen and up the stairs to shower and change before her mother could delay her.

"Best be gettin' on, Elizabeth! I will not tolerate lateness—again!"

Lilly yelled an apology over her shoulder just before she made it into the bathroom. Being yelled at was part of her daily routine.

Every morning, Lilly woke up at 4:30. She would bike the short way to the barns at Pimlico, groom and hot walk the horses for Mr. Malone, bike back home, and get to school by the start bell at 7:45. Most days she made it without a problem; recently, however, being on time had become a little more difficult. It was Preakness week; the corporate tents were going up, and the contenders were arriving daily. Lilly was doing all she could to remain an asset around the stables, and if that meant being a little late for school, then so be it.

As she showered, she thought about her morning. The Derby winner, Attribute, had just arrived the day before, and Lilly had spent her morning watching him work out. He had traveled so smoothly over the freshly raked track, his copper coat reflecting the early morning sun. His exercise rider barely moved on his back. Lilly let the hot water wash the conditioner from her hair as she imagined herself on the back of the beautiful horse.

There was a sharp knock on the door and an unintelligible warning from her mother. She sighed. Why did she have to worry about geometry? How was learning the area of a square really going to help, when all she wanted to do was ride a racehorse?

She stepped out of the shower, threw her school uniform on, toweled-dry her long, blond hair, and threw it in a sloppy ponytail. Lilly ran down the stairs and slid into the chair at the kitchen table.

Her mom's back was to her as she cooked up breakfast: her famous pancakes. Thin as paper and slathered in butter. Lilly's favorite. She grabbed a piece of the crispy bacon from the pile already on the table.

"This is the third day in a row you've had to rush to be ready for school on time. I don't know why you need to go to the track every morning, Elizabeth. You have finals soon, and I don't know when you have time to study," her mom commented as she flipped the pancakes on the griddle. She slid a plate in front of Lilly, who dug in—no syrup necessary, not with the butter dripping off each piece.

"Mom, Attribute got to the track yesterday and I needed to watch him gallop this morning," she said between bites. Her mom turned to face her.

"As a fifteen-year-old, you should be studying, hanging out with your girlfriends, going to the mall and movies, meeting boys. Not hanging out with old men and horses."

Keeping her eyes on her plate, Lilly sighed heavily. *Here we go again,* she thought.

"Your father works hard, and I do too, to send you to private school so you can get the education that we were not blessed with. School is so important! It was cute to love ponies when you were seven, but I really thought you would grow out of this horse-loving phase at some point, and—"

That's when Lilly zoned out. This part of the speech was so well known to her that she had dreams about it. Her mother stood there, arms folded across her chest, love and frustration battling for dominance in her demeanor.

Lilly more than appreciated the life her parents worked so hard to give her. She knew that school was important to them, and she wanted so badly to make them proud of her. The problem was, Lilly hadn't grown out of loving horses. In fact, in the year since she'd started working for Mr. Malone, her infatuation had only increased. She worked with all twenty of Mr. Malone's horses, brushing up their coats until they shone prior to their workouts, and then hand-walking them when they returned from the track afterwards. She was never happier than when she was with horses, and there was no easy way to tell her parents that their ideas and dreams for her future were ones that she didn't share in the slightest.

"Elizabeth. Are you listening to me?" Her mother cut into her thoughts.

Lilly pushed back her chair, placed her dish in the sink, and grabbed her backpack from the hook on the wall.

"Gotta run to make the starting bell. Thanks for breakfast, you're the best!" Lilly kissed her mother's cheek and ran out of the house.

———————

Lilly ran to the corner of Northern Parkway, her backpack hanging from one shoulder. A Lexus pulled up beside her, and Lilly jumped into the backseat.

"Hi!" Lilly greeted the two girls in the car, Macy, her best friend since first grade, and Angela, Macy's older sister.

"In trouble again this morning?" Macy asked.

"Not too much, just the normal 'your father and I work so hard,' like she doesn't realize that I know I am on financial aid!" Lilly said, exasperated. She laid her head back against the headrest.

Macy and Angela were part of the upper crust of Baltimore. Their dad was a patent attorney and their mom was a heart surgeon at Johns Hopkins. Angela was about to graduate and head to Johns Hopkins University, following in her mom's footsteps. They never flaunted their money, but Lilly knew it was hard for them to sympathize with her. They did well in school because they could. Lilly did well because she would feel guilty if she didn't.

"You're their only kid. Your parents have to say the same things to you over and over again. If they didn't, who else would they talk to?" Angela was good at making Lilly feel better.

"Yeah, well if she wants to throw on some knee socks and write a paper about WWII, I'm not gonna stop her. She's the one who wanted this fancy education, not me." Lilly looked out the window and saw their school entrance coming into view.

The Bryn Mawr School was one of the oldest all-girls high schools in the country, and it was located just three miles from Lilly's house. She and Macy were just about to finish up their freshman year there.

"No offense, but I think if I ever saw your mom in knee socks, I would have a hard time picking myself off the ground in hysterics!" Macy said. All three girls burst out laughing, and the stress of the morning lifted from Lilly's shoulders. The Lexus pulled onto campus, and Angela pulled into a parking spot along the tennis courts.

The girls got out of the car and grabbed their backpacks. As they walked along the sidewalk of the quadrangle in the center of campus, Angela teased Lilly, "There's your building!"

Lilly looked up at the "Garrett Building," named after one of the founders of the school: Mary Elizabeth Garrett, no relation to her, Elizabeth Marie

Garrett. It was a big joke among her friends, and even Lilly's mom liked to say her name helped her get into the school.

Lilly smiled. Although she would have been happy at the track all day long, she did enjoy coming to school. She liked the learning and her teachers, and she liked being with her friends. Even if her parents didn't understand her passion for horses, her friends supported her.

"Come on, let's meet up with Julie before math class," Macy said.

Lilly smiled at her best friend, ready for another day. Finals were in two weeks and she had to make sure she was on top of her game. She was determined not to give her parents anything to be upset with her about. The Preakness was on Saturday, and there was no way she was going to miss it.

 # A Career in Riding

Lilly was sitting on an upturned bucket, pages of science notes on her lap and a highlighter in her hand, staring into space. She needed to study, but her mind refused to focus on school. The Preakness was over, and Lilly had spent almost every moment since the race in a state of awe. She'd seen the Preakness run before, but she'd never been more than just a spectator. This one would be forever burned in her brain. She had spent every waking moment from Friday after school at the track watching the horses. Lilly payed close attention as they galloped around the track, and tried to over-hear what the trainers told the jockeys. She helped where she could, and enjoyed learning when she wasn't needed. And when the time came for the race, Tom made sure she got a special seat.

The Derby winner Attribute had tried to pull off the win, but he tired in the stretch. There would be no Triple Crown winner this year. Lilly rev-eled in the knowledge that a year ago, she wouldn't have known even half of the technical stuff she knew now. She'd been able to listen to the trainers and jockeys talk about strategy and she had actually understood what they were saying. It was more than she could have hoped for, being involved in such an amazing race. She knew without a doubt that she never wanted to do anything else with her life.

"That marker's gonna dry out if you don't put the lid back on it soon."

The voice startled Lilly and she let out a small yell as she fell off the bucket into the hay at her feet. She looked up to see Tom laughing at her, and felt a sheepish smile spread across her face.

"I've got finals coming up. I thought I should use my break to study," she explained as she stood and collected her papers.

"I remember my first time being behind the scenes for a big race like that. It's an incredible thing, don't you think?" Tom asked her.

"Oh, absolutely! Mr. Malone, I can't thank you enough for letting me be a part of that." She was so overwhelmed with gratitude that she felt like she could have cried.

"It was my pleasure. I think I enjoyed watching you take it all in almost as much as you enjoyed watching everything else. You didn't let a single detail past you," he commented, leaning casually on the side of the barn.

"No, sir," Lilly smiled, "I would have followed them all out onto the track if I could!" Lilly, now off her break, grabbed the pitchfork and continued to pick at the manure in the stall she'd been cleaning before. She was meticulous about a clean stall for all the horses she was in charge of.

Tom was silent for a moment, watching her closely. "Do you have any experience riding horses?" He asked.

"Well, I rode a bunch at summer camp. I actually got to help train some of the new horses that came in," Lilly told him.

"That's a start. How would you like to ride something a little quicker than a lesson pony?" Tom asked.

Lilly stopped her pitchfork in mid-toss and the manure missed the wheelbarrow she'd been aiming for. "You'd let me ride a race horse?" She was frozen, afraid that if she moved, he would come to his senses and realize that she was just a scrawny girl who had no business with horses.

"Not just *a* racehorse. Lilly, I'm looking to hire an exercise rider and I think you fit the bill."

"But…" Lilly stammered.

"But, what?" Tom raised his eyebrows.

"Gosh, Mr. Malone. Riding a racehorse is beyond my wildest dreams. I guess I just thought dreams happen somewhere in the future, not, like, RIGHT NOW! Am I old enough?" Lilly blurted, her voice lowering with excitement.

"You're fifteen, right?" Tom asked.

Lilly nodded her head.

"The best riders start early; usually they are up on a horse much younger than you. Most get involved because their parents are in the business or they grow up riding show horses or doing pony club. They are around horses their entire lives. I know a rider who started exercising horses at the age of thirteen. Sure, you are a bit on the younger side and you haven't had the exposure, but I like how you handle yourself and my horses on the ground. I'd like to see what you can do when you're riding one of them. You want to give it a go?"

―――――――――――――

"Absolutely not," Lilly's mom retorted.

"But riding horses is what I want to do, and I am good at it!" Lilly stammered.

"Good at it? How do you know you are good at it?" Her mom quietly asked. Her dad sat in his recliner, listening to their conversation, but his eyes were focused on the Pirate game, which was heading into extra innings, on the TV.

Lilly had been planning this conversation for weeks. Macy and Angela had helped her during their drives to and from school. Lilly knew her mom had been so set on Bryn Mawr because of her aspirations of Lilly becoming a doctor or lawyer or engineer. Yes, Lilly had received a partial scholarship from the school based on her grades, but her parents still worked long hours at their corner store deli to make sure their daughter had the best education.

It was one thing for her to help out at the track in the mornings, cleaning stalls. It was a completely different thing for Lilly to actually be riding a thousand-pound animal running fast around a track. It was a big step forward, and as excited as she was about it, she knew it was also a giant leap away from the future her parents wanted for her. Her mother knew it too. The more involved Lilly got at the track, the less time there would be for other extra-curricular activities, which looked good on a college application.

"Well…" Lilly stopped and took a deep breath. Her only hope was to ease them in using rationality. Her parents would never take her seriously if she whined about what she wanted to do for the summer. She placed her hands firmly on her knees and started again, this time focusing her attention on her dad.

Her mom was emotional, while her dad wouldn't say much until he heard all sides of the argument. Neither of her parents liked change, and she was proposing a big change in their plans for her. She didn't want an internship in an uptight corporate office environment. She didn't even want to work for the local pool or deli with her friends. She wanted to continue working at the track for the whole summer, not just in the mornings, but all day.

"Mr. Malone has asked me to work for him all summer and learn to be an exercise rider." Her mother stared at her with a blank expression. Her dad's eyes continued to focus on the game; in the bottom of the 11th, one of the Pirates hit a walk-off home run to end the game.

"Yes!" He clapped his hands in celebration. Lilly looked at him silently.

"Robert, please!" Joyce reprimanded her husband. Lilly's dad hit the off button on the remote and turned to face her.

"What is an exercise rider?" Joyce stared at Robert, her mouth slightly ajar, shocked that he would entertain the conversation at all.

"It's the person who helps work and train the racehorses in the morning. You've seen them. The ones we would watch when we used to walk by the track to get your coffee in the mornings." She smiled. It was many years ago now that Lilly and her dad would stop to peer though the fences and watch the horses gallop by. It had always been a special time for her, just her with her father, and though he didn't talk much, they had a special bond.

His lips curved into a smile, and Lilly's heart skipped a beat.

Exercise Rider

Lilly's alarm sounded at 4am. Her arm reached out from under the covers to hit the snooze button. It crawled across her bedside dresser and came to a sudden stop. The alarm continued its buzzing, loud enough to wake the dead. She pushed the covers away from her small body, sat straight up in bed, and quickly slammed her hand down on the alarm to turn it off so it wouldn't wake her parents.

It was finally the day. Her sleepy, groggy mind came to full attention and adrenaline shot through her. It was finally the day Tom said she could exercise one of the horses for him. Just one to start with, but one was all she needed.

Lilly pulled her slippers on her feet, grabbed her riding clothes from where she had set them the night before, and ran to the hall bathroom. She softly closed the door before turning on the light so as not to rouse her mom, whose bedroom door was slightly ajar. She could hear her dad snoring.

Did she look any different? she asked herself as she looked in the mirror while brushing her teeth. She was about to become an official exercise rider. Her heart thumped in her chest. Thank goodness her dad had supported her. With school out, she could focus all her attention on becoming the best exercise rider she could be.

That had been the one stipulation her dad had put on her. She couldn't start this 'crazy idea,' as her mother referred to it, until after school was out for the summer. Classes had ended the day before. She had confirmed all her year-end grades with her teachers; all "As", another stipulation—this one from her mother.

Because Bryn Mawr was a private school, they got out earlier than the public schools in the area. It was the second week of June and she would have the entire summer, June, July, and August, to be at the track. They hadn't addressed what would happen when classes resumed in the fall, but she would just cross that bridge when she had to.

After getting dressed in her britches, tall boots, and blue collared shirt, Lilly pulled her long, blond hair into a tight ponytail and pushed it under her baseball cap. Sometimes it was easier to fit in with the boys when you looked like one. She wore no makeup and wore the tightest fitting bra she could find to keep her breasts from being too pronounced under the shirt. Luckily, she didn't have much to hide in that department and her safety riding vest would cover her when she rode. Lilly thought briefly that this whole thing would have been easier if she'd been born a boy.

While she was busy working on a plan to convince her parents, Lilly was also working with Tom to figure out the plan for her to start riding. She would have to get the signoff of at least one other trainer, an outrider, the starter, and the steward to become a full-fledged exercise rider. Lilly used her afternoons at one of Tom's training farms to get herself back in the saddle and ride some recently retired horses, as well as some horses that were training to return to racing after an injury.

Tom had pulled some strings to get her out on the track. She had to be there ready to go at 5:45am sharp, prior to when the other horses would be entering the track to workout. She was going to have her own "working interview" to demonstrate she was ready for this next job. The next step in her plan to become a jockey, she thought to herself.

She opened the bathroom door, threw her jammies into her room, and tiptoed down the stairs. At the bottom, she stopped short.

"Good morning, Elizabeth," her mother said as she cracked eggs into a bowl on the counter. Lilly was silent; the shock of seeing her mother up so early in the morning had made speaking seem impossible.

"Well, you certainly can't control a beast ten times the size of you without a good breakfast, can you?" she said to Lilly, her eyes shiny with unshed tears.

Lilly knew her mom wasn't happy about her going off to the track to ride, but she hadn't realized until that moment, watching her mom's hands shake as she held the spatula, that her mom's unhappiness was rooted in fear for her only child.

Lilly quickly closed the distance between them and hugged her mother fiercely from behind. Her mother was strong and Lilly knew she wouldn't let the tears fall.

"Come on and eat. The eggs will be ready in a minute. You can start on the sausage and oatmeal," her mom said as she whipped the eggs into a scramble and poured them into the frying pan. Lilly sat at the counter next to her. She grabbed the mug of coffee her mother had already set out for her.

"Thank you," she said quietly, not knowing what more to say. She squeezed the mug between her hands, staring hard at the creamy brown liquid. Using the thumb and forefinger of her right hand, Lilly pulled her lower eyelids away from her eyeballs, forcing her own tears that had gathered there back to wherever they came from. She hadn't expected to see her mom this morning and was surprised at the emotion that overcame her.

"Promise me you will be safe and not take undue risk, Elizabeth. Promise me," her mother said to her.

"I promise, Mom," Lilly replied. "Tom isn't going to let me ride anything crazy."

Her mom looked at her directly and said, "You will be the most talented rider out there. I know that. It is the way you are with all animals. They relate to you and those trainers will all learn that eventually, so please don't be a show off and take on anything over your head."

Lilly thought that making such a promise was the least she could do. "I won't, I promise. Thank you for trusting me, Mom."

Her mother looked back down into the frying pan, breaking their eye contact.

"Eat," she said, spooning the scrambled eggs onto Lilly's plate.

Lilly rode her bike down the backstretch road to Tom Malone's barn. Her muscle memory took her where she needed to go. She had been working for Tom for over a year; Lilly smiled as she thought back to how she'd gotten involved with his operation. It had happened by chance.

As a child, Lilly had asked repeatedly for riding lessons. Her parents, unsurprisingly, had said no. She realized later that they just didn't have the money for a sport that was so very expensive.

All her school friends had various sports they were involved in: soccer, basketball, lacrosse. Her parents didn't have a problem signing her up for those sports, and she tried several of them. No other sport made her feel the same as when she would walk by the track and watch the horses working out.

She saw the jockeys lying low on their backs as they ran by and knew she wanted to become one. The little hairs on her skin would stand on end, she would hold her breath until it felt like her heart stopped beating. Time stood still to her when she was around the horses. Becoming a jockey was her dream, and she was going to find a way to become one.

After school one day, when all her friends were busy, she finished her homework and told her mom she was going to take Angel, their dog, for a walk. They walked toward the racetrack and wandered around to the backside of the track where the horses were stabled.

Though she couldn't get past the security gate, she could get close enough to watch the activities going on. From where she stood she could see that some horses were being walked and bathed, while others were getting ready to run in the next race. She could hear the workers talking to the horses and talking to each other, and she was overcome with a sense of camaraderie that she ached to be a part of.

After that day, each afternoon Lilly walked Angel around to the back of the track. Her friends would ask her to hang out after school or go to the movies. Lilly gave them excuses: too much homework, studying, or that her mom had her doing chores.

One afternoon as she was watching the horses parade past, heading for the start of the next race, Angel spotted another dog beyond the security gate. In a split second, the leash slipped from Lilly's hand and the dog was gone.

"Angel!" Lilly called after her. Without thinking, she ran past the security gate and into the stabling area, calling after her dog. She could hear the security guard yelling after her.

Angel had run down an aisle to the left, and Lilly followed behind, trying desperately to catch up with her. A Rhodesian Ridgeback was hard to miss. Several other dogs joined the ruckus and now there was a pack of happy, tongue lolling dogs running around the stabling area.

Lilly didn't know what to do. Many of the grooms and trainers had already started to call for their dogs and corral them in a stall. Angel had finally stopped at the end of one of the barn aisles and was puppy-bowing and rolling on her tummy to encourage a massive, stoic German Shepherd dog to play with her.

Lilly ran up to them and grabbed Angel's leash.

"Angel, bad dog!" she said sternly.

A tall man dressed in khakis, a white button down, and cowboy boots walked out of the tack room to her left.

"Whoa, now, who is a bad dog?" he asked her. He dropped his hand to the head of the shepherd, ruffling his fur. The dog closed his eyes and dropped his ears, appreciating the attention. Lilly stood silent. It suddenly hit her that she was in the middle of the backstretch without any authorization. What had she been thinking, running in here and causing such an episode?

As Lilly and the man stood looking at each other, the security guard pulled up in his golf cart.

"You are not allowed to be back here, little missy," he said to her sternly as he got out of the cart. "I hope they didn't cause any harm to your horses,

Mr. Malone." He directed his last comment to the tall man.

"No, all is fine. This young lady and I were just having a conversation," he said, winking at Lilly.

"Well, *young* lady, get yourself and your dog into the golf cart and I will escort you off the premises," the guard said. Lilly dropped her head and looked at Angel.

"I'm sorry, sir. My dog got away while I was watching the horses walk by for the next race. She usually stays right by my side while I'm watching, but today…something must have caught her attention that was more interesting than I am."

"That's just as well, I was looking for an excuse to invite you back here anyway. I've seen you watching the horses." He reached out to pet Angel.

"You have?" Lilly didn't know whether she was about to be chastised or not, but felt it better to err on the side of caution.

"Well, after three weeks of watching the horses, I figured you might like getting a little closer than that fence out there. Am I right about that?" He smiled. The question was rhetorical, but she answered anyway.

"Oh, yes, sir! I love horses! I have been watching the jockeys, too," Lilly said, the excitement in her voice hard to miss. "I want to be a jockey one day. I've been studying each one and learning how they ride. Each jockey rides differently, which is so cool, and I keep track of their riding styles and the outcomes of their races."

"Mr. Malone, I'm sorry, but she's not allowed back here…" The security guard was clearly annoyed at being overlooked, and made a move to usher Lilly and her dog toward his vehicle.

"It's okay, Joe," Tom interjected, "she can be my guest for the afternoon. Please put…what's your name?" he looked at Lilly, raising his eyebrows.

"Lilly. I mean Elizabeth Garrett," Lilly told him, her hand sweating as she held on for dear life to Angel's leash.

"Please put Elizabeth Garrett as my guest on the sign-in sheet," Tom finished.

"Yes, Mr. Malone," Joe relaxed at this, but gave Lilly a firm look. "Keep your dog on its leash though."

"Yes, sir," Lilly said, with Angel still straining at her leash to engage the shepherd in some play time.

After that, Tom put Lilly's name on the security list every day, and it wasn't long before he'd hired Lilly on to help the grooms in the barn. And so, Lilly started working for Tom Malone, trainer extraordinaire. She owed everything to him. He was the reason she was now about to take her first step in becoming a jockey.

She had spent the last year hot walking and grooming the horses, getting to know each one of the twenty horses that Tom had in training. They were owned by various people, but they were all Tom's responsibility. He cared for and trained them to hopefully become winners. Some came and went, but Tom never had a shortage of owners who wanted his services. He had a waiting list; he would only take up to twenty at any given time. And today, after a lifetime of waiting, he had agreed to let Lilly ride one of them.

Lilly leaned her bike against the fence outside the tack stall. It was still dark, with just a small sliver of light along the horizon. The moon was setting on the other side of the sky and the stars were beginning to fade. Lilly took a deep breath to calm her nerves and opened the door to the tack room.

Gus, Tom's senior groom, looked up at her, his dark wrinkled hands working on the leather of one of the bridles. Gus had worked at Pimlico since he was a child, his dad before him. He'd grown up tagging along with him around the backstretch. Lilly loved sitting with Gus while he worked his love into each piece of leather and listening to his stories of days gone by. He had never wanted to be anything more than the reliable and trustworthy groom that he was; it was God's Calling, he liked to say.

The backstretch couldn't survive without the hardworking souls that tended it. Many lived their entire lives in run-down apartments on the backside of the track, usually located directly above the stalls of the horses they were in charge of. Gus had been Lilly's direct boss when it came to grooming duties, along with three other grooms. Each one of them was responsible for four horses in Tom's string of twenty. Gus took care of his own four horses, the ones that were considered his most prized trainees.

"How was everyone this morning?" Lilly asked him.

"They're all spit-fires." Gus winked at her. "Me and the boys will have a lot of work to take up with you moving up the ranks, Lil. Who am I going to find that can bandage legs like you can, or someone who can find the way a horse likes to be brushed? You have a talent like no other, my friend."

Lilly blushed. Gus had taught her so much in the last year. Little did she know when she started her grooming responsibilities that she not only was responsible for feeding and brushing the horses and cleaning their stalls, but she also had to learn how to bandage legs, pack feet, look for behavior that was out of the ordinary, and be the main communicator between her horses and the trainer. Anything that was amiss could impact the horse when he went to race. Tom relied on all his grooms to keep him updated on the horses entrusted to them. Most information funneled through Gus, but each groom had to be ready if Tom asked them a direct question on how his or her horse was doing.

Gus took pride in the grooms he hired and he was clearly sad to see Lilly move up the ranks, but she knew he wanted to see her succeed, and he'd told her plainly that he couldn't keep a girl with her talent as just a groom.

"Ready for your first ride?" He smiled warmly.

Lilly forced a smile to her face, the joy fighting through her nausea. The butterflies in her stomach had become angry bees. She would not let Gus see how nervous she was. She had been looking forward to this day for months.

"I can't wait," Lilly replied confidently. "Who did Tom put on the board for me to ride?"

"See for yourself," Gus motioned towards the board with his head, all the while his hands working their magic to soften the tough leather of the bridle laying across his lap. He dribbled a few more drops of olive oil onto the reins, working it into the braiding while keeping his eyes on Lilly.

Lilly walked toward the white board. Instead of seeing her name under the grooms with the horses she cared for, like usual, her name was listed under the schedule of exercise riders, along with which horse she would be riding. She looked carefully at the board to make sure she didn't misread anything.

Lilly—Hank

Her shoulders dropped a little. She would be riding tough, old Hank. The plodder no one ever wanted to ride. Hank wasn't one of the horses that she had groomed, but she did know him. She had helped out a few times and given Hank his bath and cooled him out. It never took very long, as he never worked up much of sweat. He was a sweet horse and didn't demand his treats like some of the other hot heads.

At four-years-old, Hank wasn't known as the pride of the horses that Tom worked with. His owner kept him in training in hopes he would turn a corner; he had brought him to Tom earlier in the year, but they all knew he just wasn't cut out to race. Nothing Tom did could get Hank to run faster.

"Penny for your thoughts?" Lilly could feel Gus' eyes on her back, waiting for a response. Lilly stood up straight, turned, and smiled at Gus.

"Just thinking how Hank and I are going to turn it on today out on the track," she replied, hoping her voice sounded as sure as she was attempting to make it.

"You go, girl," Gus replied. Lilly grabbed her helmet and started walking out of the tack room to retrieve her mount.

"Forget something?" Gus called after her. Lilly's face was blank. Gus pointed to the far wall where the chest protectors hung.

"That will save your life one day," he said.

"Oh my god! I'm already messing up. Thanks Gus." Lilly grabbed her black vest and headed out the door, her face red with embarrassment for forgetting a crucial piece of riding equipment.

Lost in her thoughts, Lilly walked down the length of stalls. She patted each head that reached out over the half doors as she passed. As she got to the end of the row, she turned the corner, talking to herself. She was so self-absorbed that she didn't notice the boy standing in front of her, talking to Tom, and proceeded to walk right into him.

"Oops," Lilly stammered as she backed away from the two of them.

"Here you are," Tom said to her. He walked around the other rider and put his arm around her shoulders. "All ready for your first gallop?"

"Yes, sir. Hank and I are going to have a good run out there," Lilly replied.

"Good, glad to hear it. This here is Buck. Buck Wheeler. He's come down here from New York and is going to do some jockeying for me." Tom introduced the young man that she had run into.

Lilly looked at the smooth-faced boy in front of her. He couldn't be much older than she was.

Lilly held out her hand. "Nice to meet you."

"Likewise," Buck said, shaking her hand.

"Buck's been jockeying for a few years now, making his way up the charts. I'm glad to say I have the opportunity to have him ride for me in a few races over the next couple of weeks. Congrats on taking the title down in Florida, by the way," Tom directed toward Buck. "Buck here won the jockey title with most wins during the racing meet at Gulfstream this past winter."

"I'm only as good as the horses I get put on, Tom," Buck replied, flashing a smile of straight white teeth. Lilly stood there trying to guess how old Buck was as he bantered back and forth with Tom. His smooth face and white teeth put him about nineteen, she guessed. *Nineteen and cute,* she thought to herself. She felt a blush creeping up her cheeks and leaned down to check her boots, hiding her face. When she was sure there was no trace left and all the heat had drained from her face, she stood up.

"Well, I will see what I can do for you," Tom directed his next comment back to Lilly. "Buck is going to take out Wolf at the same time you take out Hank this morning. I'll pony you with Midget for a bit until you feel settled, and then you both will gallop for a mile. I want you to pull up once your mile is done. Buck is going to breeze out Wolf for a quarter mile to tune him up for next week's race," Tom instructed.

"Let's start your education now, Lilly. Do you know how fast I expect Wolf to go during his breeze workout?" Tom asked her.

Lilly cleared her throat, nervous with the new jockey standing there; she didn't want to look stupid. She looked directly at Tom and recited what she knew about breezing. "A breeze is used to condition the horse to prepare for his or her next race. It is faster than galloping and the time is published by the clocker. These reports are used by the handicappers to assess how horses compare to each other in each race. A fast breeze is expected to be around twelve seconds. In this case, since you instructed Wolf's jockey to breeze a quarter mile, that would be two furloughs, and you would expect a time of about 24 seconds."

Tom looked at Buck and said, "Didn't I tell you she knew her stuff?"

Buck smiled. "We will see if Miss Smarty Pants can translate her words into her riding."

Tom laughed. "Yes, we will see. Ready to go?"

"Yes, sir," Lilly replied, letting the breath out that she had been holding, relieved she had passed her first test. She put her helmet on her head and walked towards Hank's stall. She was aware of Buck's eyes following her as he leaned lazily against the wall, and was thankful he couldn't see the blood rush to her cheeks again.

"Where are you going?" Tom called out.

"To get my ride," Lilly called over her shoulder.

"But that is what the grooms do," he commented. Lilly pulled up short. She wasn't the groom anymore. She was the rider.

Lilly perched on Hank's back, light as a feather. Tom was on Midget, holding the leather strap looped through Hank's bridle. The two of them trotted down the outside of the racetrack. Lilly concentrated on Hank's rhythm. She was nervous and secretly thanked God that Tom had arranged for her to ride early, without all the activity of other horses on the track.

There were a million thoughts going through her mind, overshadowed by the sheer thrill of being up on a horse. No matter how many times she threw a leg over the saddle, each time she got on she was in heaven.

Usually during the summer she went to camp with all her private school friends. She was able to go only because she received financial aid, so she took full advantage of the camps and participated in every activity possible.

Inevitably, she gravitated to the stables each summer and wound up being offered a counselor position. She had been assigned to the riding camp, which meant she spent most of her time working with and training the horses to make sure they were well behaved for the campers.

Even still, no one would have guessed that Lilly would be out riding a real racehorse this summer instead of overseeing a bunch of giggling girls. *Things happen for a reason*, Lilly thought. If she had never attended those camps, she would never had gotten the experience in working with so many different horses and personalities. She tried to relax while Hank stretched his legs.

"Been doing all those exercises I told you to do?" Tom asked her.

"Yes, sir," Lilly said through her breathing. She didn't realize how short the stirrups were going to be. The riding she had done at Tom's rehab farms wasn't on a track or on tightly wound, ready-to-race horses, nor had she jacked her stirrups up so high, as she had been focused on getting to know the horses she rode. No amount of squats or weight lighting could prepare her for the amount of energy she needed to stay poised like a cat on the back of a horse. Her inner thighs were starting to burn. She posted to the rhythm of Hank's trot.

Buck and Wolf were trotting up ahead of them. Lilly was a little perturbed that he got to ride without a handler, but she had to accept the fact that he had much more experience than she did.

"Now, when we make the turn up here, I am going to let go of you two. Buck knows to stay trotting until you reach him. Once you draw abreast with him, both of you will go into the gallop and work a mile. Once you pass the quarter pole, heading for home, Buck has the go ahead to breeze the last quarter mile like we discussed. You will be fine, Hank won't care to keep up with Wolf. I still haven't figured out what makes this horse tick. Just gallop through the finish pole and I'll meet you on the far turn." Tom finished up his instructions.

"Thank you, Tom," Lilly said quietly. She didn't know what else to say. Tom looked over at her. She could almost hear his thoughts; the doubt on his face was plain as he took stock of her small frame, her long, blond hair in the ponytail that made her look even younger than she was, a sixteen-year-old naïve girl sitting atop a thousand-pound steam engine. Suddenly, she was not so confident herself. Sure, Lilly had a way about her with the horses, but was this going to work? Tom shook his head, and the doubt disappeared from his face.

They reached the turn and Tom let the strap run through Hank's bridle to release him.

"You've got this, Lilly. Go have fun." Tom pulled Midget out to the outside rail. Lilly was all business as she concentrated on moving up into a canter to catch up with Buck and Wolf. Buck glanced behind him and saw them approaching. He eased Wolf into a gallop as Hank pulled aside him. Lilly stared straight ahead, intent on following Tom's directions to the letter.

The horses galloped two abreast around the track and entered the homestretch. Lilly counted the strides Hank was taking, one, two, one, two. She wanted to make sure he didn't miss a beat, indicating something was off or possibly wrong with one of his legs.

Lilly was in heaven, lost in the power of this beautiful animal below her. Even if they were only galloping, Lilly had never gone so fast in her life. She moved her arms along with Hank's head as he reached it forward and dug his hooves into the soft dirt. She no longer thought about the searing pain in her thighs. Her adrenaline kicked in and all her focus was on being one with Hank, being a part of his effort.

They hit the quarter pole and Buck seemed to momentarily forget that he needed to breeze his horse. He stole a look at Lilly and yelled, "See you back at the barn!" He chucked his reins at Wolf and gave a cluck, encouraging him on. Wolf, thrilled to be free of his constraints, leapt into the bridle, grabbing the bit. They pulled away from Hank and Lilly.

For a few seconds.

Before Buck knew what had happened, Hank came swiftly alongside Wolf and, with a petite, blond-haired girl tucked tight on his back, overtook them as they crossed the finish line.

Oh boy. She's going to be trouble, Buck thought as he eased Wolf up.

Lilly approached Tom, where he waited for them on the far side of the track. Tom had his cell phone to his ear. He expertly looped the leather strap through Hank's bridle and continued to listen in his cell phone as they walked back to the stables.

"Nice ride," Buck said next to her.

"I'm going to be fired. I didn't listen to Tom's instructions at all. I got caught up in the moment, you know?" She looked over at him, tears that didn't fall welling in her eyes. "It was just the best experience of my life and I couldn't stop myself. I saw you move on and go faster, and I...I don't know. I guess my instincts just kicked in and I encouraged Hank to catch up with you," she sputtered.

Buck could relate; though it had been so long since his first real ride on a fast thoroughbred, he could still recall the freedom of it. Now, as much as he loved being a jockey, it was a job. A hard one at that. He didn't have the freedom to just enjoy the moment. There were the trainer's instructions and owner's wishes, as well as trying to predict what other jockeys were going to do during a race with their horses. There were all these other things that needed to be considered when riding in a race. The sheer joy of riding a racehorse was a novelty that he couldn't afford to experience anymore.

It was refreshing to see the newness of it all written all over Lilly's face.

"You are definitely *not* going to get fired," Buck said to her and he trotted ahead of them back to the barn.

Hanging Out

Lilly sat on the prickly bale of hay and spread out her lunch.

A slice of cheese, an apple, and a protein shake. She had eaten her mom's big breakfast of eggs and bacon and it was a good idea to try to offset those calories. In reality, gaining weight wasn't something Lilly had to worry about. She was a smidgen over 5 feet tall and weighed 150 pounds.

It had been a month since her first exercise ride, and Lilly was still on cloud nine each time she got onto one of Tom's horses.

Tom had actually told her she should put on some muscle weight, which would help her balance in the saddle and be able to stick on the back of a rowdy Thoroughbred. Acknowledging the fact that she was on an unpredictable animal that weighed more than 1,200 pounds, which she was controlling through a bridle around its head and a bit in its mouth, was a necessity in the world of working with racehorses. There was no way she could control the horses through brute strength; a horse would win every time. Lilly liked to think she was successful at riding the horses Tom had given her through her emotional connection and intuition, as well as the long hours she had dedicated to riding at the training farm. She did think the additional muscle would help give her the strength she needed in her legs to keep her butt out of the saddle on the long gallops around the track.

Buck rounded the corner of the barn and stopped short.

"Hey." Lilly looked up at him.

"Well, hello," Buck replied. "What do you have there?"

"Just a quick bite to eat before I finish up with Sulu; he banged his leg on the starting gate yesterday. The swelling's gone down a bit, but I want to change the wrap one more time before the afternoon races," Lilly said.

"I thought you weren't a groom anymore, Miss Exercise Rider," Buck commented, eyeing her food.

"Old habits are hard to give up. Gus doesn't mind the help anyway. He hasn't been able to find a replacement for me, and I enjoy staying in touch with my horses," Lilly said. "Want a slice of my apple?"

"Just a slice," Buck held out his hand, in which Lilly placed the piece of red apple. Buck put it in his mouth and sucked on the apple.

"Don't want to miss a race?" Buck asked through the apple in his mouth.

"I gotta make sure I learn as much as I can before I head back to school," Lilly replied. The fact was that ever since Lilly started her job as an exercise rider, she never missed a race. Summer was coming to a close and she would be heading back to school. She wanted to absorb all she could before she had to start back with biology and calculus. She wondered for maybe the millionth time in two months why she needed to go back to school. She wasn't going to become a doctor or a lawyer. Her education was at the track. Her parents had agreed to allow her to continue exercising the horses in the morning when school started. She would address the education piece at a later date. One step at a time with them.

"Do you want anything else to eat?" Lilly asked Buck.

Buck spit the rind of the apple slice into his hand after sucking all the juice out of it. He walked over to Wolf's stall and offered it to the big brown horse. He gave the horse a pat and then ran a hand through his own brown hair, which was cropped short on the side but kept long on top. Lilly noticed it was the same color as the brown horse he stood next to.

"Gosh, no," Buck replied. "I don't have the same luxury as you, skinny-minny." Lilly pursed her lips, unsure if she should be offended. Buck laughed.

"Don't get all worked up. Take it as a compliment. You don't have to work like the majority of us jocks to make weight," Buck said, patting his flat stomach as he sat down next to Lilly on the hay bale. "Do you even know what some of us do to make weight? It's tough for a guy to keep to 110 pounds, max 115. Especially when we have pretty girls like you, offering us a bunch of food." He winked at her.

Lilly blinked at Buck, ignoring his comment. She hadn't really thought about "making weight" as it pertained to a jockey.

"What weight do you need to be at to ride in a race?" she asked him. The crucial piece of information had escaped Lilly's attention entirely. She hadn't even considered that aspect of the job in her dream to become a jockey. She had spent her days reading glorified fiction novels about jockeys, but they never talked about the specifics of what it took to actually become a jockey. Was she living in a dream world? Would she even qualify?

"It depends on the race. The Derby and such for the three-year-olds require a weight of 126. And you need to remember that your tack adds about seven pounds. So to ride in those races, I can't weigh any more than 119 pounds. Though most of us aren't going to risk being that close and being kicked off a mount due to weight. I like to keep my weight under 115. Sometimes I need to sweat off a pound or two more than that, depending on what type of races I am riding in on any given day. Each race has its own weight requirements," Buck replied.

"What happens if you weigh more than what is allowed?" Lilly asked.

"You'd find me running my tail off back here on race day," Buck answered with a smile. He noted the curiosity in Lilly's eyes. "Boy, you are innocent when it comes to this stuff, aren't you?"

Lilly dropped his gaze in embarrassment. "Sorry."

"Hey, no, I'm sorry. It is refreshing to have you around. Someone who isn't jaded about some of the stuff that can go on around here." Buck grabbed her hand. Lilly looked back up at him in surprise. He playfully air-kissed the back of her hand and placed it back down on hay bale.

"Okay, so seriously. Some jocks may use any kind of means to make weight. Have you heard of a hot box?" Buck asked.

"Like a sauna?" Lilly replied.

"Exactly. Well, there is one of those in the jockey's room. Some guys will sit in there all morning to sweat out any unwanted pounds. How about a heave bowl? Have you heard of one of those?" Buck asked.

"A heave bowl? That sounds disgusting," Lilly said, wrinkling her nose.

"Well, it is. And it is used exactly as it sounds. The jockey's room can be a vomit factory sometimes. At some racetracks, there is a special stall in the bathroom where the heave bowl sits. Jockeys who have eaten too much during the morning make themselves throw up so they don't retain the food they just ate. Or some may take diuretic pills to force themselves to pee out the retained water in their bodies," Buck answered honestly.

"It sounds like a bunch of middle-school girls with self-esteem issues and eating disorders," Lilly said.

"Pretty much. Some of my best friends in the business suffer from bulimia and anorexia. Sometimes it also leads to drug abuse, which I'm sure you know doesn't go well with trying to control a 1,200 pound animal racing at 40 miles per hour. A few years ago, a friend of mine fell right off his horse in the post parade because he was so dizzy from not eating and dehydrated from not drinking for twenty-four hours just to make weight."

"Why don't they raise the weights that the horses carry so you don't need to worry about making such a low weight?" Lilly asked, mildly horrified.

"Don't know. It's been this way for 100 years. Other sports require bigger, stronger, faster athletes, but horse racing requires us to be smaller, skinnier, lighter, and maintain our strength to actually ride."

"That's horrible," Lilly said. Buck shrugged.

"Maybe it is. This isn't a sport for the easily deterred though, Lilly. Being a jockey has the highest mortality rate of any professional sport. On average, there are 2,500 injuries and two deaths per year. But we all still ride, mostly for the love of it, some because they don't know anything else and need to make a living to support their families."

"So, on the off-chance I don't accidentally starve myself to death, I could still randomly die if a horse under me has a bad day and decides to throw me off?" Lilly briefly thought that her parents had been right to keep her from the sport for so long.

"Yeah, basically. Sure you still want to be a jockey, Lilly?" Buck finished, raising his eyebrows. Lilly looked straight into his eyes.

"You haven't scared me off, if that was your intention," Lilly said. "I appreciate the lesson, but like you said, we ride for love. Now that I have been on the backs of these beautiful creatures, there is no place else I would rather be. I just know I wouldn't be happy doing anything else."

"That's exactly what I thought you'd say." Buck smiled lightly. "Let's go check out your Sulu's leg before I have to hustle over for the start of the races. It will help me burn some more calories to walk there and back."

Farm Call

Buck drove them down the long tree-lined driveway. When he'd asked her to run an errand with him, she'd jumped at the chance, and not just because he'd promised to introduce her to a man who was very influential in the racing industry. Lilly enjoyed their time together tremendously, as Buck was so easy to talk to and was teaching her so much. Having someone to talk at length with about her passion was something she never had. Macy and the girls at school didn't get it and preferred to talk shopping and boys. Her mom got so anxious hearing about Lilly's riding that she avoided the topic entirely in the evenings, instead preferring to hear about the deli and customers that had come in that day.

Buck had told her, warned her, about the grandness of Doug Walker's Shamrock Hill Farm. She thought she had prepared herself, thinking big paddocks and large barns, but nothing could compare to what unfolded in front of her as they turned into the farm.

In the distance rose several barns painted white with red trim. Several outbuildings dotted the landscape. Off to her left sat the large training oval, complete with a large lake and fountain in the center. The poles along the inside rail, marking the eighths of a mile or furloughs, were painted a rich green and white. Off to the right of the oval down the shoot sat a four-horse training gate.

The landscaping was impeccable, with red Knockout Rose bushes blooming everywhere, complementing the red roofs of the barns. Several workers were tending to the flower beds full of impatiens and begonias around the entrances of the barns. Lilly knew her flowers from the many years she had helped her mom in the gardens in the back of their house.

She watched the gleaming white fence go by and looked beyond it to the band of broodmares and their babies. The grass had returned a rich green from the late summer rains and the heat of mid-summer was starting to abate.

Thoroughbred breeders planned as best they could for foals to be born as early in the year as possible to take advantage of the January 1 birthdate for all Thoroughbreds. Given it was late August, these four- to five-month foals were getting bolder and venturing further away from their moms. In a couple more months, usually around six months of age, these foals would become "weanlings," separated from their mothers into a group of their own. Fillies would be separated from the colts, and the mothers would be moved to a far field on the other side of the farm to help with separation anxiety.

"I don't think I would be able to stand all the calling and squealing when they separate the mommas from the babies," Lilly said, looking out the window.

"It's not as drastic as you think," Buck replied. "Doug cares a lot about the emotional state of his horses, so he takes a bit longer than others to make sure both the mom and foal are okay."

"Really, how does he do it?" Lilly asked, then exclaimed, "Oh my gosh, stop the truck!"

Buck pulled his big blue Ford F-450 to the side of the driveway. Lilly opened her door and climbed down. She walked slowly over to the fence so as not to spook the foals that had been playing on the other side of the fence. Lilly watched as they nipped at each other, spun around and kicked up their heels. As Lilly leaned her hand on the fence, the foals stopped their play and all four heads turned to look at her.

Lilly started to hum softly. One of the foals, a big white blaze down the center of his forehead, pricked his ears and nudged his nose towards her. He took a step forward and then hesitated. His three friends hung back, appraising the stranger in front of them, not bold enough to step forward but not scared enough to run back to their mommas.

Lilly continued her soft hum as she leaned down and slid through the two lower slats in the fence. She sat on the soft grass and crossed her legs. Playing follow the leader, the foals as a pack moved forward one step at a time, curiosity overcoming their fear. They walked together like a wall, shoulder to shoulder, none of them wanting to be the first to reach the stranger, but not wanting to be the last either.

The foal with the white blaze reached his head down and blew on Lilly's knee. Though she didn't move, he quickly moved his nose away. He repeated his attempt at getting to know who this person was, sitting cross-legged in his paddock. Lilly put out her hand, palm side up. The colt nestled his chin into her cupped hand and nibbled at the soft flesh pad at the base of her thumb. Lilly made no other movements to scare off the foals.

They moved around her one by one, blowing at her head, causing her hair to softly float around her face. She took in their attention and one by one laid a hand on the side of each one's head, looked into their eyes, and assessed their personalities.

Like a cat getting up from a nap, she slowly raised herself to her feet. Standing, the foals were about eye level with Lilly. She moved her hands over their necks and their backs, acclimating them to the feeling of a new person and showing them that they shouldn't be scared. Lilly lost herself in the sensation of socializing with the young horses.

"Unfortunately, we need to go, oh horse whisperer," came a voice. Lilly looked over, surprised to see a man standing next to the open window of Buck's truck. She had been so involved with the foals that she hadn't heard him arrive.

"Which one do you think will be the next winner?" he asked her. Lilly slowly retreated back towards the fence and lowered herself through the rails. As she straightened, the bolder colt pushed his nose through the fence and grabbed at Lilly's shirt. Without a reprimand, Lilly gently removed her shirt from between his baby teeth.

"I think they all have potential. Their pedigree is already set in stone, it's the trainer's job now to surround them with the environment in which to thrive," Lilly commented, still rubbing her hand up and down the blaze of the colt's face.

"Do you favor nature or nurture, Lilly?" the man asked her. Lilly was struck momentarily by this stranger's use of her first name, but a quick glance at Buck's reassuring expression was all she needed to continue the conversation with the man she now realized was Doug Walker, the man they'd come to see.

Lilly thought for a moment and said, "Nurture, absolutely. When a foal is born, its pedigree has done all it can. Once it hits the ground, success or lack thereof comes down to the work of the people who surround him or her. You can undo a great pedigree by poor training and you can overcome a so-so pedigree by great training." Lilly shrugged and looked back at the colt by her side. Doug turned to Buck.

"I like her already," he said, smiling. He called back to Lilly, "Come on, let's see what you think about my two-year-olds. I'll hitch a ride with you back to the barn." Lilly walked around the truck, jumped into the passenger side, and slid in close to Buck as Doug slammed the door closed. Doug held out his hand to Lilly. "Doug Walker, pleased to meet you, horse whisperer." Lilly smiled, shaking his hand with her own. As Lilly sat sandwiched between Buck and Doug, she marveled at where her life had taken her. She couldn't be any happier than she was at that moment.

"Mr. Walker, Buck mentioned you separated the mommas and the babies slowly. How do you do it?" Lilly asked.

"Call me Doug, please. It's pretty simple actually. Different people have different schools of thought. Do you rip off a band-aid or peel it off slowly? Generally, for band-aids I like the fast approach, but I don't like the trauma that goes along with quickly separating a mom from its foal. Instead of removing all the mares from the foals at one time and forcing them to 'get over it'—like when a baby 'cries it out' before falling asleep—we remove one mare at a time. That allows the foals to still have other moms around to lean on and they form closer relationships with the other foals. After a period of time, only one mare remains with the herd of foals. They have gotten so used to being without the other moms that they barely realize when the last mare is removed," he finished.

"How do the mares take it?" Lilly asked.

"They are pretty strong; many have been through the process year after year. It's the new moms that take a bit more time. We put them in a far paddock with other mares, far enough that they can't hear the calling of the foals. Keep in mind, the mom has, in most cases, already been bred back and she's focused on growing a new baby," Doug said.

"So soon? Why?" Lilly continued her interrogation. Doug smiled and Lilly blushed. "I'm sorry, you don't have to answer that."

"Never apologize for wanting to know all you can about something you love doing. It's knowledge that gets you ahead, gives you something to fall back on, makes you a better rider, which is your goal from all that Buck has told me." Lilly looked quickly at Buck, smiling in the driver's seat, and then back at Doug, and smiled. Doug gave a short nod and then answered her question.

"The best time to breed back the mare is within thirty days of giving birth. The mare and new foal are loaded onto a trailer and taken to the stud, wherever he is located, and the process starts all over again. Given the eleven-month gestation period, breeders want to breed back as soon as possible or the timeline slides further away from the January 1 birthdate. A foal born in May isn't as developed as a foal born in January or February when it comes to the three-year-old Classics."

Lilly was silent as she absorbed the details of the Thoroughbred breeding industry. It was more intricate than she had ever imagined. She hoped that the breeders didn't lose sight that each foal born was a living and breathing soul, versus an asset just to make money off of. Or that the mare was an animal that had done her job and wasn't just a breeding machine.

"I didn't confuse you, did I? I'm not always great at explaining things," Doug chuckled. Lilly smiled back the best she could.

"No, I understood it all. I was just wondering if owners really related to these beautiful creatures or if they just see them as money making machines," Lilly mused. Buck stomped on the brakes a little too quickly, causing the truck to jerk to a stop. "Oh crap, did I just say that? I am so sorry, Mr. Walker, I didn't mean to insult you," Lilly quickly said.

Buck had pulled the truck up to a building that had a sign that read "Office" outside of it. Before opening the truck door, Doug turned in his seat, throwing his arm over the headrest; the honesty in his eyes was all Lilly needed to see to know that this man was one of the good ones.

"Lilly, horse racing has been around for centuries, dating back to the ancient times of Greece, Syria, and Egypt, and was part of the Greek Olympics in 648 BC. Its premise—to identify which of two or more horses is the fastest over a set distance—has remained unchanged since the earliest of times. We have had our distractors for sure, as well as the bad seeds that the media seizes, making the entire industry look bad. But I can guarantee there are many more owners, breeders, and trainers who want the best for these animals than there are bad people involved in the sport. Horse racing is a vast industry that employs millions of people. Think about the grooms, exercise riders, vets, farriers, and chiropractors: all those people work around the horses and make a living at it. It's not an easy job, but these people, for the most part, love what they do and love the animals that they work with.

"For most of us, it is not about the big time millionaires, noted racetracks, or the 'Classics', which is all that the general public usually sees. It is about the racetracks in the far corners of the country, the breeding farms that have been around for generations in the smaller states where the sport has been declining for a while now. It'll never die though, because asking people to quit this industry or trying to shut it down would be no different than asking cattle farmers to quit raising cattle or Perdue to stop raising chickens. This is an agricultural business and it has supported thousands of families over hundreds of years.

"The best we can do is continue to educate people and do the right thing when it comes to caring for these great creatures. They work hard for us and we all work hard for them."

Lilly sat looking at her hands, feeling the passion behind Doug's words. She'd never heard anyone talk about it like that. Even Tom, who'd worked in the industry for most of his life, had never sounded so passionate about the animals and the work that he did.

"Come on, I'll show you," Doug said, opening the door to the truck and stepping out. Lilly looked over at Buck, wondering how he'd reacted to Doug's speech.

"Doug loves to talk about the changes in the industry and prove people wrong. He also loves strong people who aren't afraid to say what they are thinking," he said, grabbing her hand and pulling her out of the truck. Doug walked towards the door to the building, opened it, and stood aside to let Buck and Lilly walk into the office of Shamrock Hill Farm.

The first thing that Lilly took in was a trophy shelf behind the desk. The next things she took in were all the trophies on shelves around the room. Doug was clearly not an unsuccessful breeder, Lilly mentally noted.

"Hi Buck!" a woman shouted from across the room. She stood up from the massive mahogany desk that was the centerpiece of the room.

"Hey Molly, great to see you!" Buck said in reply, striding over to the desk to give the woman a large hug. She was a bit taller than Buck, with brown hair that was cut in a bob around her soft, round face. Lilly saw the resemblance to Doug immediately.

The woman looked over Buck's shoulder at Lilly. "Who have you brought with you?"

Buck motioned Lilly over. "This is my friend, Lilly. She's making quite a name for herself at Pimlico. I figured she'd be a better source than I to assess Doug's latest projects."

"Well, that is a big compliment coming from you." Molly held out her hand. "Nice to meet you, Lilly."

Lilly held out her hand and the grasp she found that awaited her was one of strength, one that could be interpreted as 'don't mess with Buck, he is a good guy,' but her smile was warm and welcoming.

"I couldn't run Shamrock without the help of Molly, my sister, if you haven't already guessed. She and her husband, Steve, are the backbone to everything that goes on here. You can't run a business without a great back office person, and Molly keeps us all in line. She's magic with the computer, and when it comes to spreadsheets, she's second to none. She also ensures we document each and every detail on each and every horse we own, on site here as well as at the tracks."

Molly moved back around the desk and sat in the big leather chair. "Well, being related to the owner has its perks." Molly leaned down and lifted a car seat on top of the desk.

Lilly saw a sleeping baby nestled in the seat, buckled in but content to slumber in his innocence.

"Hello, Sammy," Doug whispered softly, running his finger along the baby's cheek. Lilly was drawn to the baby and Molly, who stood proudly, one hand on the car seat and the other resting on his little foot. The look on her face was one of pure joy for her son.

"We can't sit here all day being enamored by a baby, there is work to do and horses to ride," Doug said, squeezing Sammy's foot and turning toward Buck and Lilly.

"Wait one little minute." Molly stopped them. "Have you given me the information on Lady Rock I asked for?"

"See? We may be family, but she is a slave driver," Doug said. "I will come back in a little bit and go over it with you. Right now, I need to show these two around and get them on a couple of feisty two-year-olds."

"Nice to meet you," Lilly said.

"Nice to meet you, too," Molly replied. She walked around the desk and placed a hand on Lilly's shoulder, "Don't let these two get out of hand. It's not often Doug brings a new rider to the farm. He must think you have something special. Don't let him trick you into getting in over your head."

"No, ma'am," was all Lilly thought to say. She caught up with Doug and Buck before they'd walked halfway across the parking lot. The two men were walking side by side, so Lilly decided to stay back a little and not interrupt what they were discussing.

"Good to see her up and moving again," Buck said.

"Yeah, she had a hard time there for a while. They both did."

"Sam's in the clear now, right? He's twice as big as the last time I saw him," Buck chuckled.

"Yeah, the doctors gave him a clean bill of health a while ago. Molly took a little longer because she refused to focus on her own health when little Sammy needed attention." Doug sounded mildly annoyed.

"That sounds like Molly all right." Buck clapped Doug on the shoulder and looked over at him. "They're both in the clear now. Nothing left to worry about."

Doug nodded in affirmation as they reached their destination. Buck looked around and saw Lilly. He smiled and waved her forward to join them.

The rest of the day, Lilly was on cloud nine. She rode horses and gave opinions and actually felt as though she belonged. It was almost a shock to her when they said their goodbyes and started back down the grand driveway. Lilly couldn't wipe the smile from her face. Just before they left, Doug promised to use her as often as he could. She was moving up in the industry already.

As Buck drove them back to the track, Lilly thought about the conversation she had overheard about Molly. "Is Molly okay?" she asked.

Buck looked sideways at her. "She's fine."

Buck was silent for a few moments, "Molly can't have any more kids. She had a bunch of issues during her pregnancy with Sam and during delivery. Doug told me they were all thankful that they both are alive. Sadly, Molly had always wanted a house full of kids. But she will say how blessed she is with Sam."

Lilly recalled the look on Molly's face as she gazed upon her son. She hoped that she would feel the same towards any child she might have in the future, but right now she couldn't even imagine having children. She loved riding and horses way too much to sacrifice her dreams for a needy baby.

Back at School

"Well, how was your summer hanging around the track? Were you bored? I would have been so bored. You should have come with us, Lilly. Paris was just awesome!" Macy continued her chit-chat as they walked to their first class of their junior year.

Lilly walked quietly beside her friend, trying desperately to appear interested in everything that Macy had to say. They had exchanged letters while they were apart, so she'd already been briefed on the important things anyway.

"Well?" Macy nudged her shoulder.

"Well, what?" Lilly replied as innocently as she could.

"I have known you way too long, Lilly Garrett. You are not listening to me at all. Tell me what is up, and hurry because we only have fifteen minutes before the first bell," Macy urged.

Lilly sighed. She had to tell someone or she would burst. Of course there had been other, minor crushes over the years, but nothing had come of them. She knew Buck was something special.

"I had an awesome time working at the track, of course. Did you get my letter about starting to be an exercise rider?" Lilly asked her.

"Yes, and how it's fun and scary at the same time. That's not what you're thinking about now though," Macy said. She pulled them both over to the stone bench on the side of the sidewalk to get out of the way of the other students walking to class.

"Well…" Lilly stammered.

"What?" Macy said determinedly, "Elizabeth, you tell me right now!"

"I may have met someone special," Lilly said softly.

Macy looked closely into her best friend's face. "What? When?"

"My first day of riding. He's a real jockey, and he's been helping me all summer with my technique. He's so nice, and he knows about horses like I do, and he's funny, and—"

"And he's attractive?" Macy probed.

"He's older than us," Lilly said, avoiding the question.

"Okay, so that's a yes. And you didn't mention him in any of your letters, which means you wanted to have a real conversation about this, which means this is not just a basic crush." Macy's grin had grown slowly as she spoke.

Lilly gave her a soft smile. "He is quite the catch."

"So, tell me everything! And don't you leave out a single moment, missy. I want to hear about every little detail, including if you have kissed him yet! "

Lilly could feel the heat rushing to her face at Macy's words.

Macy squeezed Lilly's hand. "Tell me!" She met Lilly's eyes with complete sincerity. Lilly broke into a wide grin, lowered her voice, and began to speak eagerly. Sitting there with Macy before class, Lilly felt for the first time like the kind of normal teenage girl her mother had always wanted her to be.

"Mom, I'm home!" Lilly set her book bag on the table and filled a glass with water.

"Oh, hi dear, can I make you a snack?" Lilly was about to turn down the offer, but an idea struck her.

"Yeah, I'd love that. Maybe I could help you, like I used to." Lilly grabbed the spare apron off the hook by the fridge and smiled at her mom. It almost broke her heart how excited her mother looked at the prospect of spending time together.

"Of course! I would like that a lot." Her mom grabbed her own apron and a recipe book from the shelf by the oven and began instructing Lilly on the ingredients they would need.

"I signed up for that math class you wanted me to be in," Lilly said

"Oh, good! That will look so good on your college applications, dear. Now you just need some extra-curricular activities." She measured out some flour and dumped it into their bowl.

"Well, it's funny you mentioned that, actually. I talked to my counselor about that today as well…"

"Did you now? Well that's good. I'm sorry to hear that you won't be doing your horse work anymore, but—"

"Actually, she said my work at the stables will look great to colleges. She said that the discipline and the responsibility it takes to work at a stable will look amazing on my resume. And she also said that the fact that I've had a paying job for most of my high school career will look good to the more expensive colleges; they'll see that I've always worked hard and kept my grades up, so it'll be less risky to give me loans." Lilly stirred the ingredients in the bowl. She could feel her mom's eyes on her, but she refused to look up.

"She said all that, did she?"

"Yes, she did. And she also said that if I wanted to count my work at the stables as my extra-curricular, then she would put my study hall period first so that I could still work with Mr. Malone until I graduate. That is, if it's alright with you."

"Well that's just great," her mom said, but she sounded as though it was anything but great. Lilly flinched as her mother brought her knife down on the cutting board, slicing the strawberries.

"Mom—"

"Lilly, you're getting too involved in this horse stuff," she practically spat the last two words and Lilly stiffened. "I want you to be involved in activities that actually pertain to your future career! I don't want you wasting your time working somewhere that means nothing in the end!" Lilly squared her shoulders and met her mother's eye.

"It's not just 'stuff' to me, Mom. I love what I'm doing, and it has more to do with my future than you think!" Her mother opened her mouth to speak and Lilly realized her mistake. "I'm making good money with Mr. Malone. I can help pay for my own college now. I don't know any other kids who are making money, getting straight A's, AND working at an extra-curricular activity that will impress colleges."

"I don't want you worrying about how we'll pay for college," her mother said.

"Well I am! Mom, come on. You and Dad work so hard, and I'm not a kid anymore. You want me to be a normal girl and go out with my friends, but I don't have the money to go out with my friends! I won't have the money to rush a sorority or buy extra school supplies I might need."

"Lilly—"

"Mom just listen. I know you don't like it, and I get where you're coming from, I really do. I have some points that I think will help you, if you will just agree to hear me out." Lilly sat down at the table and motioned for her mother to sit across from her. There was a moment of silence, and then a chair scraping across the floor, and then her mother sat, hands folded, at the table.

"Alright, I'm listening."

"Okay, I know you want me to be a normal teenage girl. I've talked to Macy, and she's agreed to come by twice a week and take me out to do normal, teenage girl things, like walking around the mall or hanging out at the movie theater with everyone else from school. I won't be spending all my time at the barn. I promise to spend some of the money I make on useless junk or seeing meaningless movies, and not be hyper-responsible and save it all."

"Let me get this straight. You're saying that if I let you keep working at the barn, you'll spend less time on homework, and waste your money?" Her mother looked skeptical.

"Well…yeah. I'm really trying here, Mom. In the history of the world, what is more normal for a teenage girl than wanting to do something that her parents don't agree with? And like a boy she doesn't tell them about?

And have friends that help her waste time and money?" Lilly stood up and paced next to the table. "I'm not asking for you to agree with me forever, I'm just talking about until I graduate!"

"You like a boy?" Lilly stopped pacing and her face flushed.

"What?"

"You mentioned a boy."

"I just…that was just an example. I was trying to make a point," Lilly stuttered.

"Tell me about him." Her mother's expression became inviting, and Lilly sat down.

"His name is Buck. I met him at work," she said to her lap, twiddling her thumbs.

"Is he nice?" Lilly looked up. She was struck again by the joy her mother seemed to feel, sharing time with her only daughter. Lilly smiled and decided discussing Buck was the least she could do.

"He's extremely nice. A real gentleman. He's 19 and he's a professional jockey." She saw her mother's brow furrow. "He regrets not finishing school, and he's told me repeatedly that if I even think about dropping out, he'll never speak to me again."

Her mother's expression eased. "That's quite a threat," her mother said, and Lilly laughed and rolled her eyes. "When did you meet him?"

"My first day of riding. He's a professional, so he's not there all the time, which means I don't get to see him all that much, but when he's at the track, we talk."

"That's nice." Lilly was surprised to hear the tremor in her mom's voice.

"Mom?" Her mother had stood and walked to the counter, her back to Lilly, stirring the mixture they'd started.

"I don't care if you do your horse stuff, Elizabeth, if your counselor really thinks it will look good on your applications." Lilly was in shock. She'd spent so much time thinking that her mom was uninterested in her whole life, that she'd never considered the idea that her mother was just upset that they didn't have more to talk about.

Lilly walked up behind her mom and gave her a hug.

"I love you, Mom."

"I love you too, Elizabeth."

Point of No Return

Lilly met up with Macy for lunch in the dining hall. She took out her slice of cheese, apple, and protein drink.

"Is that all you are going to eat?" Macy asked.

"I have to make sure I maintain my weight or I won't be asked to ride," Lilly informed her.

"You sure you want to pursue this thing, Lilly?" Macy asked her, eyeing the sparse contents of her friend's lunch bag.

"Totally. And actually, I need your help. I really need to convince my parents to let me become a real jockey. They are not going to be very supportive, you know them, but maybe together we can think of a way to get them on board," Lilly said, taking a bite of her cheese.

"What do you mean, 'real jockey,' Lilly? Like not go to college, not have a real job?" Macy asked.

"Being a jockey *is* a real job, Macy. Buck makes a decent living, and he just started riding in some of the bigger races," Lilly smiled.

"Just because your parents like your boyfriend doesn't mean they want you to have the same job he has." Macy rolled her eyes and nudged her friend.

Lilly and Buck had been dating for a little over a year; they'd made things official during winter break the year before. Interestingly enough, her parents had been less anxious about her riding since she'd started seeing Buck. Perhaps they were hoping that his involvement in the racing world would be enough for her and she'd lose interest in becoming a jockey herself.

Since her first ride the summer before her junior year, she'd been rising up the ranks at the stables and now, five months from graduating, she was well on her way to becoming a professional. The only problem was that her parents had no idea. They still thought she was just an exercise rider. The extra time she'd been spending at the track, they assumed, was because she wanted to see Buck.

"Your parents have wanted you to become an engineer ever since I have known you," Macy commented. "Ever since you put together that gas grill on your back patio when you were thirteen-years-old."

"Okay, there were instructions; it wasn't really the feat that everyone made it out to be. I don't want to ruin their dream for me, but I don't want to live their dream. I want to live mine! I love what I'm doing now, and after being so involved in racing like this, I can't imagine giving it up for more school and a boring desk job," Lilly said tiredly.

"I get it. I really do. I just don't want you to do something you'll regret. I mean, what if you go to school and keep working? Just so you have a back-up. I don't want you to give up on your dream, but...what if you get hurt and you can't ride anymore? You'll have nothing to fall back on."

"If I get hurt riding, there is still a lot I can do around the stables. Or I can go to college then. Trust me, I've thought about that. I'm willing to take the risk. School will always be there but the sooner I start racing professionally, the better my chances are of making a good living at it."

"Lilly...your parents are never going to go for this. I'm saying this as a friend. They will most likely kill you if you tell them you're not going to college."

"I know, it's not gonna go well. But I'm 18 next week, and I won't exactly need their permission. They'll be pissed for a while, but they'll have to get over it. Right?"

"Would you get over it if they somehow kept you from riding?" Macy asked. Lilly sighed. She knew the answer to that, and it was like a punch in the gut to realize that her parents would never be okay with her decision.

"Then I wait. I graduate like I planned, and then I leave." The thought made Lilly sick to her stomach. She couldn't see any way around someone getting hurt, but her need to ride outweighed her need to spare her parents.

"Catch!" Lilly looked up just in time to catch the grape that was flying at her in her mouth. She smiled and bit down in triumph. Buck chuckled and kissed her briefly.

"Welcome back," Lilly said, wrapping her arms around his neck. "What did you bring me?"

"Oh, so I'm not enough now?" Buck joked, attempting to pull away. Lilly laughed and tightened her grip.

"You'll do, I suppose." She kissed him. "I really missed you."

"Back 'atcha." He deepened their kiss and for the next few minutes, Lilly's worries evaporated. They were startled apart by a whinny from close behind them. When their laughter died down, Buck suggested a walk around the track and Lilly, eager to get his opinions on her predicament, agreed.

It was a perfect night. The stars were clear in the sky, there was a warm breeze blowing, and the moon gave them enough light to easily walk a path around the track. Lilly listened in awe as Buck told her about the races he'd been in while he was away. Each little detail made her heart skip a beat, and she gripped his hand tighter.

"You'll get your turn, Lilly. Before you know it, you'll be bored of my stories because you'll have so many of your own." He put his arm around her shoulders and planted a kiss on her head.

"I highly doubt I'll ever be bored by you, Mr. Wheeler." She pulled him to a stop by the starting gate and leaned back against the railing. "And as for having my own stories…I hope so. My parents—"

"Lilly listen to me. You were made to do this. I've never met another person so in tune with horses. You're so incredibly passionate about every aspect of the race, and that is what makes a good jockey. Your parents will come around when they see how amazing you are at what you do."

"But Buck, what if they don't? They're my parents, I can't just...I'm all they have! It would break my heart to hurt them." Buck brushed the hair away from her face and rested his forehead on hers.

"I know. You have an amazing heart. That's one of the things...one of the reasons why I...I'm glad I know you." Lilly's arms tightened around him, and she pulled her face away so that she could look into his eyes. He sighed and closed his eyes. Lilly smiled.

"I'm sure glad you're my guy, Buck Wheeler." She rested her head on his shoulder. After a moment, Buck pulled away, grabbed her hand, and began leading her back toward the stalls. He sat her down on an upside down water bucket, instructed her to close her eyes, and told her that he would be right back.

As she waited, she took in the smells of the building around her. There were some good and some bad, but together they made up her favorite smell in the world. She thought again about her parents and the idea that following their path for her would mean giving up this smell, and this life. She sighed.

"That wasn't a yawn, was it? Are you bored?" There was a slight tremor in Buck's voice that Lilly assumed was laughter.

"No, I'm not bored. Are you going to tell me what's going on? Why are my eyes closed?"

"I wanted this to feel more dramatic. You can open them now," Lilly opened her eyes and saw Buck standing in front of her, his hands behind his back.

"What are you up to?" She stood up and stepped toward him. He put one arm out to stop her advance and she raised an eyebrow in question.

"If I'm not mistaken, your birthday is fast approaching. Being the good boyfriend that I am, I got you something." The tremor returned to his voice and Lilly recognized it this time as nerves. "I was going to wait to give it to you, but now seems like as good a time as any." He lowered his arm and closed the distance between them.

"You didn't have to get me anything," Lilly said.

"Well I did, so just open it." He held out a small parcel of newspaper. "Sorry it doesn't look nicer on the outside." He attempted a joke, but his voice shook as he watched her unwrap the square. Lilly's hands were steady, but when she removed the last layer and saw what lay at the heart of the wrapping, she gasped.

"Do you like it?" Buck asked, taking the ring from the paper in her palm and grabbing her hand.

"Buck, it's gorgeous," she said, and it was. It was a beautiful band with several sapphire colored gems that glinted in the dim light of the lanterns above the stalls.

"It's a promise ring. Some of the guys I ride with get them for their girlfriends when they are in different places. It just means that...I'm committed to you, Lilly, even though I'm not always here to show it."

"I don't know what to say." Lilly looked into his eyes and the sincerity in them made her weak in the knees. "Can I wear it now?" Buck's face immediately broke into a smile and he slipped the ring onto her finger.

"There's one more thing," Buck said, his grip on her hand tightened.

"No, you've already done more than enough, I can't—"

"I love you, Lilly." His eyes were closed, as if shielding himself from a bright light. She felt the tears well up in her eyes, and did the only thing she could think to do: she kissed him. She put all of her feelings for him into that kiss, and he responded with equal vigor.

"I love you too." She barely had time to get the words out. He smiled against her lips and pulled her closer. They stumbled backwards into the free stall behind them and let themselves be overtaken by the feelings they'd both shared. She barely noticed when he laid her gently in the hay, enveloped in the heat of his skin after she slipped his shirt over his head.

He drove her home when Lilly thought her parents would be worried and left her at her front door with another deep kiss and a whispered, 'I love you.' She watched him drive away before she closed the door behind her. All the way up to her room, she twisted the ring on her finger and smiled. She fell asleep that night feeling loved and happy and like she could take on the world.

The Argument

The Steelers were playing on TV. It seemed like déjà vu to Lilly. She had sat in this same room on this same chair and explained to her parents that she wanted to be an exercise rider.

Now she was sitting there about to burst the bubble, the perfect future they had planned for her.

Lilly pretended to watch the game. Her mom was flipping through an article in *Good Housekeeping* while her father's eyes tried to fight off the afternoon nap. The Steelers were up on the Bengals by three touchdowns, so her dad didn't have much need to watch the game anymore.

Lilly stood up and turned down the volume on the TV and then decided to turn the TV off entirely. Her dad's eyes popped open.

"What do you think you are doing, Elizabeth? I am watching the game," he said.

Lilly stood in front of her parents. "No you weren't. You were about to take a nap and the Steelers are winning by a landslide. I need to talk to you both. Seriously."

Her mom closed the magazine and put it in her lap, keeping her finger in it so not to lose the page she was on. "What is it, dear? Something wrong at school?

"No, it is not school. That is all fine. My classes are easy. I need to talk to you about my career in riding," Lilly said.

"Career in riding? But you are riding, dear. You ride every morning, even though I dare say I don't know why it needs to be every day. My rosaries are getting rubbed down from all the praying I do to keep you safe," her mom smiled at her.

Lilly could feel her hands go ice-cold. How could she break the hearts of the two people she loved the most? She looked at the floor to steel her resolve. This was her life and she was going to live it the way she wanted to. She was tired of being the perfect only child.

"I want to ride for my career. I want to be a jockey when I graduate from school," she blurted.

Lilly's dad watched her calmly. "Elizabeth, we know you love to ride, but you will be busy with job offers and deciding where to live after you graduate from college. I am sure you will have time to ride once your engineering career takes off. With your smarts, you will have all the major companies knocking at our door." He smiled over at his wife.

Lilly could see the pride in their eyes, and hesitated. Her heart was about to burst out of her chest with the pain she was about to inflict.

"I don't want to go to college," she said quietly.

"Of course you are going to college, Elizabeth," her mom said incredulously.

"No, Mom, I am not. I have made up my mind. I love riding, I am good at it and I want to do it for a living," Lilly stated.

Her parents sat frozen in their chairs. Lilly stood frozen in place in front of the TV.

"I don't believe that is your decision to make, young lady," started her mom. Lilly's dad put a hand on her mom's arm.

"Joyce, Elizabeth is seventeen years old and she has her own thoughts and opinions. The least we can do is hear her out," her dad said.

"Okay, Elizabeth. If you indeed think this is what you would like to do, please elaborate. Please tell us all about this job, this career you would like to pursue. What do you get paid, what health insurance will you get, where will you live?"

Lilly hesitated. She needed to sound professional, like she knew exactly what she was getting into. The problem was that she didn't know all the answers herself. She just knew she needed to spend her life on the back of a horse. No four-walled office with a computer was going to make her feel like she did when she rode. And not only when she rode, but when she rode a racehorse.

She drew back her shoulders, and forged ahead. "I am going to spend the time during the rest of my senior year continuing to ride horses in the morning. I promise to get all As and continue my school work. When school gets out, I can start my apprenticeship. Tom said I would have more than a year of galloping and breezing horses and that I will be ready to ride in races. I will gallop horses in the morning for Tom and ride in races in the afternoon. Hopefully it won't take me too long to win enough races and I'll qualify to become a full-fledged jockey."

"And what does a 'full-fledged' jockey get paid?" her father asked.

Lilly looked directly at her dad. He wasn't going to be too impressed with her answer. "Well, if the horse I ride finishes 'in the money', which means first, second, third, or fourth, I would get 10 percent of what the horse wins for a first place, and 5 percent of what the horse makes for second, third or fourth."

"And if the horse doesn't finish 'in the money'?" her dad asked.

Lilly let her glaze slip a bit. "About $100 per ride."

Her mom gasped, "You want to give up on a career where you can potentially make hundreds of thousands of dollars in order to ride horses that may make you $100 per ride?"

"Buck told me the average jockey makes between $35,000 to $40,000 per year, and if you are really good, the top jockeys make six figures," Lilly tried to convince her mom. "And I think I can be really good," she added quietly.

"Buck, Buck. Is he the one filling your head with this pipe-dream?" her mom asked her sternly.

Lilly hardened to her mom's line of questioning. "Buck has been nothing but supportive, which is more than I can say about you both."

"Now, Elizabeth," her father tried to interject.

"No, Dad, don't 'Elizabeth' me. I am going to become a jockey with or without your blessing!" Lilly yelled at them.

"Not under our roof you won't, young lady. You will finish up high school and go to college, just like we have always planned," her mom said in a low tone of voice. Lilly knew from years in this house that when her mom stopped yelling or crying and her voice dropped, there was no arguing with her.

"So you can have it your way," Lilly calmly said back. She looked from her mom to her dad, whose eyes were looking a bit damp with unshed tears. "It doesn't have to be this way, but if you can't support me, then I will have to do it alone."

Lilly turned her back on her parents and calmly walked up the stairs to her room, softly closed her door, and promptly burst into tears into her pillow.

After she had spilled all the tears that she had, Lilly slowly lifted her exhausted body from her bed. She grabbed a duffle bag from the closet and started throwing some clothes in it. She yanked her cell phone out of her back pocket and texted Buck *Come get me.*

A knock on the door drew her attention.

"What!" she hissed, still burning with anger. "There's nothing to talk about."

"Please open the door, Elizabeth," her father called through the door. Lilly stopped short her packing. Her dad knocking on the door was the last thing she expected.

Lilly slowly opened the door. Her dad stood in the hallway, her rock when things were rough with her mom.

"May I come in?" he asked.

Lilly opened the door wide for him to enter her bedroom. He took in the half-packed duffle and she noticed his shoulders slump a bit.

He turned to look closely at her. "I need to side with your mom on this one, Elizabeth. We both believe you are too young to be making this decision and feel you will regret it for the rest of your life."

Lilly had been certain he would have talked to her mom and convinced her otherwise. She felt the ball of rage filling her chest cavity again. She was about to blurt at him, but he held up his hand.

"I don't want to argue with you Elizabeth, and I certainly am not a yeller, so I wouldn't be able to compete with you on that front. We have been extremely accommodating with you riding daily and we expect you to return the favor and respect our wishes. When you graduate from college, you can make whatever decisions you want with your life. Until then and while you live under our roof, you finish out your high school year, continue your application process, and go to college."

Lilly couldn't focus and she felt the air closing in on her. They wanted to stomp on her dreams. She couldn't let that happen. She closed her eyes and took several long breaths in and out.

"Elizabeth?" her father said gently, touching her arm.

She opened her eyes and with all the strength she could muster she said, "I appreciate all you have done for me Dad, both you and Mom. I love you both to death, but I can't let you prevent me from following my dream." With that, she grabbed her half-packed duffle bag, ran down the stairs, past her mother who had been rubbing her rosary at the bottom of the stairs, and out the front door.

In front of her, Buck was just pulling up in his pickup truck. He pulled to stop and was about to open his door to get out when Lilly yelled to him, "Don't get out, we are leaving!" She jumped into the passenger seat.

"ELIZABETH!" her mom called from the open front door.

Lilly looked solemnly at her mom, seeing her dad walk up behind her. She saw the look of shock, as well as disdain, in her mother's eyes as she turned to look at Buck. They would of course blame him for her decision, and she couldn't live with that either.

Buck pulled the truck around to the backstretch of Pimlico and up to

Tom's barn. He was waiting at the bottom of the stairs that led to the apartments above.

"Didn't go so well, huh?" he asked as Lilly got out of the truck. She shook her head, spent from yelling, and didn't say a word. Tom wrapped his arms around her bereft body and she shook again with another bout of tears.

"Don't worry, dear girl, we are a team. I'll take care of you," Tom said softly.

Buck had grabbed Lilly's duffle bag from the truck and the two men led an exhausted Lilly up to her new home above the stalls.

Settled In

Lilly had come to love her small apartment, a small efficiency with a bed, bathroom, and kitchen area all in one. She loved smelling the horses below her and listening to their breathing in the middle of the night.

Being on her own wasn't too bad, and she loved the freedom that came with it. She could afford to eat on what Tom paid her, and that was all the money she really needed. Her life now was centered here in the backstretch and she rarely left it, except to go to school. School was done now and she had kept her end of the deal and graduated with high honors.

The hurt was still there and she wasn't ready to forgive her parents, but she'd looked for them in the crowd during her graduation ceremony. They'd all smiled at each other tentatively, and for a moment, it felt like everything was back to normal; but then she saw Buck, a few rows back, and her resolve returned.

Lilly's phone had buzzed constantly in the few weeks after she stormed out of the house. It alternated between her mom and dad, but she never picked up. Mostly because she was afraid they would convince her to come home, and she didn't want to turn back from the path she had decided on. On several occasions she had seen her dad's old Cadillac drive up to the security gate, only to turn around and leave. The security guard had strict instructions from Tom not to allow her parents access to the backstretch.

At times, Lilly missed them, but she pushed those emotions to the back of her mind. No time for that, she would tell herself, and get busy working with the horses. Because she lived above the barn full-time, Gus had allowed her to take on some of the groom duties, like cleaning stalls, feeding horses, and wrapping legs. She loved being the first one to walk along the shed row in the early morning hours before the bulk of the workers got there. She would check on each of the horses and get their feed buckets ready for distribution.

With all the time now at the track, her riding had improved dramatically. She had finished her chores earlier and was nervous in anticipation for tomorrow. She paced her small apartment in anticipation of the fulfillment of her dream of finally riding as a jockey in her first race.

Her phone rang and she grabbed at it and launched her tiny body on to her bed. "Hi!"

"Hey Lil, I am so sorry that I can't be there with you tomorrow," Buck started.

"Don't be silly. You're riding in the Belmont! How is everything there?" she asked him, trying to turn her thoughts from her first race the following day.

"Oh, it's buzzing for sure. The first chance for a Triple Crown winner since Affirmed! Of course, I wish I was riding Pisano, but if anyone can get him home first, it will be Pat," Buck said.

"Gosh, he is a legend around here," Lilly commented. "Every time Pat Day gets on the back of a horse, he has a chance to win. I hope I can have that reputation one day."

"Not everyone likes his style of riding, you know. He's known as Patient Pat to some, as he likes to have his mounts wait until the last second to make their moves. It drives some of the trainers crazy. But he must be doing something right with all his winning. Did you know some years ago, he won eight of nine races in a single day? That is unheard of!" Buck exclaimed. He knew she was nervous about tomorrow as he continued to try to distract her with tales of Pat Day.

"Well, I'm sure you will ride a fabulous race regardless of the great Pat Day," Lilly said, shakiness in her voice. Buck picked up on it.

"And so will you, tomorrow," he said.

"I'm so nervous, Buck," Lilly confided in him. Buck had turned into her most trusted confidant. Their friendship had only grown with their relationship. He and Lilly would spend their time dissecting each horse in every race they saw. They would argue over what the jockeys could have done differently to get their horses to win.

They were each stubborn with their own perspectives. Lilly would side with what she interpreted as the emotions of the horse and Buck would point out the jockey's perspective. They had fun egging each other on, but these conversations always left Lilly with another nugget of information on how she would ride her first race.

"Lilly, I've told you a million times. No, a billion times. You were MADE for this! You are going to do so great, and I am so proud of you, and I better get a play-by-play the minute you're finished." Lilly laughed lightly and breathed deeply.

"I love you," she said. She was lying on her side and could see her reflection in the mirror that hung above the sink across the tiny space.

"I love you, too."

She watched her reflection smile wide at the words that came back at her across the phone. "I better go, I have to be ready to go pretty early in the morning."

"Stop worrying, eat protein for breakfast, pee before you get on the horse, and remember to have fun," Buck said. Lilly laughed out a goodbye and hung up the phone.

The Jockey Room

Lilly hadn't slept as well as she would have liked. At 3:30 she couldn't take it anymore, got out of bed, and got dressed for the day's work. She would be riding in her first race this afternoon, but she still had to get her morning chores done and exercise the horses Tom assigned to her. It would be a long day, but well worth it.

At 10:30, Lilly ran upstairs and took a quick shower. She looked at herself in the mirror and whispered to herself, "Today's the day."

She allowed herself a brief moment to let it all sink in, taking big breaths in and out to calm her beating heart. She walked down the stairs and into the tack room to grab her helmet.

Gus was sitting in his customary spot, shining up one of the well-worn bridles. He watched her, a toothpick sticking out the side of his mouth, working it along his teeth as he worked the cleaner into the leather of the bridle.

"Gotta go, Gus," Lilly said to him as she made her way out the door of the tack room.

"Come back in one piece, you hear me? Don't let those boys push you around," Gus called to her as she heard the door close behind her. *Oh great,* Lilly thought, *just the words of encouragement I need.* But that was Gus, honest to the core, and sugar-coating words was not his strong-suit.

Lilly walked around the big oval towards the imposing grandstand on the other side of the track. She and Buck had made this walk many times over the last year and had toured every inch of the property, sneaking in different spots to steal a kiss, but today was different.

Lost in her own thoughts of her dream and Buck, her feet made their way along the track. She pushed the thoughts of her parents to the far recesses of her mind, not wanting to ruin her big day. She turned towards the large open garage door that led her into the bowels of the grandstand. In front of her were fourteen empty saddling stalls of the track's indoor paddock area.

"This is so weird," Lilly had said to Buck when he first showed her the race track's unique paddock.

"Yeah, I can't say I have seen any other indoor saddling area at any of the other tracks I have ridden," Buck replied.

"But how can anyone watch the horses getting saddled? There is barely any room in here," Lilly mused.

"Well, most can see from up behind those windows," Buck pointed out, walking around the perimeter on the clubhouse side of the building. "Remember, this is one of the oldest racetracks in the country, maybe it couldn't fit anywhere else so they needed to put it under the building?"

Buck pulled her around the end of the paddock. "Now, close your eyes."

"What?"

"Close your eyes," Buck repeated.

Lilly smiled and did what she was told, closing her eyes as Buck guided her slowly, making sure she didn't bang into the end of a stall wall. He stopped her. "Now open them."

Lilly opened her eyes and in front of her was a sign that read "Female Jockeys Only." She stood still as a rush of pins and needles covered her body. "You want to go in?" Buck asked.

"No way!" She took a step back. "That will jinx it." Buck laughed. Lilly punched him in the shoulder.

"How about the jockey room over there?" Buck asked, pointing to the door up the short set of stairs on the other side of the paddock area.

"No, I am not going into any of these rooms until I am riding in my first race," Lilly said, and grabbing Buck's hand, she pulled them out of the shadows of the dimly lit paddock area underneath the massive grandstand and into the sunlight of the day.

Now, Lilly stood once again in front of the door that read "Female Jockeys Only." She had kept her promise and hadn't entered the paddock area since Buck had shown her around. She was superstitious and she wasn't going to let anything sidetrack her dream.

She reached a shaky hand out to turn the handle. It wouldn't turn. A lump in her stomach started to grow. She tried harder and still it didn't turn. It was locked. Lilly could feel her anxiety starting to get the better of her, and her hands grew cold and clammy. She looked around frantically. Now what was she going to do.

Maybe she was too early. She didn't ride until the second race. No, that wasn't it, Buck had told her the doors are always open early, because the jockeys started to arrive at about 10:30 to get ready for the day.

The paddock area was deserted. She looked through the windows of the clubhouse on the opposite wall, and could just make out a few workers setting up for today's races. Should she knock on the window?

As she stood there pondering her next move, she could hear whistling, and a uniformed security guard walked into the paddock from a door that read "Administrative Offices."

He looked at Lilly inquisitively. "Hello there, can I help you?"

"Um, well, yes…..sir," Lilly stammered.

The guard held out his hand. "Captain Russell."

"Um, Captain Russell," Lilly started, reaching out to shake his hand with her clammy one, "you see…um….I'm-I'm riding today and I can't seem to get into my jockey room."

Captain Russell raised his eyebrows. "And you are?"

"Oh, sorry, yes, I am Lilly Garrett, Elizabeth Garrett, sir…Captain," she said.

"Why, yes, Ms. Garrett, of course. I am head of security here at Pimlico. I had instructed one of my men to open the door for you today. We don't have many female jockeys here, so we generally don't keep this door unlocked, for security reasons. Can't have someone hiding in here and then popping out when the horses walk by, given the room is right here in the paddock area. I guess they couldn't find a better place for a separate area from the boys. I still don't know why they couldn't carve out a small room upstairs adjacent to the main jockey room," he said apologetically. Captain Russell pulled a large ring of keys from his pocket. "Now, let's see which one of these works."

After trying a few different keys, he finally found the one that worked, unlocked the door, and opened it for Lilly to enter. Lilly didn't move, her feet frozen to the floor.

"Ma'am?" Captain Russell encouraged.

Lilly looked up at the large man standing next to her, said, "Um, okay," and stepped across the threshold of her new world.

The room in front of her was empty and sparse of furniture. The walls were a pale yellow, with a brown utility rug throughout. *To hide the dirt,* Lilly thought to herself.

"Anything else I can do for you, Ms. Garrett?"

"Um, no, I'm fine. Thank you so much." Lilly turned a bright smile to Captain Russell.

"Now, if you need anything, you head on up to the main jockey room where you will find the rest of the jockeys hanging out, as well as the kitchen, which serves up the best grub in the whole place," he finished.

"Okay," Lilly said to him, turning back to the lonely room in front of her.

A brown frayed massage table was directly in front of her, with a few random chairs tossed around. Brown laminated lockers lined the walls and the blank screen of a TV stared at her from across the room. Holding the prominent position in the room was the scale, a big black platform to stand on with a black digital reader that stood a few inches taller than Lilly.

Lilly dropped her helmet and stood on the scale, which read "105." She let out her breath, but made a small promise to herself that she would not allow herself to get obsessed with her weight and develop an eating disorder. She stepped off the scale and did a quick walk through of the small area.

The first room led to a second room with more lockers and a few faux leather office-type bucket chairs. Through a door was the bathroom with a couple of toilet stalls and a shower. A steam tub used to sweat off extra pounds was squeezed into the corner, another piece of equipment Lilly hoped she would never need.

Another scale was present in this room, but this one reminded Lilly of the scale that she had to stand on in her doctor's office during her annual physicals for school. The one with the two sliders along the top, one for the 50-100-150 pounds and the other to track the individual pounds. Lilly stood on this scale and slid the bottom slider to 100 and jimmied the top slider until it sat on the 5.

"Well, at least, the scales are consistent," she said out loud. The words echoed off the bathroom walls.

Lilly opened another door and peered into a room with two bunk beds. *Sleep, who had time for sleep?* she thought. Then again, if she was going to be in here all day long, the beds may come in handy for a cat nap.

"I guess I should get comfortable," she said. Sitting in one of the chairs in the room all by herself, Lilly's anxiety started to return. She couldn't just sit here for two hours until her race was called.

Lilly pulled out the Daily Racing Form and reviewed the entries in her race for the umpteenth time. She sat on down on the massage table and tried to meditate. She paced the length of the room to try to calm her nerves. Her footfalls echoed off the pale-yellow walls. She was used to being around a lot of activity in the backstretch, and being in this jockey room all alone was starting to feel unbearable.

Lilly peered out the door into the paddock and glanced at the black iron stair case up to the sign that read "Jock's Room, Employees and Jockeys Only." The paddock area was starting to fill with people waiting for the horses to arrive for the first race.

Well, Captain Russell said I was welcome to hang up there too, she thought.

She looked at her watch, 12:30pm. Still another hour until her race, she needed to do something.

She silently slipped out of the female jockey room, closed the door behind her, making sure it didn't lock, and walked across the paddock and up the stairs. She pushed open the door, which led to another set of stairs in a dark stairwell. She made her feet move up each step to the top to another door.

Lilly paused before pushing the door open. She took a deep breath and wiped her sweaty hands on her legs. The dark stairwell was closing in on her.

"You can do this!" she whispered to herself. Her heart was pounding in her chest. Lilly took another deep breath.

The cell phone in her back pocket vibrated. She pulled it out and glanced at the screen.

"Stay true to your instincts, Lilly. You have what it takes to be great. Go get 'em! B."

Lilly smiled, as her eyes welled up with tears. She fought them back, utilizing her habit of pulling her lower lids away from her eyes to make the water go away and not fall down her cheeks. She didn't reply as she knew he didn't need to. But she kept the text on the screen of her phone as she hit the off button and slid it back into her pocket. She was on her own now.

Steeling herself for what might lie beyond the door, Lilly pushed it open and stepped inside. She hoped she could remember everything Buck had told her about what to expect.

The easy-going chit-chat came to a stop. She could feel all eyes turn to her. Lilly straightened her back, took a deep breath, and looked around the room, which served as the jockey's lounge.

Jockeys were in various stages of undress, relaxing before the afternoon races. Several sat on old couches in front of televisions. Two were playing ping pong, their game momentarily forgotten as she entered. A group playing cards had also stopped to look at her.

At the far end of the room, Lilly could see the kitchen and the cook busily preparing various food choices. Buck had laughed when he told her that the best food was made here in this kitchen, right in front of the same people who ate it the least. But the kitchen was open to all the track workers, so there was a lot of activity in this part of the building.

Through the open door to her right, Lilly saw a man sitting at a desk and beyond him, down a hall, she saw rows and rows of vibrantly colored jockey silks. She had commented to Buck that silk was such a flimsy fabric that she was shocked that they didn't tear during the race. He then informed her that the silks, while originally made of silk, were now mostly nylon or lycra, making them more aerodynamic.

Lilly felt glued in place, her feet like cinder blocks. She took in the small group gathered around a TV, awaiting the start of the first race of the day. Several held the Daily Racing Form in their hands in order to mark the results.

As the activity returned to normal in the room in front of her, she walked a few steps through the door on her right.

Her eyes rested on the scale. Just like Buck had described. It wasn't like the small square scale that had sat on the floor of her mother's bathroom and it seemed bigger than the one in her jockey room. The large white dial stood at the same height as her face, rimmed in grey, along with a big platform on which to stand. It was the first stop for every jockey entering the room, Buck had told her, so they would know how much time might be needed in the steam room to make weight for the day. Most jockeys could lose one to one and half pounds in thirty minutes just by sweating it out.

The scale was also the last stop for jockeys before heading out of the room for a race. *No wonder it had such prominence in the room,* thought Lilly, *these men had to live their lives depending on what this piece of equipment told them.*

Toward the back of the room, she noticed the same kind of massage table that was in her locker room. Lilly had joked with Buck that she was looking forward to her weekly massage, but it certainly didn't look like any spa that she had imagined Angie and Macy frequenting. The brown fabric covering was frayed and didn't look at all comfortable. She supposed the jockeys didn't mind though. It was just a table on which jockeys stretched out to get sore muscles loosened and tense minds relaxed.

Around the walls were brown wooden cubicles, which served as lockers to house the jockeys' equipment. Each jockey owned several saddles of various weights, along with boots, vests, and goggles—the gear of their career. Running in front of the cubicles were wooden benches, and in the center of the room was another storage area holding the protective vests.

A half-dressed man sat on a nearby bench, the Daily Racing Form in his right hand, and a green highlighter in his left. The other jockeys had turned back to their own activities, their chatter again filling the adjacent room.

"Good day, Ms. Lilly," a voice called out to her, "thank you for coming up here to get me. I apologize for not meeting you downstairs."

Lilly turned towards where she heard the voice coming from, and a slender man about a foot taller than her was striding toward her holding a set of red and white silks. She couldn't find her voice.

"I have all your equipment ready to go, if you will follow me, please." He gently laid a hand on her arm and turned her around, guiding her back down the dark stairwell. When they reached the bottom of the stairs, Lilly stopped and looked at him, questioning.

"Buck asked that I look after you. I am his valet when he is in town. Roy's my name, pleased to meet you," he said, holding out his hand.

Lilly held out her hand for him to shake. "I was down here earlier but the empty room was making me batty."

"Yes, I imagine it would, being the only girl right now. We do get some others around here occasionally for the big races, but haven't had a resident female jockey here in a while." Roy pushed open the door for her to enter.

"We don't have much time. Once the first race kicks off, it seems like it is one right after the other. I have all your equipment ready to go. The weights are in pockets of the saddle pad for when you go to step on the scales. Can I have your helmet, please?" Roy held out his hand. Lilly passed her black helmet over to him and watched him expertly pull on the red and white silk cap.

"Now, let's get you dressed for your first race," he said.

He handed Lilly a pair of bright white jockey silk pants. Lilly slid off her athletic pants, thankful for her compression shorts, and slid the pants on. The pants were baggy around her upper legs, but tightened around her lower legs and calf muscles in order for the pants to fit inside her riding boots.

Roy then held out her protective vest, as well as a white compression athletic short sleeve shirt. "You will be more comfortable with this shirt under the silks."

Lilly pulled at the T-shirt she had on. "I can't wear this one?"

"Unfortunately, no. I have already accounted for all the weight, and if you wear that one you will throw off the weight I have put in the saddle pad." Roy continued to hold out the shirt in front of him.

Lilly grabbed the shirt out of Roy's hand and turned away from him towards the locker. With her back to him, she pulled off her cotton T-shirt and quickly yanked on the nylon one. Luckily, she had worn a white bra this morning, she thought to herself. She turned to Roy and he was holding out her protective vest so she could slide her arms into the armholes.

"Quickly now, your boots have been all shined up," he said as he pulled them from the locker behind her.

Lilly sat in the chair in front of her, took one of her boots from Roy, and stopped short. "Oh my goodness, they are so shiny!"

Roy smiled. "That's my job."

"I would never have been able to get them to look this great." Lilly marveled at the reflection off the black toe of her boot, as well as how the few inches of brown leather around the top of the boot looked brand new. Not a scrape could be found, yet she had worn these boots every day for over a year.

Roy helped Lilly slide her feet into each of her boots.

"Here, please put these on while I grab your equipment." Roy left the red and white silk top and her helmet on the bench next to her. Lilly slid her arm into the soft silk of the shirt. Her heart started to beat quicker as she buttoned it up. She twisted her ponytail into a bun and stuffed it all into her helmet.

Roy returned with her saddle, girth, and saddle pad.

"I didn't realize I would need this much help," Lilly commented to him.

"Every jockey has a valet assigned," Roy said to her as they made their way to the large scale in the corner. "It's my job to make sure you have the appropriate silks for each race, that your equipment is spick and span—boots, saddle, goggles—and I also make sure your horse gets saddled appropriately for your race. I'll meet you after the race as well to take your equipment from the race back to the jockey's room."

"Wow, that's great. Thanks for the help!" Lilly said innocently.

Roy smiled at her. "Here you go, get up on that scale."

Lilly grabbed the saddle, girth, and saddle pad from Roy and stepped onto the scale. The scale bounced up to 116. Lilly stepped off the scale.

"Whew," Roy said to her, "I'm always a bit anxious heading into the weigh-in of a new jockey. I haven't lost my touch." Roy took the equipment from Lilly and led her out the door and into the paddock for her first race.

 # First Race

Lilly closed her eyes before pushing the door open that would lead her to the paddock and to the life she had always dreamed about.

Her first ride on Hank seemed so long ago. So much had happened since.

Lilly had been on a whirlwind of rides since that morning when she let her instincts take over and pushed Hank to a gear he had not previously exhibited. Buck had been right, Tom had taken her under his wing. Lilly had become his go-to girl for all his morning exercise rides. Under his tutelage, Lilly's learning curve grew exponentially.

Tom taught her the difference between a speed horse, one that liked to break first and run out first in a race, and the plodder and closer, who came from way back in the pack during a race to finish strong. Sometimes Buck joined them during their morning workouts to work on Lilly's racing strategy; he showed her how to come around a horse on the turn or cut inside to take up a hole left on the rail by a drifting horse.

In many cases, Tom and Buck would turn to each other and raise their eyebrows in unison, realizing that Lilly's intuition was the best teacher and that there wasn't much more they could impart to her. They knew she would get her next level of training on the big stage, in a real race.

Lilly's reputation in working with the hot-heads as well as the plodders was growing throughout the backstretch of Pimlico. Other trainers noticed her and asked her to work with more challenging horses. She would do more than just exercise them; she would spend time with them, groom them and figure out their nuances, finding out what exactly made them tick and not tick, as the case may be.

Lilly spent time talking to their grooms and learning about their routines. Many times, it was through these conversations that Lilly would find out the most about a horse and its habits. And it was because of Tom that all of that had been possible.

Lilly owed everything to Tom. He had taken a chance on a naïve waif of a girl, and now here she was, about to ride in a real race.

After leaving the jockey room, Lilly approached Tom where he waited for her to provide last-minute instructions. His words of wisdom were limited, as he knew she was the only one who could get Hank running so he could possibly be competitive in the race. With a brief hug, he dropped his hand around Lilly's knee and hoisted her into the saddle. Once she was settled, Tom squeezed her leg.

"You be safe out there."

She wondered if he told all his jockeys to be safe.

The whole episode had been a blur, from the jockey room to the paddock, but now Lilly found herself in the post parade just minutes away from the start of her first race. Sweat ran down her forehead from the edge of her helmet and threatened to drop into her left eye. Lilly blinked. She could feel the wetness. Her pupil could just make out the edge of the droplet hanging from her eyebrow. She blinked again, trying to get it to drop.

"Come on!" she whispered to herself as she grabbed both reins in her right hand and swiped the sweat off her forehead with her left.

Lilly was a wreck, sweating like it was the dead heat of August versus the coolness of the first week of June.

Tom had planned everything to hopefully ensure her success, though he couldn't control her emotions; Lilly needed to do that.

"You okay, little lady?" the outrider asked her. Lilly didn't take offense to his words. She was a girl and she was the tiniest one of all the jockeys around her. It came with the territory of working in a sport that was primarily run by men.

"Yes, fine," she replied, giving him a shaky smile. "Actually, no."

"The first one is always the hardest. But each race and horse you ride will give you a new experience—each and every time. The thrill of riding a race never gets old," he told her.

The outrider grabbed the leather strap that ran through Hank's bridle as they proceeded into the post parade for the first race on June 6. Lilly's senior year at school had ended the previous week. Even though she had moved out of her parent's house, she had kept her promise to them and graduated. Now it was time for her to keep her promise to herself and make this first, most important step in her dream of becoming a professional jockey.

She had worked so hard over the last year, both in school and at the track, and her dream was coming true today! Lilly's hands began to shake. Overcome with emotion, tears started to well up in her eyes. She tried to distract herself. She couldn't let Hank get all wired up just because she was dealing with a case of the nerves. Lilly shook her head.

"Were you a jockey, sir?" she asked the outrider. Lilly could see the elderly man smile slightly as he urged them all into a trot.

"You could say that," he answered. "I had a few winners, but I rode a lot of horses. I enjoy this part of it now that my old body can't support itself. The knees just can't hold that position anymore." He nodded to her legs positioned at a tight 45 degree angle.

The parade in front of the grandstand was over, and it was time to stretch out Hank's legs before they entered the starting gate. They jogged down the lane together. Up ahead, the outrider would let them go and Lilly would be responsible for galloping Hank a bit to settle him down. Hank didn't really need to be settled down, Lilly thought, but she certainly needed the time to calm her nerves.

"Is it worth it?" she asked him.

"You'll never want to do anything else," he replied.

There was no more time to ask any further questions as they had reached the turn. It was time for Lilly to be on her own.

"Good luck, little lady," the man said to her. "Try to appreciate every moment. Your first race will never happen again."

Lilly looked into his weathered face. His wrinkling eyes sparkled with a knowledge she only could dream of attaining. Lilly gave him a quick smile and directed her attention to Hank.

Lilly glanced up at the grandstand. Macy and Angela were there somewhere. They had promised to come to her first race. Thoughts of disappointing her parents entered her mind. She had so wished they would have come around and would have been watching and experiencing her joy with her. Lilly pushed the thoughts from her mind. She had avoided them for a reason. She hated confrontation. She had been their perfect child for her entire life.

Macy and Angela had tried to talk her out of becoming a jockey, but after riding in the car with them day after day, year after year, they knew the extent of Lilly's passion. Macy had spent hours counseling Lilly on the drastic decision to move out of her parent's house, but Lilly wouldn't back down. Her parents had forced her hand and had criticized her passion for both racing and the boy she had fallen in love with. "A toxic choice," they'd called him.

Lilly shook her head, needing to focus on the task at hand.

Hank's easy gallop could lull anyone to sleep, but Lilly knew beneath his easy-going nature there was a beast to be set free. Only she had found his trigger point and now, together, they were being put to the test. This was her first race and Hank's first race since he had been moved to train with Tom. Tom had invested a lot of time in her and Hank. He had been her support both emotionally and financially when she packed her bags and moved to the track. She would do him proud.

Lilly turned Hank around and headed for the starting gate in front of them. Even though it was the same gate they had practiced in, it looked like an entirely different creature today. A big green and white monstrosity. A line of tiny stalls, barely two feet wide. In just a few moments, as all the horses were loaded, the starting gate would become a shifting mass of horses, jockeys, and starting crew. Luckily, Hank didn't have any adversity to the gate. All the commotion was new to Lilly, however.

Lilly laid her hand on Hank's shoulder. "It's okay, buddy," she said, though she knew she was the one who needed calming. Tom had told Lilly to stay to the back as they approached the gate. Hank was a pro, but Lilly's nerves were frayed. She concentrated on the gate handler who approached to lead Hank into the stall.

"Ready to go, Lilly?" he asked.

"First time for everything, right, Jim?" Lilly croaked out of her dry throat. Jim had been there every morning the last few weeks helping to teach Lilly to break out of the gate safely and effectively.

"Remember what I taught you and you'll be fine. Keep your knees tight against Hank's sides so they don't get banged up on the sides of the gate." What he didn't mention was no matter how much training they had done, the gate always felt smaller and more claustrophobic in a race.

Jim led Hank into the number 4 stall of the gate, which had barely enough room for his hindquarters to fit. The two green butt gates slammed shut behind them. Lilly jumped a bit. Hank was the fourth horse in, and she had to wait for the other four horses to her right to load. The white bars in front of Hank's head loomed large, as neither horse nor rider could see over them, but had to look through them. Lilly breathed slowly in and out, trying to calm her racing heart. She felt palpitations, and her anxiety started to overcome her. The gate was starting to close in on her and the expanse of racetrack in front of her blurred. She wrapped her hand into Hank's mane to steady herself.

"You okay, Lilly?" Jim asked, standing on the platform to the left of Hank's head.

Before she could answer, the starter hit the button and the gates split open in front of them, and the dragged dirt before them awaited fresh tracks.

Thank goodness for Hank, her hand wrapped in his mane, and Jim's advice to keep her knees tight, or else Lilly would have been left sitting on her butt in the dirt of the starting gate.

As Hank took his first strides out of the gate, it was like slow motion. He didn't jerk out of the gate to gain his footing. Hank sat back on his hind and pushed off like a cat ready to bounce in one smooth motion. This hesitation helped Lilly snap to attention, while leaving them behind the others. Within just a few strides, Hank was in full flight, running with the other horses in front of them.

After riding any and all horses thrown at her, Lilly had gained a strong intuition and auto reflex as it came to dealing with the unexpected. She had horses try to unseat her by rearing or bucking or moving sideways in the blink of an eye. She had developed a second sense in anticipating a horse's movement. Thankfully, it was that intuition that kicked in when her anxiety was at its highest.

Lilly settled herself over Hank's withers, balancing on the balls of her feet, the muscles in her thighs keeping her butt high out of the saddle. As she did with all her rides, she listened for Hank's rhythm. Focusing on the four beats of his stride helped her stay in the zone instead of getting overwhelmed with what was playing out around her.

Lilly took stock of her situation. Hank was towards the back of the pack, but not dead last. There was a horse running to her right, its head bobbing next to her leg.

The white track rail was a blur to their left, and a horse raced directly ahead of them.

Oh boy, thought Lilly. She had yet to be in this situation, running with seven other horses. All her training had been with, at the most, two other horses. As much guidance as Buck and Tom had given her, she had to develop her own racing strategy as the race developed. A trainer can provide information and instruction prior to the race, but it's the jockey who needs to make the final decisions as the race actually unfolds.

Think, Lilly, she admonished herself. Hank was running smoothly. Tom had put her in a longer race so she would have the time to settle in and decide what to do. The race was a mile and an eighth. She would have almost two minutes to think before the finish line. *How do I get Hank to the front? I guess that's better than one minute*, Lilly thought to herself, which is all she would have had in a sprint race.

Lilly stole a glance up to the leaders ahead of her. Two were running neck and neck, with two more behind them, then the horse in front of her and the horse to her right. From her perched position, Lilly glanced under her arm and saw the last horse running right behind them.

She was boxed in. How was she going to get out of this mess? Hank was waiting for her to do something. The half mile pole whizzed by them. They had already run through half the race. Lilly tried to take Hank off the rail a bit.

"Hey, hey!" the jockey yelled to her right. She couldn't go that way or she would impede the path of his horse and possibly cause a fall, or at a minimum an inquiry into her unsafe riding.

The horse in front of her was going nowhere. In fact, she felt Hank's stride shorten as the horse in front of them slowed a bit. The horse to her right now raced at her shoulder. She could see the jockey urging him on, but then not moving any further to go by them.

"Come on, guys!" Lilly screamed to the riders around her. They weren't budging. Were they boxing her in on purpose? Did they have a plan to embarrass the new girl? Lilly's mind reeled. How was she going to get out of this mess?

She thought about what the outrider had said to her. She would never have a first race again. She didn't want to be known as a reckless rider, but she had to earn her fellow jockeys respect. They were testing her. This was her initiation.

The horse in front of Hank veered out a little from the rail, and Lilly saw her chance in an instant.

"Come on, Hank!" She threw her hands up his neck and rocked him into the tiny space that emerged in front of them. It was the action Hank had been waiting for. He accelerated instantaneously. As they surged through the hole at the rail, the jockeys looked over at them in surprise. They hadn't expected Lilly to take the risk of coming up on the rail in her first race.

The horses came around the far turn into the homestretch. The field spread out along the track as each jockey made their move to bring their horse home first.

Lilly continued to urge Hank on, through the hole, past the horse to his right and between two horses in front of him. He ran at the lone horse ahead of him as they raced for the wire. Suddenly, the horse that had been racing behind them at the start entered her peripheral vision, racing down the center of the track.

Lilly pumped Hank on with her entire body, moving her arms with the motion of his head, urging him to go on.

Hank tried valiantly, stretching out his long body with each stride, but he was running out of steam. As they crossed under the wire, the horse in front held on to win and the horse coming down the center overtook them for second.

Lilly finished third.

Lilly threw her arms around Hank's neck. She had done it. She was a jockey. Her adrenaline rushed through her veins. *If this is what it feels like to race and come in third, god knows how it feels to win a race,* Lilly thought to herself. She couldn't stop smiling as she turned Hank around and trotted back toward the grandstand.

Tom came up to them and took hold of Hank's bridle. Lilly jumped to the ground. Roy was right behind her, and stepped forward to unstrap the girth and pull her saddle off Hank. "Great first run, Ms. Lilly," he said as he handed her the tack.

As she turned to head to the scale to get her weight rechecked, Tom pulled her into a bear hug.

"Great job, Lilly," he whispered into her ear.

Lilly looked up at him, her cheeks flushed red with her excitement. "Oh, thank you so much, Tom! Thank you for giving me a chance to do what I love. It was awesome. I owe everything to you."

Lilly turned to walk to the scales and didn't see the flash of pride mixed with obsession in Tom's eyes, a response to the words she had just uttered.

A Bug's Life

"How does it feel to be a bug?" Buck joked.

Lilly punched his arm, laughing. She was still basking in the light of her first race.

"Jealous?" she retorted.

"Nah, I would have to get my weight down even further to go back to my days of being a bug," he replied seriously.

She ran her arm through his as they leaned against the rail and looked out onto the track.

"Where does the term 'bug' come from anyway?" she asked.

"It's the asterisk next to their weight assignment in the program," he told her.

"Well, lucky me, I get to be ten pounds lighter for all those trainers who are going to be knocking down my door," she said sarcastically.

Buck tightened his hold on her arm. "You sell yourself short, Lilly. Trainers of horses that are assigned to carry a weight of 125 are going to come running. Your 'bug' status allows their horse to carry ten pounds less. Those ten pounds carried around for a mile on the back of their horse may mean the difference between first and last.

"The weight assigned in a race includes not just the jockey but everything that will be riding on the back of the horse, including the saddle, stirrups, helmet, whip, goggles, everything. You're 100 pounds soaking wet. You don't have to be constantly monitoring your weight, so the trainers won't have to worry if you are going to be over the weight allowed for the race. Roy will just have to make sure he is on his game to make sure the added weights in the saddle pad add up to what the horse is supposed to carry," Buck smirked. "On top of that, you actually know how to ride."

Lilly looked down at the ground to hide her smile. Buck's compliment meant the world to her. She focused on the conversation to keep her sanity and not just melt here with love right in front of him.

"How many races do I get to keep the weight allowance?" she asked.

"Until you win five races, which won't take you long, I'm sure. Then you get seven pounds usually up until 30 wins. Depends on the state. If you are a superstar and win 35 races prior to end of your first year, then you get five pounds for one year from the date of your fifth winner," Buck finished.

"Can I be a bug indefinitely?" Lilly asked.

"I think you either win out of it or after four years, but since I rode through my bug status within 18 months, I didn't really pay attention to how long I had," Buck replied. "The lower weight requirement for a bug really helps a jockey get their business started. If they carried the same weights as the pros, the trainers wouldn't want to risk the stupid mistakes that a newbie is going to make. They basically trade lack of expertise for lower weight," Buck continued. "But given your natural ability and instinct, I'd wager any trainer is getting both."

Lilly was speechless for the second time on the heels of his compliment. She was the luckiest person in the world, doing what she loved and being around the person she loved the most.

 # First Win

With a rush, they broke out of the starting gate as a group. All six horses were the same color, bays with no distinctive markings. It took the announcer a second to iron out who to call out in first. He made out the silks of Morehead Stables and surprised even himself.

"It's Tremely Hot breaking first with Lilly Garrett aboard, shooting to the early lead by a head, closely followed by Quicksilver. Bunched tightly with them is Brown Bill, Fashion Sense, My Dream, and Worrisome. Barely a length separates them all. In this short of a race at five furloughs, no one is giving way. This sprint is anyone's race."

Lilly pressed Tremely Hot, or Hottie, as she liked to call him. Mr. Morehead had given her the ride at Tom's recommendation. Hottie was a sprinter and needed to break first to have a chance to win. The problem was that none of his jockeys could get him to settle enough in the gate to break fast. The horse was always distracted by the goings on around him: the other horses being loaded and the handlers. He would nudge at the gate in front of him in his anxiety and was never prepared for the opening.

Lilly hadn't had a lot of time to work with Hottie, just a workout earlier in the week. Tom had noticed how the horse responded to her quiet demeanor. Even though he only had one chance to watch them together, he called up Mr. Morehead to encourage him to give Lilly a chance.

Lilly thought back to all her talks with Buck about what the life of a jockey entailed.

She would have to maintain a certain weight and be stronger than an ox to control an animal ten times her weight. She'd have to sit in a locker room next to her competitors in every race. In each race, there is only one winner and then the jockeys all have to go back to the same space, sit a few feet from each other getting ready for the next race, and do it again. Day in and day out, up to ten times a day. She imagined having to deal with that rush of adrenaline over and over again, and then having to be nice to the guy sitting next to her after he just whipped her butt in the previous race.

But she loved this feeling of riding with the wind atop these beautiful animals that gave their heart each and every time they stepped onto the racetrack.

With Lilly sitting tight on his back, Hottie continued his onslaught towards the finish line. Tom had been right, he only had to break clean and in first to have a chance.

The horses all around started to press at them, and Lilly moved her hand slightly up Hottie's neck. That was all he needed as they raced toward the finish line, six horses spread out across the track. Lilly held her breath for a moment. Her heart was beating right out of her chest as they rushed over the finish line. She closed her eyes as they raced past the finish pole.

She knew it.

Hottie had won. Lilly had just won her first race. The buzz in in her ears was loud and her hands were shaking.

Oh my god! I did it! Lilly thought to herself. "Actually, you did it, Mr. Hottie." Lilly patted the horse on his neck and slowed him to a bouncy trot. She turned him around and trotted towards the winner's circle.

"Congrats, Lilly," a call came from behind her.

"Thanks, Scott," she called to the jockey over her shoulder. Her voice was shaking.

Don't you cry, she scolded herself, but she couldn't wipe the ridiculous grin off her face. Tom approached with a lead rope to take Hottie and walk them towards the winner's circle.

"Great job, Lilly, I knew you would get your first one," he said to her. Lilly couldn't speak. She just continued to smile at him.

Mr. Morehead walked slowly up to them, leaning on his cane. An elderly grey-haired woman stood next to him, looking at Lilly closely.

"Nice job, Lilly. I wasn't sure about putting you up on him, but Tom convinced us." He smiled at the woman standing next to him. "Didn't he, love?"

Mrs. Morehead smiled at him and looked up at Lilly sitting on Hottie's back. "I think we have found our regular rider, Simon. Now let's smile for the picture."

Lilly jumped off and grabbed her saddle from Roy as he took it off of Hottie. As she turned, Tom caught her off guard and wrapped her in a big bear hug. "You deserve it."

"Thanks Tom," she finally could muster and walked towards the scales.

Lilly walked quickly back towards the jockey's room. As much as she wanted to relish her win, she had the next race to think about. She didn't ride in many races each day, as she hadn't built up a clientele, but today she was in back to back races.

Lost in thought, Lilly didn't see it coming.

Out of nowhere, jockeys descended on her. They covered her in anything they could get their hands on. Some had run to the kitchen and grabbed ketchup and mustard, as well as a carton of eggs. Others had grabbed what they could find in the locker room, Vaseline and shaving cream.

"No, Greg, not the shoe polish," she heard a familiar voice say.

Buck stood in front of her, laughing.

Lilly angrily wiped the shaving cream from her face. "What is all this about, I need to get ready for my next race!"

"Pipe down, missy, everyone gets 'creamed'" when they win their first race." Buck said, adding more shaving cream to the top of Lilly's head for good measure. "Congrats on breaking your maiden!"

The jockeys surrounded her, laughing. Lilly realized they were not laughing at her, but laughing in the excitement of welcoming someone into their midst as a winner.

She finally heard the comments they showered on her. "Great job, congrats, you're on your way."

She wasn't an outsider anymore.

Buck walked with Lilly as she made her evening rounds to say goodbye to the horses. It was her nightly ritual before she went up to her apartment. She was still on cloud nine after winning her first race. After she had quickly showered to rid herself of all the yuck the other jockeys had creamed her with, Lilly rode in the next race and finished second. Not a bad day for riding.

Her compatriots cheered her on today, but she knew tomorrow they would be watchful. She had become another credible competitor they had to beat when they were all out on the track.

Buck held her hand. He was so worldly, yet only two years older than her. They slowed as they reached the end of the row of stalls, standing next to an empty one. Its occupant had been shipped out that morning. Lilly leaned against the wall next to the half door.

"Hey," Buck said softly.

"Hey," Lilly answered back.

"I am so proud of you, you know," he said to her, running his thumb along her jawline.

Lilly swallowed. The sun was setting behind his head. The glare made it hard to make out the other features of his face. She got lost in the dark of his eyes.

"How did you feel?" he asked her, still rubbing her face.

Lilly raised her eyebrows, her thoughts in a jumble.

"How did you feel," he asked again, "when you won?"

Oh right, Lilly thought. She paused for a moment. How could she possibly put that feeling into words? She closed her eyes, recalling the rush of adrenaline as she was coming down the last of the homestretch and running under the wire in first.

"Like when I was a kid and my dad took me on my first roller coaster ride. You truly don't know what to expect as the coaster goes up the track, you can't breathe in anticipation. Then it peaks and you race down the first big hill, screaming at the top of your lungs. Your stomach drops out and your heart beats out of your chest as you race around the track. Then, when it is all over, it takes several moments to get your heart to slow down and return your breathing to normal." She smiled up at him.

Buck's eyes grew darker. Lilly's breath caught in her chest, all the feelings she felt this afternoon rushing to the surface. She could feel her heart pounding in her chest. She reached up and wrapped her hand around his neck and pulled him close. She didn't want this feeling to end.

Buck leaned in against her, pressing her to the barn wall. Lilly couldn't think. His kisses were everywhere, on her lips, on her neck. She loved the feeling. She always had to be in control. It felt great to let it all go and lean into the feelings Buck was bringing out in her.

She pulled at the stall latch and opened the door, dragging Buck behind her. They fell onto the deep fresh straw that had been put down after the last occupant had left. The setting sun streamed through the half open door, the rays glowing on the far wall above their heads.

Buck lifted his head. "You are so special, Lilly." He pulled a bit of straw from her hair as she looked up at him.

"I'm not sure what to do about you. I am usually so confident and certain about my life, but you have thrown a wrench into my thoughts. I had my whole life figured out. I was going to travel from track to track and win the top jockey award at each one. Now all I want to do is stay here with you," Buck continued.

"Oh Buck, you would do that for me? Give it all up?" She looked him in the eyes, saw the flash of uncertainty.

"Yes, I would," he said. His voice was steady.

"You are so full of it," she laughed. He looked hurt and turned his face away, so she put a hand on his cheek and turned him back to face her. "Do you know how incredibly bored you would be if you quit racing? Do you really think I would EVER let you do that? Your dreams and goals are what attracted me to you in the first place. Well, that, and your eyes," she smirked.

"Lilly—"

She moved her hand from his cheek to his mouth so that he couldn't interrupt her.

"I will not allow you to sacrifice any part of your career for little old me. Besides, I plan on winning the top jockey award at each track, too, so we can travel all around together." She removed her hand from his mouth.

"Oh, I can speak now?" He sounded annoyed, but his eyes registered none of it.

"Yes, as long as you don't say anything else as ridiculous as you did before," Lilly teased.

"You, Lilly Garret, are one of a kind." He smiled and brushed a bit of hair back away from her face. She pulled him close, kissing him deeply. Buck returned the kiss with abandon, rolling Lilly on top of him, holding her close.

No one noticed Buck and Lilly leaving the stall hand in hand several hours later.

The World of Racing

"How's business?" Buck asked Lilly.

They were in their customary evening spot, leaning on the rail and looking at the track as the sun set.

It had been a long day, but Lilly relished each moment.

She had been up since 5. After she galloped her assignments for Tom, she had spent the morning introducing herself to other trainers, trying to drum up rides for later in the week. She was finding out that most trainers weren't ready to put a girl up on the back of their horses in a race. It was okay that she galloped their horses in the morning, but a race was a different story.

"Have you found an agent yet?" Buck asked.

"I'm not sure I want to go that route, Buck. I want the trainers to get to know me, not someone working for me. I think I will have a better chance of getting a ride if they meet me in person. Plus, I'm not sure the agents want a girl client either," she confided.

"No matter the sex, they are supposed to work on your behalf," he said.

"Yeah, but I haven't proven myself yet. I've only ridden in a few races, and only on Tom's horses. If an agent reps two jockeys, one a guy and one girl, he's going to put forth the guy first. I am also competing against Reed and Kyle," she sighed. Reed and Kyle were also apprentices who were trying to get rides.

"Ah, you've got more talent in your little finger than those two," Buck said.

"Oh, you're just being supportive of your girlfriend," she said, though happy with his comment. "Plus you've never ridden against me in a race, so how do you know?"

"Gut feeling," he smiled at her, "and I've ridden against those two and they don't have what it takes. They will be low level jocks at low level tracks for their entire careers."

"I wonder how other female jockeys made it in this world of men?" she asked thoughtfully.

"By sleeping with the trainers," Buck quipped.

"What?" Lilly stammered. Buck just raised his eyebrows. Lilly pushed at him and he grabbed her into a bear bug.

"You beguile me, Lilly Garrett," Buck said.

"Well, that's a big word, Mr. Wheeler," she replied giddily, enjoying his physical presence.

"Just because I'm a jock, doesn't mean I'm not educated, Lilly," he said to her seriously.

"I didn't mean anything..." she stammered, pushing against his chest.

"No offense taken," Buck replied, not letting her go. He leaned in for a kiss.

The kiss deepened as Lilly leaned back into him. They were so lost in their embrace they didn't notice Tom looking on from the side of the barn, a frown on his face.

Buck and Lilly sat down at Lucky's, a local eatery not far from the track.

"Back to the topic of females in a man's world," Lilly started.

"Oh, I thought I silenced all that feminism talk a bit ago," he smiled at her.

She kicked his foot under the table. "Seriously, I want to find out how other female jockeys made it."

Buck leaned back in the booth, realizing he couldn't avoid the topic. "Well, I guess you need to start with knowing the names of the female jockeys that 'made it,' as you put it."

"I know Julie Krone," Lilly said defiantly, and then paused. "I guess no other names come to mind," Lilly said.

"Well, it's easy to know of Julie Krone, she was the first woman to win a Triple Crown race—the Belmont on Colonial Affair. I think it was 1993. Did you know she was on the cover of *Sports Illustrated*?" Buck informed her.

Lilly raised her eyebrows. "Really? Awesome!"

"She placed ninth in the Belmont on Subordinated Debt in 1991 and sixth on Colony Light in 1992. She kept getting closer and closer to the winner's circle, that's for sure. Julie has always been quite determined."

"You certainly know a lot about Ms. Krone," Lilly retorted.

"Jealous?" Buck smiled at her.

Lilly swatted at his hands folded on the table and he grabbed at them.

"I make it my business to know all I can about my competition," Buck said, looking so intently into Lilly's eyes that she blushed.

In an effort to stay composed, Lilly asked, "Have you ridden against her? Where is she riding now?"

"I have ridden against her. She is hard as nails. She won't give you an ounce of racing room if she thinks she can win. And I mean it when I say tough as nails. She has seven aluminum screws and a metal plate in her forearm from a fall at the Meadowlands. Last year, she had a horrible fall at Saratoga and broke several bones in her ankle. If it weren't for her safety vest when a horse's hoof landed, well…" Buck's voice faded off. He held Lilly's hands more tightly.

"You don't need to explain," Lilly said softly.

"Yes, yes, I do, Lilly. This is a dangerous sport you want to do. Jocks fall and get injured, sometimes terribly. Horses breakdown right from under us and the force of the speed at which we are traveling—close to 40 miles an hour—propels us to the ground like a torpedo, all while trying to avoid a tumbling mass of 1,200 pounds of horseflesh, to say nothing of the horses running up behind us." Buck paused and looked at Lilly to make sure she was really paying attention, and then continued, "We don't talk about it, the risks and dangers we face every time we get up on the back of a horse to race. If I thought about them, I would never be able to do what I do."

"Then why do you?" she asked.

Buck raised his eyebrows.

"Why do you ride?" she asked.

Buck looked down at their hands intertwined and rubbed Lilly's fingers.

"Because I can't not ride. It's in my veins. I fell in love with riding the minute I sat on a horse on my grandpa's back forty. He had a big ranch in upstate New York and kept a few horses. Not racers, just ones that he and grandma could trail ride in the Catskills. I was about nine years old and grandpa sent me out to collect the horses one afternoon so we could all go for a ride.

"The herd was a bit far out in the field so I had to walk a-ways to get them. Being nine, I didn't want to walk more than I had to. Once I haltered up two of the horses, I pulled one to the side of the fence and jumped on its back. He didn't know what I wanted him to do, so he turned his head, seeing this pistol of a boy on his back, and decided to teach me a lesson. That darn horse dropped his head and took off for home with his partner in crime trailing behind us, followed by the rest of the herd. The best thing was that I wasn't scared. The adrenaline that shot through me as the horse gathered speed was like nothing I ever felt before, or since. Each race it pumps through my veins—like a drug, I guess." Buck smiled. "I couldn't stop if I wanted to."

Lilly squeezed his hand. "I know exactly how you feel. Which is why you would never be able to talk me out of following my dream."

They sat in silence for a few moments reflecting on each other's comments. The waitress walked over with their food. As Buck started to put his fork into his salad, a voice rang out, "Hey Buck, how have you been?"

Buck jumped up and hugged the man who approached their table. "Great to see you, Doug!"

"Crazy meeting you here! I am only in town for a couple of days, I have been meaning to get in touch. I have a couple of horses for you to take a look at. Nothing ready for the big time yet, but they're at my farm, and I would love for you to sit on them and give me your opinion," Doug said, looking at Lilly.

"Miss Lilly, I see you're still hanging out with this riff-raff. Is he behaving himself?" Doug pulled Lilly into a hug as well, and she laughed.

"As well as can be hoped. You know these jockey boys," she smiled. They both looked over at Buck, who rolled his eyes and then spoke, trying to ignore Lilly's comment.

"Sure, Doug, I would love to help out. Hey, did you hear that Lilly won her first race? She's a good one, Doug. You should sign her up while she's still available." Lilly blushed and shot Buck a glare.

"Actually, I had heard that. And forgive my belated congratulations. I do have a few horses that could use a rider like you, Lilly. Why don't you come up to the farm with Buck and I'll introduce you to a few of the owners that like to hang around the stables."

"I'd love that Doug, thanks!" Lilly said excitedly, looking at Buck. He winked at her. Riding for Doug Walker would be a big boon to her business.

Women Jockeys

The next day, Lilly didn't have any races on her calendar. After she finished her morning gallops, she helped Gus bathe the last of the horses.

"What are you up to today, missy?" Gus asked while Lilly dunked the large sponge into the soapy water and swiped it across the sweaty back of the big chestnut horse he held.

Her conversation about women jockeys with Buck had left her wanting to know more. "I'm going to head over to the library for a bit, I think."

"Oh yeah, watcha looking for?" Gus asked, the chestnut tossed his head as the soapy water washed down his face.

"Anything I can find about women jockeys," she told him.

"Won't be much," Gus replied. "There just ain't that many."

"I know, but Buck and I talked about Julie Krone last night and I realized that I need to find out all I can about the women who have done what I am doing and what obstacles and challenges they had to overcome," Lilly said, dunking the horse's long tail into the bucket and swirling it around.

"Ah, Lilly, you don't need to worry about the past. You got your future. Don't worry yourself with what others have had to deal with. You make your own path…you have done a great job so far." Gus wasn't one to throw compliments around, and Lilly almost dropped the bucket.

"Thanks, Gus, that means a lot." She didn't turn to look at him as she grabbed the hose and sprayed the last bit of soap from the horse's legs. She didn't want him to see her scrunched up face as she fought the emotions building up at his compliment. "He's all done."

Gus led the horse back into his stall, clipped the stall guards, and hung his halter and lead shank on the hook next to the door. "Now you're done, get outta here before I find something else for you to do."

Lilly gave Gus a quick hug and jumped on her bike.

The ride to the library at the school was short, but it allowed her to get her emotions in check. She hadn't been on campus since the school year ended. Even though she graduated, she knew the library was open for the summer—the librarian wouldn't mind if she utilized it. Lilly and Macy had spent many days studying here in the weeks leading up to finals.

"Hello, Miss Garrett, what are you doing here? Didn't get enough of school while you were here?" Mrs. Dillon, the head librarian, called to her from behind the counter.

"Ah, well, I have one last project I am interested in. Fortunately, one that has nothing to do with school. I am done with that!" she laughed, leaning on the white counter.

"Shouldn't you be getting ready to head off to college, dear? Shopping and packing and all that?" Mrs. Dillion asked.

Lilly's smiled dropped a little and she tensed. "Ah, I am done with all that right now. I have a bit of a break and there is a topic I am interested in. Can you help me, Mrs. Dillon?" She figured distracting her from the line of questioning about college was the best tactic.

No one knew that Lilly wasn't going off to college, as far as she was aware. She had pretended the whole thing during the final semester of school, not wanting to have to deal with all of the questions. The only people who knew were Macy and Angela, as well as the college counselor. There had been a lot of pressure from her to fill out applications and make sure she followed the financial aid deadlines. Lilly had had to tell her that she wasn't going to college to stop all the hounding and pressure.

"A project? Sure. Is this something your college wants you to get started on before you get there?" Mrs. Dillon returned to her line of questioning. Lilly decided to play along.

"Yes, of course. Because I live so close to the racetrack, they asked that I do a research paper on women jockeys," Lilly told her.

"Women jockeys? Really. Well, that sounds like a challenging one!" Mrs. Dillion replied.

"They think so too, which is why they want me to do it. There probably isn't much to find, so they want me to document anything I come across and build a case study," Lilly said more confidently.

"Okay! I can certainly see what I have in the library. Have you checked online? This Yahoo search engine is becoming quite popular," Mrs. Dillon suggested.

"I don't have any online access, Mrs. Dillion, which is another reason I am here," Lilly said.

"Alright, let's start by looking at what I have on the shelves and we will go from there," Mrs. Dillion said as she turned to a computer to type in "women jockeys."

"Well it seems I actually have one book in the system. Let's go hunt it down," Mrs. Dillion wound a path through tables where students would normally be seated to study. She turned down a row of book shelves and went all the way to the back. "Let's see, it must be here somewhere. I can't imagine too many students are looking for it." She ran her index finger across the row of books.

"Ah-ha, here it is." She pulled out a slim hard-covered book with a red book jacket. She handed it to Lilly.

Lilly looked at the cover, *Great Women in the Sport of Kings. America's Top Women Jockeys Tell their Stories.*

"Perfect," she exclaimed.

"Glad to be of help. You want to go look online?" Mrs. Dillon asked as they walked to the front of the library.

"No, ma'am. Unfortunately I don't have the time," Lilly replied; this book was all she needed and she wanted to dive right into reading. "Thanks so much for your help."

"Well, good luck in college, dear. I will miss seeing you around," Mrs. Dillion called to her as Lilly made her way out of the library.

Lilly flopped herself on her bed and spent the next several hours absorbing the stories within the little red book.

She read about the first jockey licenses being awarded to women in 1969 after a long process of working their way through the many stumbling blocks put up by the states' racing commissions and Jockey Club. The male dominated sport believed women weren't strong enough and would panic during a race; that they did not have the lightening reflexes to make adjustments in the heat of a race and would endanger male jockeys. Finally, on February 7, 1969, Diane Crump was the first woman to ride in a race at Hialeah Park in Miami, Florida. She finished tenth out of twelve, but the significance of her achievement opened the doors for future woman jockeys.

Lilly turned the pages as she absorbed the stories of Diane Nelson, Jill Jellison, and Donna Barton, along with several other stories of the women who had made their way into the limelight of Thoroughbred racing throughout the country.

Her cell phone buzzed next to her and she jumped. She looked at it slightly annoyed to be distracted from her reading, then she grabbed at it and hit the answer button. "Did you know that Diane Nelson was breaking horses and exercising them at fifteen years old??" she blurted into the phone. "That was younger than me when I started riding at the track!"

"Whoa, missy, what's going on there?" Buck asked.

"And Jill Jellison was doing it at fourteen and fifteen; she even dropped out of school. At least my parents should be happy I finished high school!"

"Doing a little light reading?" Buck asked her.

Lilly took a breath. "After we talked the other night, I realized I didn't know anything about the history of women as jockeys, so I went to the library at school. I got this book that has a chapter about ten different female jockeys and how they got into racing. It is fascinating."

"That's great, Lil." She could feel Buck's smile through the phone. "What else have you read?"

"So far, they all pretty much grew up around horses in some capacity, mostly because their parents had horses. Although, I am just starting the chapter about Donna Barton, and did you know her mother was one of the trendsetting female jockeys in 1969 when they started getting licensed? She won 179 races her first year, a record that stood for nineteen years, until 1988. That's when your crush, Julie Krone, along with Patti Cooksey, broke the record in the same week."

Buck laughed at her comment. Lilly grew somber, missing him terribly when he traveled to other racetracks.

Sensing the change, Buck asked, "Now, what's wrong?" He knew their time apart was tough on Lilly, although he didn't want to avoid the topic. He was a talker and knew he didn't want her to keep emotions inside.

"It's just…just…." Lilly sniffled and squeezed her eyes shut, "it's just, all these stories, these women, they have supportive families. Moms and dads who encouraged them and cheered them on when they decided to become jockeys. Regardless of the circumstances."

Buck was silent, not wanting to stop her from talking through her emotions.

"My parents, well, they don't give a crap about me and my dreams. They could have been supportive, but they wanted their perfect little girl, following their perfect little dream!" Lilly threw the book down on the floor next to her bed. Pulling her legs to her chest, she curled into a ball and nestled the phone against her ear.

"Listen, Lilly, I didn't get to know your parents very well, but I am sure they wanted the best for you," Buck replied.

"Right, the best for me as long as it was what they wanted," Lilly retorted.

It was the first time Lilly had really opened up about her feelings on leaving her parents' home. Buck had tried to get her to talk about it, but Lilly had said it was just easier not to think about it and move on. This book she had been reading had opened her wounds, and Buck knew it was heathier for her to keep talking. He knew it hadn't been easy for her to leave, and he wanted to make sure that she didn't blame him somewhere down the line.

"I just feel like I'm in the eye of this storm, Buck," Lilly said quietly. "You know, the center of a storm where you made it through the wind and rain, the weather calms and the sun comes out briefly, but you know that you have to endure the backside of the storm and all its fury.

"I love you and I love riding. I feel like things are perfect. But for some reason I can't shake the feeling that this can't last. The front side of my storm was the craziness of fighting with my parents and moving out. I am so afraid of what the backside of this storm might be."

Buck was silent on the other end of the phone. He had the same feeling.

PART TWO

 # Leesburg, Virginia

Charlie Jenkins sat at the table looking out at Genuine Storm in the field, a mug of coffee between her hands. Storm would grab a mouth full of grass and then raise his head to look around. *Looking for someone to mess with,* she thought. Sarge and Hershey were getting their fill, without a care about the goings-on around them. The weather was warm and the grass had come in lush. They wouldn't be out on it for too long today; Charlie was wary of Storm getting colic from the richness of the grass.

Charlie was still on cloud nine. The Kentucky Derby winner was right out there grazing in his paddock.

She loved that their story was getting so much attention, but she was greatly enjoying her time outside the public eye. The media presence had been overwhelming in Kentucky for the couple days they were there after they won the Kentucky Derby. The questions about where Storm came from, questions about her kids, and about Doug and Lilly.

Charlie couldn't remember how many times she'd had to tell and retell the story of how she'd come upon Storm in the claiming race. The more she told the story, the more astounding it all seemed to her: meeting Doug, making it to the track office in time to claim Storm, Doug being willing to help, Doug just happening to know the only jockey who could make Storm run.

The fates, Charlie thought, were clearly on her side.

The reporters had been kind enough to Charlie when she'd asked that they respect her past and her children's privacy, but they had given no such courtesy to Lilly, whom they'd grilled about her semi-recent departure from racing and the reasons behind it.

Lilly. More information was being brought up about her past each day. Her days at Pimlico, how she got into the business, her successes, as well as her disappearance from the sport. Journalists were interviewing anyone who would talk about Lilly. There was a growing question as to why she left racing. It seemed no one but Lilly could give an answer to that, and she wouldn't divulge any information. She had ended up refusing any interaction with the press, which only made them more curious.

Reporters continued to call Doug and Charlie, trying to pry information about Lilly from them. Doug had stopped answering his phone altogether, while Charlie had decided to let her daughter, Skylar, handle the rude interruptions. It was some of the best entertainment Charlie had had in a long time: Skylar, bless her heart, didn't have a bad thing to say about the hero who helped her horse win the race. Charlie smiled as she recalled a particularly long conversation Skylar had had with a reporter, which ended with, "—and Lilly is just so nice, she sometimes lets me sit on Storm while she's walking him back to the barn! Hello…? Mommy they hung up again!"

Charlie hated to admit it, but she couldn't have given the reporters any insight into Lilly's past even if she'd wanted to. Charlie was realizing that what she knew about Lilly would fit comfortably on a Post-it note.

And now, she might never get to know Lilly any better.

Almost immediately after the Derby ended, Lilly told Charlie that she would not be riding Storm in the next leg of the Triple Crown, the Preakness Stakes. In fact, Lilly had told her she wouldn't be riding in any races anymore, that her deal was one and done.

Charlie knew that Lilly hadn't wanted to ride in the Derby in the first place, and that she had had to overcome a lot of anxiety and personal issues in order to go through with it, but Charlie had been sure that Lilly would change her mind about continuing to ride Storm once she got through the Derby.

In fact, Lilly had not changed her mind, and said her goodbyes on Sunday after she made sure Storm had come out of the Derby in good health. Doug seemed to be the only one not surprised by her decision to leave. Skylar was close to hysterical.

"Goodbye, what do you mean goodbye?" Skylar asked, her eyes filling with tears.

"Well, Skylar, I promised your mom, and Storm, that I would take you as far as the Derby, and I did. I gave your mom a list of very talented jockeys that I think would be wonderful with Storm." She pulled Skylar to sit down on a bale of hay. "Storm will have his pick of jockeys; they will all want to ride the Kentucky Derby winner," she said softly.

"No, he won't run for anyone else!" Skylar said anxiously, wringing her hands in her lap.

"Yes, he will," Lilly replied, "it's just another phase of his training. He's been getting better and better with his exercise riders." Ryan, Charlie's teenage son, leaned against Storm's stall door, his face unreadable. He'd heard enough. Thrusting his balled fists into his jeans pockets, he turned and walked down the aisle and out of sight.

Lilly detached herself from a crying Skylar, shook hands with Charlie, hugged Doug, and left the barn. She was all packed and headed back to Laurel racetrack, where Charlie had first met Lilly. There was nothing Charlie or Doug could say that would change her mind.

Lilly was hiding something, that much Charlie knew. Charlie had seen her a few times when Lilly thought no one was around. There was a sadness that seemed to come from within her, that was evident in every aspect of her being. Charlie knew that Lilly was hurting and desperately needed help, but she also knew that she was practically a stranger to Lilly. Charlie had been determined when all of this started that she wasn't going to lose sight of the important things in life, and aside from being an awesome jockey, Lilly was a woman in desperate need of help.

She took a sip of her coffee. Charlie made up her mind that she was going to get to the bottom of what happened to Lilly. She didn't have much time: only two weeks separated the Derby and the Preakness. It was now Monday afternoon, and in just a couple of days, the whirlwind of the lead up to the Preakness would start, and that would mean most of her free time would disappear. However, she owed Lilly a lot, and even if Lilly never rode again, Charlie wanted her to know how important she was to their little family.

On Wednesday they would take Storm to Doug's Shamrock Hill Farm to resume his training and preparation for the second leg of the Triple Crown. Although some Derby winners went directly to Pimlico after the Derby, Storm was most comfortable at either Charlie's farm in Leesburg or Shamrock Hill Farm with Doug and Ben, his devoted groom. Therefore, they had decided to give Storm a few days to stretch his legs in Leesburg and then head to Shamrock. Doug's farm had a beautiful training track, and it would still provide some buffer to the media storm that would take place once they arrived at Pimlico.

Charlie outlined the next two weeks in her head: two days here, Wednesday to Shamrock for a week of galloping, and then on to Pimlico on Wednesday the following week. At Shamrock, Jenny, Doug's niece and go-to exercise rider, would gallop Storm. They were okay on the jockey front for the next week.

Charlie would need to have a permanent jockey named by the time they got to Pimlico to ensure enough time to work with Storm before the big race if it wasn't going to be Lilly. She hoped she wouldn't have to use the list Lilly had given her, but she had been keeping it close, just in case.

She took one last look at Storm, Sarge, and Hershey in the field, refilled her coffee, and walked into her office to sit at her computer. She expected Ryan home from school shortly, and they had a lot of research to do.

Dinner Conversation

"Charlie, you're worse than all those reporters! She doesn't want to talk about it," Doug said as he put plates on Charlie's kitchen table. It seemed an unspoken agreement that their break from the racing world would in no way mean a break from each other.

"I wouldn't ask if it weren't important, Doug." Charlie handed him silverware and watched as he placed it around the table. Doug was closer to Lilly than anyone else Charlie knew. While Ryan was in charge of doing all the online research, Charlie had decided that her job would be to convince Doug to join their mission.

"It's not our business. She's a grown woman, she can make her own decisions, and she doesn't want to ride in races again. She gave you a gift, can't you leave it at that?" He stopped to consider the job he'd done, seemed satisfied, and turned to Charlie. "I love Lilly, I do. She's important to me and to Shamrock, and to this team, but we can't force her to race again, Charlie."

"Doug, she's hurting. I see it every day I'm with her. Something happened, and she's scared, and she just needs to know that someone is there for her! I couldn't care less whether she rides again. Lilly helped me out when no one else could. She took a chance on me, on my family. And I don't care what it takes, I will help her in any way I can."

"What if she doesn't want to be helped in the way you're offering? What if she really wants to just go back to riding problem horses?"

"If that is really what she wants, then no one will stop her. All I'm saying is, I saw her face when she crossed that finish line the other day. She was happier than I've ever seen her. I don't think she wants to give it up." Doug crossed the room and wrapped his arms around Charlie. It was impossible to mistake the sincerity in her voice. He sighed.

"I can only tell you a little bit," he said, hoping that would be enough to satisfy Charlie's curiosity.

"Every little bit helps." Charlie kissed him deeply.

The mudroom door burst open, and Skylar yelled into the kitchen, "Mom, everyone's inside and fed. Should we turn Sarge and Hershey out overnight or leave them in with Storm?"

"Oh, um…definitely leave them in. Storm will be a basket case if you separate him from them. I'll check in on everyone again when I do night check. Both of you come in and wash up for dinner, please," Charlie told her as Skylar turned to run out and tell Ryan to leave the horses inside.

"How would you feel about a kid-free evening?" Charlie asked Doug. He raised his eyebrows and smirked.

"You mean like just a 'you and me' kind of evening? Where I could kiss you and not have to worry about anyone barging in?" Doug asked, pulling Charlie closer.

"That's exactly what I mean." She leaned in and kissed him lightly. His grip on her waist tightened. As she moved her arms around his neck, the back door flew open for the second time, and Skylar ran in with Ryan close behind.

"I just wanted to help you!" Skylar shouted. Charlie moved over to where they were and put one hand over each of their mouths, before Ryan could retort.

"I don't care what it is you're fighting about, but it stops now. You're not to talk to each other anymore. Go wash your hands and come back down for dinner," Charlie said.

"But, Mom, she—" Ryan started.

"Nope. Not entertaining the argument tonight. We can talk about it in the morning if you are still upset, but right now, we are going to have a peaceful dinner. Ryan, you go shower, Skylar, hands. Now," Charlie demanded, knowing that separating them physically would be the best way to defuse the situation.

It was clear that Ryan wanted to continue their argument, but he thought better of it and trudged up the stairs to the shower. Skylar's attention span allowed her to forget the fight almost the second Ryan was out of sight, and she too left to wash up.

"One day the sibling rivalry will stop. They had been getting along so great while we were away. Now back to the same routine," Charlie said, rubbing her temples. Doug laughed behind her and she turned to see him smiling.

"What was that you were saying about a kid-free evening?" Charlie shook her head and moved the casserole to the middle of the table. "How about you grab that bottle of wine and refill our glasses?"

———

After dinner, Charlie followed her kids upstairs to usher them to their bedrooms.

"No playing your iPod, missy," she reprimanded Skylar as she stood in her doorway.

"I won't, Mom. But can I just tell you that Ryan was not being nice to me all of a sudden tonight," Skylar confided.

"I'm sorry, honey. Teenage boys tend to pick on their younger sisters, so I will have a talk with him about it. I also know that he is taking Lilly not riding Storm pretty hard, just like you are. It's not easy for him to let it go."

"Why won't she ride him, Mom?" Skylar asked for what Charlie thought must have been the thousandth time.

"She has her reasons. Now you can read for a bit, but lights out in thirty minutes." Charlie kissed Skylar on her forehead and quietly closed her bedroom door.

Charlie slowed outside of Ryan's closed bedroom door. She lifted her hand to knock, and then lowered it. It would be better if she gave him some space this evening and talked to him tomorrow. He probably needed to cool off. Charlie decided it was time for her to stop asking him to help her with research on Lilly. He wanted to be involved, and she wanted to spend time with him, but she wasn't sure what she would find, and for all their sakes, it would be better if Ryan started doing normal, non-sleuth activities again. They had all spent so much time on the Derby trail that Ryan had stopped hanging out with his friends at school. She would talk to him about the information she had received for the summer hockey league.

As she walked down the stairs, she also decided to see if Jenny could drive out tomorrow and spend some time with him after school. Seeing her would definitely cheer him up.

Charlie walked to the kitchen to help clean up. Doug had already begun putting dishes into the dishwasher for her. She smiled at how helpful he was, sure that he had some ulterior motive for wanting the job done quicker.

"Do you think Jenny would be okay with coming out tomorrow after Ryan gets home from school?" she asked him. "I think Ryan needs a distraction from all this Lilly stuff."

"Not a bad idea. Once I'm done here, I will send her a text," Doug replied, cleaning the last frying pan. "Why do you use every pot and pan you have in the house when you cook?"

"I don't!" Charlie replied, pulling a small pan out of the cabinet, "See, I didn't use this one." She proceeded to swat Doug on his butt with the back of the pan.

"Hey!" Doug swiped at her with his wet hands. Charlie moved out of the way. Doug cupped his hands and filled them with a mound of soap from the sink,

"Two can play at kitchen wars." He moved quickly before Charlie saw it coming and placed his hands on the top of Charlie's head, covering her head in bubbles. Before she could shriek, Doug covered her lips in a deep kiss that left Charlie dazed.

Doug slowly moved her backwards towards the mudroom bathroom and the shower beyond. "I think we need to clean you up."

"The kids..." Charlie whispered, pushing her arms against his chest, without much conviction.

"They are in their bedrooms, and I've never seen them come back down after Skylar has her nose in a book and Ryan puts his earphones on."

Charlie let Doug guide her backwards and she locked the mudroom door as it closed behind them.

———————

Later, as they sat on the couch in the living room, looking for something to watch on TV, Charlie turned to Doug.

"So, what can you tell me about Lilly?" Doug continued changing channels looking for a movie to watch, and Charlie repeated her question, thinking he hadn't heard her. Doug had heard her and had hoped he had distracted Charlie from this line of questioning. Obviously, he was wrong, so he needed a few minutes to get his thoughts together.

Doug needed to decide what he was going to say that wouldn't break the promise he had made to Lilly so many years ago, and wouldn't ruin the relationship he was building with Charlie.

"I can tell you that she is an amazing jockey. Lilly's been working with horses in a professional capacity since she was a teenager. Started with a trainer named Tom Malone. I don't know him that well, but my understanding is that they made a good team. When I first met her, she was close with Buck Wheeler. You know, the jockey who rode Duke in the Derby." Charlie nodded, anxious to learn more.

"I started using Lilly to evaluate my two-year-olds and she was great at it. She started making a name for herself and one thing led to another as her wins started adding up. She took some time off before deciding officially not to go to college, but then started up her business again and had an insane number of wins under her belt for someone so young," Doug finished.

"What about when she quit?" Charlie asked.

"It was out of the blue. One day she just stopped riding. She stopped taking new jobs, started focusing on horses that weren't ready for the track. As far as I know, there's not a person in the racing world who knows why she quit. She and Buck hadn't been close for a while at that point. I was lucky to reconnect with her, and she spent a lot of time working on several of my problem horses. Buck came to see her at Shamrock once, I think to try to convince her to come back to racing. He left in a huff, and as far as I know, that's the last time they spoke before they saw each other at the Derby."

"And there was nothing else that happened around that time that would give you any indication as to why she left? She didn't say anything in passing as she was working with your horses?" Charlie's mind was working furiously to connect the dots.

"No. Like I said, I don't think anyone knows what really happened. If they do, they're keeping it nice and quiet."

"Well, I'm just gonna have to talk to Buck. Maybe he knows more than he's letting on." She leaned her head on his shoulder. Doug had not really been much help. Charlie was banking on his information to give her a more solid place to start. Her disappointment must have been written on her face because Doug said, "I told you I didn't know anything."

"No. I guess I just…hoped…" Doug pulled her into a hug.

"I'm sure whatever it is, you'll get to the bottom of it. You're rather persistent," he said, closing his eyes above her head. She closed her eyes too, and in doing so didn't see the look of worry on his face.

Black-Eyed Susans

Charlie needed to focus on something else. The Lilly situation was driving her crazy and Doug was driving her nuts. How was she supposed to get anything done with him always trying to distract her with his visions of rainbows and butterflies and happily ever after? She had believed in that once upon a time, but now she knew otherwise. Life happens.

Her father had a saying: "You are either coming out of a problem, or heading into a problem." It was all about how you dealt with the peaks and valleys of life. Charlie knew she had just experienced a huge peak in her life; several, actually. Storm and Doug. She was getting anxious for what problem, what valley, was now coming her way.

Charlie sighed heavily and leaned back in her chair. The computer screen stared back at her with pictures of Lilly from her racing days. The days when she was the hottest jockey around, with trainers far and near looking for her special touch to get their horse into the winners' circle. She came upon articles that compared her to the golfer Jack Nicklaus, saying she had the same firm control yet soft touch with the horses she rode that the golfer used with his putter. Others compared her to the tiny spitfire gymnast Mary Lou Retton, with her balance and flexibility.

In a very short period of time, Lilly had climbed to the top of a sport dominated by men. Why had this girl given it all up? Charlie read the same news stories for the umpteenth time before finally deciding there were no hidden nuggets of information in any of them.

Charlie had built up the details of Lilly's life. She had found out where she grew up, where she went to high school, and had pieced together her early days at Pimlico. Finding stories of her accession in the sport was not that difficult. She had been a rose among thorns, the fresh face of horse racing.

Lilly's popularity had been swift, and the big players of the sport had been anxious for a poster child to combat the bad publicity horse racing had been getting—the drugs, the breakdowns, the gambling. They were looking for a rebirth, a return to the golden age of Seattle Slew, Affirmed, and Secretariat, when horse racing news was front page coverage in the newspapers and magazines and when people crowded around the TVs to watch the races and flocked to the racetracks.

In the new age of the Internet and social media, any bad news was immediately spread to all corners of the globe. PETA was always getting involved in convincing the general public that racing horses was a crime and injustice to the Thoroughbreds. They focused on the horses that were injured while racing and had to be euthanized. They lobbied against the reality show jockeys, who told the stories of what happened behind the scenes, with these athletes who partner with 1,200 pounds of horseflesh.

Lilly's quick smile and easy way with the horses had been winning over fans. And she could win, which convinced the owners and trainers that a female rider wasn't a bad thing.

Charlie closed her eyes, envisioning what it must have been like to be the lone female in a jockey's room of all males. Probably similar to those female sportscasters who go into the locker rooms of the NFL teams. Not a lot of privacy, she thought. And Lilly wasn't just some person asking questions so the players could gloat about the plays they made. Lilly had been a direct competitor, race after race, day after day. Until one day she disappeared and gave it all up.

Was the pressure too much? Charlie thought. Her brain needed a break. Charlie opened her eyes and they settled on the garland of roses draped along the back of the leather loveseat in her office. Tomorrow, she and Skylar were going to start mailing a rose to each of their investors, along with a personalized picture of Storm in the winner's circle at Churchill Downs.

Their fan following had grown tremendously. Ryan had a hard time keeping up with all the social media sites while also trying to study for finals. Charlie's friend Kate had offered to help out, given her journalistic background; so much of the activity during the day was already handled before Ryan sat down to finish up the evening comments.

Charlie recalled the stop at the grocery store where they had seen this very garland being made. They had been the underdog then. Not the case anymore. They had moved on from the Run for the Roses to the Run for the Black-Eyed Susans: the Preakness Stakes.

She put her fingers to her keyboard and began to type.

The View From Behind the Starting Gate.

I know I haven't written in a while, but as you can imagine things have been a bit hectic! For those of you wondering, Storm is settling back nicely here at the farm for a few days. I've been staring at the beautiful garland of roses that had been draped around his neck after he won the Kentucky Derby and thinking about our next adventure.

Did you know the official flower for the Preakness Stakes is the Black-Eyed Susan?

The first blanket of Black-Eyed Susans was placed across the winner in 1940. Similar to the garland of roses for the Derby, it is created shortly before Preakness Day. It takes about eight hours for four people to make the blanket, two of which are assigned the duty of cutting the stems off the bloom and inserting a wire, and then two people attaching the wire to the black matting and green felt that form the blanket. Believe it or not, this process is done repeatedly with 4,000 flowers! When it is complete, the blanket is 18 inches wide and 90 inches in length.

The secret of the garland is that it is not actually made with the Black-Eyed Susan flower, the official flower of the state of Maryland as well as The Preakness. Since the Black-Eyed Susan does not bloom until June, the makers of the blanket needed to find a similar flower to mimic it. So in reality, a Viking daisy, which has yellow petals, is used for the flower, and the centers of the daisies are daubed with black lacquer to recreate the appearance of a Black-Eyed Susan.

Another tidbit for you historians, is that the Black-Eyed Susan has 13 petals, which is to symbolize the 13 original colonies, of which Maryland was one.

She posted the short blurb and finally felt as though something productive had been done at the computer that day.

Lunch Date

Charlie was beginning to hate the internet. When Lilly suddenly dropped out of racing, everyone was an expert on why she wasn't cut out to be a jockey. The pressure had gotten to her or she couldn't get along in the jockey room; one article went so far as to detail how Lilly had bribed all the other jockeys in order to win a race. The industry had turned against their poster child out of anger that she just disappeared. The gossip had gone into overdrive. Frustrated, Charlie had slammed the lid of her computer and given the job to her friend Kate.

As usual, she was having more luck than Charlie with her research. She'd found a number of interesting articles from her early days in the business. One article in particular stuck out to Charlie: it didn't name Lilly directly, but it had to do with Tom Malone, Lilly's employer at the time of her hasty departure from the sport.

It was early morning, the kids had just gotten on the bus to school, and Charlie sat on one of the Adirondack chairs that faced the pasture where Storm, Sarge, and Hershey were busy searching for the best blades of grass. She always thought it was interesting that horses appeared to be searching as they nosed their way across the ground, not just grabbing at anything that looked like grass. One day when she was looking out her office window she saw the horses at one corner of the field, she looked at her computer monitor to type out a few paragraphs for her blog, and when she looked up they were in an entirely different part of the pasture.

One more day until Storm returned to Shamrock and Charlie would miss these quiet mornings, just looking out into the pasture at her horses. Alas, it was time to get back to work—for all of them.

Pulling her cell phone out of the back pocket of her jeans, Charlie dialed Lilly's phone number. It rang several times and Charlie was about to hang up, when her call was answered.

"Hello?" Lilly's quiet voice came over the phone.

"Hi, Lilly," Charlie said in her most encouraging tone of voice. "I was hoping we could get together for a cup of coffee or something."

"I am pretty busy back here at Laurel, Charlie," Lilly replied.

"I am sure you are, but I wanted to see if we could go over the list of jockeys you gave me in person." And then Charlie made the decision to be truthful.

"To be honest, Lilly, I am having a hard time coming to terms with the fact that you are not going to be riding Storm. I was hoping we could at least get together, just the two of us, without all the media and others around us. No Doug, no kids, just you and me. I miss having you around to strategize with, and at least you could help me on that front, right?" she finished hopefully.

Charlie didn't hear anything from the other end of the phone. She pulled it away from her ear to look at the screen to make sure she was still connected or hadn't pressed the MUTE button by mistake.

"Lilly?" she asked into the phone.

"I'm here," Lilly replied, and after a long pause she said, "I have some free time later today. I can meet at Luna's if you can come here. I don't have the time to make it over to Leesburg." Charlie could understand why Lilly would want any meeting they had to be on her terms. She agreed to the time, and said goodbye.

Lilly sat in a booth at the back of Luna's Deli waiting for Charlie to show up. She played with the apps on her phone, toggling between her email, Instagram, and Twitter, but she kept coming back to read the text on her phone, which read "If you're serious about returning to riding full time, please give me a call. I'd love to be a part of your team again. P."

She had been lucky to have Paul as her agent, back in her riding days. Paul was Lilly's age and was starting out as a jockeys' agent when they met. It was at Monmouth Park racetrack, and Lilly remembered the morning clear as day.

She had been walking around the backstretch trying to drum up some business. She had to get back in the tack after taking the year off. Tom had moved his operation to Monmouth Park for a few weeks leading up to the Haskell, and welcomed her with open arms.

"My girl, where have you been!" he had pestered her when she walked into the barn that morning.

Lilly slid from his grasp uncomfortably, looked at the ground, and replied, "I reconciled with my parents and they shipped me out of town for a bit to try to make me forget about being a jockey." The lie fell flat from her lips, but Tom didn't seem to notice.

"Well, I see that didn't work," Tom smirked.

"No…" Lilly said softly.

"Well, let's get you some work!" Tom said. "I only have a few horses here with me, so won't be able to give you much to ride. I will make a jockey change to get you in a race as soon as you're up to it."

"Thanks Tom. I need to get in the tack and get my riding legs underneath me, but I promise to do it quickly," Lilly said.

"Why don't you take a walk around and see who's looking for an exercise rider. I will vouch for you if you get any pushback. Mike Trillo is over in Barn 7 and Jack Warner is in Barn 4. They're buddies of mine and will put you up. Glad to have you back." Tom squeezed her arm, not noticing Lilly flinch.

Lilly had walked over to the barns Tom had told her about. She did her best to sound enthusiastic, but she was finding it all a lot harder than she'd imagined. Part of her was constantly worried that Buck was going to show up at the track. She knew she couldn't take that. Lilly had just finished up talking to Mike when a man walked up to them.

"Hey Mike, need any riders in today's races?" he asked. He smiled a toothy smile at Lilly.

"Hey, sorry to interrupt. I do that sometimes, in all my excitement to work for my clients," he pushed out his hand to Lilly, "Paul Ritter."

Lilly slowly gave him her hand. "Lilly Garrett."

He held her hand a bit longer, a questioning look in his eyes, "Lilly, like the Lilly Garrett from Pimlico?"

Lilly pulled her hand away, dropping his. "Yes, do I know you?"

"Not directly, but I do know you. Well, I should say, I know of you. I'm buddies with Buck Wheeler and he couldn't stop talking about you a while back. Broke his heart I think," Paul finished.

The color drained from Lilly's face. "Do you still talk to him?" she asked.

"Oh, only on occasion, mostly via text. I used to be a jock myself and we rode together for a bit in New York, but I haven't ridden with him in a few years. I couldn't make weight anymore and decided being an agent was a better path for me. I've been busy building business for my guy, Will Hackney," he smiled at Mike, "which brings me back to business. Anything, Mike?"

"Let me look at the board and I'll let you know," Mike said and walked into his tack room, leaving Lilly and Paul standing there.

"Ah, listen, Mr. Ritter—" Lilly started.

"Paul, please," Paul interjected.

"Paul. Well, I would appreciate it if you wouldn't let on to Buck that you have seen me," Lilly said quietly. Paul looked inquisitively at Lilly, but didn't say anything.

"It's just that I'm trying to start up again after being away from the business a bit. I don't want any…distractions," she said.

Paul held up his two hands. "Hey, I get it. Although I'm sure he will ring my neck if he finds out I've met you and didn't tell him. But I'll agree on one condition."

Lilly raised her eyebrows. "And what is that?"

"You become my client. I can help you get back into the business. Buck said you could ride the heck out of anything."

"You want to be my agent?" Lilly asked.

"Yes, of course. Didn't you ever have one before?"

Lilly looked to the side, "No, I didn't ride for very long before...well, before I took a leave of absence."

Paul didn't push her for more information. He knew in this business there were many secrets, and it was best to stay out of it.

Lilly crossed her arms. "And what does an agent do for me that I couldn't do myself?"

Paul laughed. "You really want to spend your time talking to every trainer, watching every race, following every horse? That's my job. I spend my days looking for the best ride for you and work my relationships with my trainer contacts to get you on them. I am here every morning ensuring my jockey is on the right horse for each race for the day. My job is to keep everyone happy, you and the trainers, so we can all be successful. I also play travel agent when you need to go to another track."

"Wow, a man of many talents," Lilly joked. Paul's laugh was infectious, and Lilly almost felt herself succumb to the urge.

"Yeah, I'm a jack of all trades! I can't really work with more than two clients at a time though, due to the work load. What I'm offering you is the chance to be my lucky second."

"Second?" Lilly asked.

"Will gave me the opportunity when I was just starting out, so I do all I can for him. But he knows I can't survive on just his earnings. The deal is that I get paid 25 percent of your earnings. For example, if you win a race, the jockeys' take is 10 percent of the purse to the winning horse. I get 25 percent of that 10 percent. Make sense?"

"I've never worked in partnership with anyone," Lilly said.

"Well, you don't know what I can do and I haven't seen you ride, so I think we are a formidable match," Paul smiled. "Deal?"

Lilly smiled for the first time in a long time. "Deal."

She hadn't thought of Paul in a long time, and there was a very good reason. Her heart skipped a beat. She berated herself and pushed the thoughts from her mind. She didn't want to think about that now; a tear slid down her cheek. She brushed it away quickly to make sure that when Charlie showed up she wouldn't see her crying.

Lilly heard the ring of the little bell on the door to the deli and looked up out of her daydream. She saw Charlie searching for her among the other patrons. She waved her hand from the booth she was sitting in.

The smile that stretched Lilly's face when she saw Charlie was genuine, but hesitant. Suddenly, Charlie was having second thoughts. The girl in front of her had desperately tried to keep her secrets to herself, and it seemed more than a little rude for her to press her for the truth.

Charlie decided she wouldn't press the matter. Not this time, anyway. She would take this time to make Lilly feel loved and missed, to show her how important she was to their family.

"Charlie." Lilly's voice held an uncharacteristic amount of hesitancy. Charlie sighed, her hand unconsciously patting the pocket with the folded article, the one about Tom Malone, and smiled.

"Lilly, I'm so glad you agreed to this." Charlie sat down, briefly squeezed the hand of the woman across the table, and picked up a menu. "I never really noticed how few women I interact with, and I miss your company dearly."

Lilly moved slowly to take her own menu, but she didn't open it. Charlie could see the question behind her eyes, and that only strengthened her resolve. This girl was family. She needed to believe it.

"When you recommended we meet here, I Yelped the place and it has great reviews. They supposedly have wonderful salads and I did see a comment specific to their protein dish, something with a lot of meat and vegetables. I thought you might like that. I think I'm going to get the chicken…

hmmm…I wonder if they substitute sides. Are you not eating?" Lilly was staring at Charlie, one hand on her closed menu, in an attitude that suggested a strong desire to get up and leave.

"I know what you're doing," she said. Charlie closed her own menu.

"And what is that?"

"You're trying to get me to come back. You just want me to ride Storm for you, and you think buying me lunch will change my mind. I'm not going to do it." She meant it. There was no sign of uncertainty in her demeanor when she spoke. Charlie was staring at a woman who had made up her mind.

"Lilly, you're wrong," Charlie said, not taking her eyes off the woman sitting across from her.

"Am I?"

"Yes, you are. Please sit down." Lilly had made a move to stand. Charlie knew she couldn't really order her to do anything, but her instincts told her that if she let Lilly leave now, there was no hope at all. "I have something to say to you, and you're going to listen. After that, if you really want to leave, you can."

Lilly eased back into her seat and her eyes dropped to her hands that she tightly folded on the table. She looked almost like an upset child, sitting in the oversized booth, teeth clenched behind tight lips. Charlie had to remind herself that Lilly was a grown woman, not much younger than herself; with age comes experience, and not all of it is good.

"Say what you need to say," Lilly said, her voice quiet but firm. Charlie flinched.

"When I first saw you calm that big black horse a few months ago, I thought you were a miracle worker. I knew you were exactly what my team needed. You were headstrong and smart, you knew how to take a good horse and make it great. I hope you don't mind me saying so…but you reminded me a little bit of myself when I was younger. What I could have been, maybe in another life. I knew you were the missing piece of the puzzle, and when you agreed to work with us, I couldn't have been happier; none of us could have."

"That's very sweet of you to say." Lilly's guard was still up, but there was a curiosity in her voice now that Charlie thought boded well.

"You know about me. My family, I mean. You know how broken we were before all this started, and you've seen yourself that there are still times when it doesn't seem like we're quite whole yet. You…" Charlie took a deep breath and tried to stop her voice from cracking. She wasn't normally a crier, but it seemed that on this occasion her body had decided to forego her usual stoic reserve, in favor of a somewhat softer approach.

"Charlie—"

"No, let me finish," She held up her hand to quiet Lilly, and saw her nod in acquiescence. "You didn't just become part of the team when you agreed to help us, Lilly. You became part of our family. We've lost family before, and it's not an easy thing. My kids love you, I love you. We couldn't stop Peter from dying and leaving us, but if I have a chance to stop you then…" She took a sip of water to ease her parched throat.

"I understand that you have your own reasons for not wanting to ride in the race. I know very well what it is like to be so caught up in the past that the future seems hardly to matter. I don't need you to tell me everything. I don't need you to say you'll ride in the race for me, but I'll be damned if I let you just walk away from this family without telling you just how much you mean to each and every one of us."

The waiter, unfortunately, chose that moment to swoop down on their table with a smile that was slightly too cheery to be real.

"What can I get for you ladies today? We've got a number of specials going on, including—"

"I would like the grilled chicken salad, please." Lilly's voice rang in Charlie's ears. She was slightly taken aback, and it took her a minute to realize that the waiter had turned his attention to her.

"Um…Oh, right!" Charlie gave her order and turned her eyes back to Lilly, who had a slight smile on her face.

"You didn't remember it was me that told you the salads at this place are great, did you?" Lilly asked. Charlie thought for a second and then laughed.

"Hah, it was, wasn't it? I guess I didn't need to Yelp the place after all."
She smiled.

Lilly opened her mouth to say something, thought better of it, and then closed it. Then, she seemed to think better of that as well, because she opened her mouth and practically yelled, "Charlie!"

A few people around them looked, and Charlie jumped slightly, but Lilly took a deep breath and continued.

"Charlie, I'm sorry. I know it is really selfish of me to leave you like this, with the next race so close, but I just…can't. And I know that I probably owe you an explanation, but…"

"Lilly, you don't owe me anything. You did more than I expected you to. I'm not going to lie and tell you that I don't want you back on the team—you're the best jockey around! However, I'm also not going to let you think that a jockey is all you are. Whether you ride Storm for us or not, we love you, and it's not okay for you to just disappear from our lives. I won't let it happen."

The rest of their meal passed rather uneventfully. It was as if the last few days hadn't happened. They spent the remainder of their lunch talking about Storm and giving each other their thoughts on how to prepare him for the Preakness, just a week and a half away.

Charlie smiled and hugged Lilly as they left the restaurant. Lilly had agreed to come by the farm and see everyone. Charlie had even told her about her plan to approach Buck about riding Storm in the Preakness. Lilly had smiled at that. Overall, it had been a success, Charlie thought, as she drove out of the parking lot and into traffic.

 # Trainer

The drive from Leesburg to Shamrock Hill Farm had become second nature to Charlie. Charlie gave a start when she turned into the long drive and realized that she had been driving on instinct for most of the way. She couldn't even remember passing most of the landmarks on the drive. She smiled slightly at the thought that her body was so familiar with the drive to Shamrock it had taken her there without question.

Cappie and Ben were waiting outside the barn when Charlie pulled up. She smiled at both of them as they went around to the back of the trailer to unload the horses.

Cappie was a short gentleman who worked for Doug and was his trusted head groomsman. He had been there the night Charlie bought Storm. It had been Cappie who insisted Charlie call Doug for help with her new horse. Charlie smiled as she thought back to the truck ride with Cappie, when she'd spent the whole time talking his ear off about her spur of the moment purchase. She wondered briefly if he'd meant for Doug to become more than a friend to her.

"Back again, huh buddy?" Ben was running a hand down Storm's nose, smiling. He'd known Storm since he was just a foal, and he'd worked hard to get Storm out of the custody of the man who had abused him. Charlie felt the familiar surge of gratitude fill her as she watched Ben lead Storm to his stall. He'd never given up, and now he would be there, cheering Storm on as he ran the second biggest race of his life.

"Where are the kids?" The words reached her ear at the same time a hand snaked around her waist, from behind. A scratchy kiss landed on her cheek.

"They are at school. They only have a few weeks left, so I told them they couldn't skip." Charlie turned to face Doug, his grip, rather than easing so she could turn, tightened, and when they were face to face, she was no more than a few inches from his lips.

"I bet Ryan didn't like that," he said, lightly brushing her hair behind her ears.

"He'll just have to get over it. I, for one, don't mind a bit that they're not here." He smiled and kissed her lightly.

Charlie heard a new voice coming from the barn. "There will be plenty of time for that after we win." His tone was light, but there was something in it that Charlie recognized. She turned to see who the voice belonged to, and took a step back in shock, almost tripping on Doug's feet.

"Hunter?" She was having trouble believing what she was seeing. Doug tensed slightly behind her, but the man walking toward them was all smiles.

"Hey, Chuck. I thought it was you." Charlie's shock turned into joy, and she pulled the man into a hug.

"So you…know each other then?" Doug was clearly uncomfortable, but doing his best to be business like.

"You could say that," Hunter smiled at his boss, one arm still around Charlie. She turned to face Doug, took one look at his face, and moved away from Hunter.

"Hunter was a friend of Peter's, back in college. I haven't talked to him in what, fifteen years?" She addressed the question to Hunter, even as she moved back to where Doug was standing, the latter man's face growing easier with her every step.

"I think so. I moved around a lot after I graduated, and Petey got all involved with his law practice and his kids and such…I was real sorry to hear about his passing, Chuck. I meant to call—" His voice took on a tone of real regret.

"He always liked you, Hunter," Charlie quickly said. Hunter gave her a sad smile.

"When Doug here told me your name, I couldn't believe it. I mean, you always talked about wanting to do something like this, but I figured with Pete and the kids…I'm real happy you're finally getting your shot, Chuck."

"Well I'm pretty thrilled about it myself. It's one thing to have a horse in a race, but it's something completely different to own a Kentucky Derby winner." Charlie couldn't hide the pride in her voice, and Hunter laughed aloud. It was a sweet, inviting sound, and it brought a ton of memories back for Charlie. A life that seemed like an eternity ago.

"Damn right it is! Doug told me a little bit about how you've been training Storm for the last few months. I've got some ideas on how to expand on all that; let's see if we can't make you the owner of a Preakness winner as well." His eyes never left Charlie, and she had the feeling he was looking into her mind, trying to find out how much the last fifteen years had changed her.

Doug, Charlie could sense, was not comfortable at all, so she tried to ease his own tension by suggesting they all go and look at the horse in question. Hunter and Doug agreed, and the trio walked into the barn.

Storm was chomping easily on the hay that Ben had put in his stall. Charlie reached over the door and scratched his ears, which he flicked in acknowledgement.

"Alright, Hunter, let's hear this plan of yours."

 # The Reporter

Hunter's plan for Storm's training had been quite simple and, as far as Charlie could tell, extremely effective. Jenny was doing a great job in Lilly's absence and Storm truly seemed to be getting over the need to have only Lilly ride him. Hunter's idea to interchange Jenny with other riders for short intervals seemed to be working.

She was enjoying watching Storm train more than ever, and her anxiety about the upcoming race was ebbing away with each passing hour. She knew, of course, that there were no guarantees, and that the calm she was feeling would all but disappear as soon as they stepped foot on the track at Pimlico.

One thing that was weighing on her mind was what she would do about a jockey. So far, she hadn't talked to anyone, and that was going to have to change if she stood any chance of getting someone good to ride Storm the following week. She reminded herself that she was offering something that no one else could: a chance to ride the winner of the Kentucky Derby. Still, time was running out. She decided that she would start making calls after Storm's training was done for the day.

She was just thinking over the list of jockeys Lilly had given her when she noticed a cloud of dust behind the barn, following a car that Charlie had never seen at Shamrock before. She stood and watched as a woman stepped out.

Clearly out of her element, this stranger was wearing a pencil skirt, high heels, and a blouse so white it hurt Charlie's eyes to look at it. The woman looked around for a moment, saw Charlie by the fence, and began to stumble her way over. Charlie decided to take pity on the stranger and meet her halfway, fearing that if she didn't, the woman would end up sprawled on her face with her shoe stuck in the grass.

"Can I help you?" Charlie asked, trying to make the politeness in her voice outweigh the slight tremor of laughter at the sight of the expression of confusion on the woman's face. Clearly, she wasn't used to being on a farm.

"I'm looking for Charlie Jenkins," she said.

"That would be me," Charlie smiled.

"Oh, hello. My name is Amanda Ault, I'm a journalist with the *Herald*; would you mind if I asked you a few questions?"

Far from reassuring Charlie, the realization that she was talking to a reporter only raised more questions. It wasn't as though she hadn't spoken to the *Herald* before—one of their people had been at every press conference Charlie had held.

"I can't think what you would ask. I have nothing to say now that I didn't say after the Derby, and I know one of your reporters was there because I read the article." Charlie did her best to hide the annoyance she was feeling. The last thing she wanted right now was for reporters to start hanging around Shamrock while she was trying to focus on getting Storm ready for his race.

"Is it true that you are looking for a new jockey? I'm trying to work the female angle for my style section, and the editor said I could make a go of it. But I guess the female owner/female trainer angle is a no-go per word on the street," Amanda said, ignoring Charlie's comment.

Charlie, taken aback, simply stared at the woman in front of her. They hadn't told anyone that Lilly wouldn't be riding. Lilly had gone back to her old job working with horses at Laurel and people were noticing that she wasn't riding at Pimlico. Charlie didn't think that would raise too many questions, as usually the exercise riders did the galloping leading up to their races, with the jockey only putting a leg over when a horse was scheduled to breeze.

Sometimes a jockey didn't even do that much and got on a strange horse in the paddock right before the race. However, Lilly wasn't that kind of jockey, and she spent the time to get know the horses she rode. This woman was probably following up on the fact that Lilly had done all the training rides on Storm leading up to the Derby. But how did she know she wasn't here now?

"I'm sorry, where did you hear that?" Charlie asked.

"We received an anonymous tip. Is it true? Your jockey quit, and you're looking for another one?" Amanda had pulled out a recorder and was holding it close enough to pick up everything Charlie said. Charlie of course, had no intention of saying anything worth recording.

"I'm not going to comment on that, I'm afraid. We're really focused on training right now, and I don't have time to answer questions." Shouting from the field added credence to Charlie's words, and she turned to see what was going on.

From where Charlie stood, she couldn't tell who was whom. Jenny had stepped in as the exercise rider, and she was standing by Storm, running a hand over his side, while one of the men was looking at the horse's foot. Charlie thought it was probably a thrown shoe or a rock. There were worse things, and it looked like Storm was okay, if only mildly annoyed.

"Ms. Jenkins, it would really go a long way with our readership if you would just give us a little inside scoop. Genuine Storm is a hometown hero, look at his beautiful grey coat over there. You and Lilly are the only female duo ever to win the Kentucky Derby and everyone wants to know what you all are doing to get ready for the…" she looked down at her cell phone to reference something, "to get ready for the race, yes, the Preakness. Well, and of course, what you might be wearing on race day," the reporter smiled brightly.

Charlie looked skeptically at the reporter. She clearly knew nothing about horse racing, and may have been ignorant about sporting events altogether. She was young, clearly trying to make a name for herself as a journalist. Still, Charlie didn't like the idea that someone was giving out information about their team to reporters, and she knew if she gave Amanda anything, it would only lead to more nosy journalists crawling around Shamrock. Charlie sighed and decided to distract her by addressing her last question.

"Storm is training very hard as you can see. So let's turn to your question about what I will be wearing on race day," Charlie said brightly.

The reporter's face lit up, and she raised her recorder closer to Charlie. Her editor had told her she wouldn't be able to get anything new from Charlie, but here she was about to get some juicy tidbits about what Charlie and that handsome breeder, Doug, were going to be wearing on Preakness Day. Her women readers were eating up the news about local bachelor Doug Walker and the female owner of the Kentucky Derby winner.

Charlie slipped an arm through Amanda's and guided her back towards her car so she wouldn't stumble, as well as to turn her away from Storm, who Jenny was walking towards them on their way back to his stall. Charlie quickly shook her head at Jenny so she wouldn't come any closer.

"Now, as for what I will be wearing on Preakness Day..." Charlie started. She spent ten minutes outlining the outfits she and her kids would be wearing and then politely answered a few additional questions about Doug and what he would be wearing. Charlie provided a few details about how they had met, but most of that was common knowledge and she figured the relationship stuff was really what this woman was after.

By the time they were done, Storm was safely back in his stall and the others had started working with a few of the two-year-olds in training.

"I really must be going, Miss Ault, but thank you for coming by and tell your readers we appreciate their support," Charlie said as she made an obvious send off by opening the car door for the reporter.

"Thank you so much for your time, Charlie, and good luck to all of you," Amanda said as she folded herself into the front seat of her tiny car. "The colors of the dress you are planning on wearing will look splendid against the grey of Genuine Storm when you get your picture taken in the winners' circle!"

Charlie smiled at her innocence and waved as the reporter spun around the circle and drove down the driveway. Amanda had been so excited about getting information about clothes and Charlie's relationship with Doug that she had totally forgotten about her original questions of Lilly not riding Storm. Charlie let out a sigh of relief.

"She knew?" Doug pushed a glass of wine over the counter to Charlie. She had told him all about the reporter.

"I don't know. I mean, I guess, yes, because she asked about it straight off, and that tells me she was pretty confident. She's got no proof though. From where we were, Jenny could have easily been Lilly, and she didn't seem like she knew enough about racing to know the difference between an exercise rider and an actual jockey. She was more interested in what I would be wearing on race day." Charlie sipped from the glass in her hand, sighing as the drink slid down her throat and warmed her.

"Who would have told?" Doug hadn't touched his own glass, but was staring off in the direction of the barn.

"Well, I wondered that, too. Only a handful of people know Lilly's not riding in the Preakness. She returned to Laurel to continue her normal work life, like any other jockey. It's not like just because a jockey wins the biggest race of the year, he or she doesn't continue to go to work every day. All twenty jockeys got up the day after the Derby at oh-dark-thirty and started hustling for their next ride. It just doesn't make sense though, you know? I can't think who it would be."

"Well whoever it was, it's not that big of a deal. Who cares if people know Lilly's not riding? That's not going to change things. I mean, it would be different if she'd left to ride a different horse, but as things stand…" Doug seemed to realize that his glass was waiting, untouched, and he took a deep drink.

"That's true. I'm going to make a call or two when I leave here, I think. I need to start talking to other jockeys. As much as it kills me, we need to make sure Storm is comfortable with whoever we get, and the longer I wait, the harder it will be to get everyone accustomed to the change." Charlie buried her face in her hands. She'd really been hoping that the complicated part was over. She'd worked so hard for months to scrape together the perfect team, and now she had less than two weeks to do it again.

She felt Doug's strong hands begin to massage her shoulders, and she relaxed into the feeling. It was nice to have someone who supported her again.

"So…you and Hunter…?" Doug's voice was calm, but his hands tightened with the question. Charlie smiled.

"He was close with Peter, like I said. They were in the same fraternity. We always got on well, because we both had an interest in horses, which Peter never really did. When we graduated, he took a job…huh…I don't remember where, it was so long ago. Anyway, he moved away, and we only ever heard from him every few months or so, and only when Peter called him first. Then the kids came, and we just sort of lost touch. We'd get a postcard every now and then, from whatever new place he was working. He sent one when Peter died. That's the last I'd heard from him."

"It didn't occur to you that my horse trainer named Hunter might be the same Hunter you knew?" Doug was clearly skeptical. Charlie snorted.

"Did I think that maybe you were employing a man that I had known as an acquaintance twenty years ago, and contrived to hide that fact from you? Is that what you're asking?"

"Is that a 'no'?" She could hear the smile in his voice, and turned to meet it with one of her own.

"It is, indeed."

"He seemed rather excited to see you, though." It wasn't an accusation, merely an observation, but one that Charlie could tell weighed on him.

"Well I think he always had a little crush on me. I mean, not many girls cared as much for his passion as I did. He used to joke about stealing me away from Peter. Obviously, that never actually worked out for him."

"Hmmm. You're not a woman easily stolen, is that what you're saying?"

"I just know what I want, I guess. And once I have it…" She pulled his face down to her and kissed him. He smiled against her lips and pulled her closer. She melted into him, letting everything else go, the stress of the last week and the anxiety that filled her at the thought of finding a new jockey.

"Have I told you yet, how much I enjoy being something that you want?"

Doug teased, running his hand through her hair.

"I don't think so, no. That's okay though, I'm the kind of girl who would rather be shown…not told." She traced her finger from his temple to his chin. He let out a breathy laugh, pulled Charlie to her feet, and guided her down the hall to his bedroom.

 # Winner Avenue

Charlie sat in her truck outside 5606 Winner Avenue.

It was Saturday and time was running out. The Preakness was seven days away and she had to make a decision on her jockey, but she had one last-ditch plan to get through to Lilly.

The house was small and non-descript, white with black shutters. The sun was just starting its descent and the shadows fell across the front yard where tidy flower beds housed blooming day lilies and azalea scrubs. A large oak tree stood in the corner of the yard with an old tire swing hanging from a branch. The rope had been tied there for so long the bark had started to grow around it.

Charlie opened the truck's door and walked across the street and up the sidewalk to the front door. She raised her finger to ring the doorbell. She took a deep breath before pressing the button, praying she was doing the right thing.

Kate's research on Lilly had led them to this address, the home where she grew up. Public records noted that this was the home of Joyce and Robert Garrett, Lilly's parents. Talking with them was Charlie's last chance to fill in the blanks and hopefully find out something that would convince Lilly to ride

Storm in the Preakness. She was running out of time—they were a week away and she needed to start considering other options if she wasn't successful.

Charlie pressed the doorbell and listened to its chime beyond the door, open and protected by a screen to take full advantage of the spring breeze blowing as the smells of cut grass wafted through the air. Charlie looked down the street towards Pimlico and could just barely make out the top of the Preakness barns that would house Storm in just a few days. How Lilly must have loved growing up in sight of one of the most important racetracks in the country, home of the Preakness.

"May I help you?" A voice came from behind Charlie. She spun around, startled.

"Yes, I hope so," she said quickly. The woman stood erect behind the screen door, not offering to open it. She was slight in build with her grey hair cut short. The hands holding the dish towel gave away the years of tending to her beautiful gardens in front of the house.

"I am Charlie Jenkins," Charlie said and waited. She had assumed her name would mean something to this woman. The woman gave her a blank stare from behind the screen door.

"Charlie Jenkins," Charlie repeated, "owner of Genuine Storm." The woman continued to stare at Charlie without any sort of recognition.

Charlie stammered, "Ma'am, your daughter, Lilly, rode my horse Genuine Storm and they won the Kentucky Derby a week ago."

The color drained from the face of the woman standing in front of her. Her hands tightened around the dish towel as Charlie heard a sharp intake of air. The screen door stood between the two women staring at each other. Charlie wanted to open it and hold up the woman in front of her who was visibly starting to crumble. The woman put out her hand and grabbed the door jamb next to her to keep from collapsing.

"Robert!" she called out. She moved her hand to the door handle and opened the screen door.

"Please come in," she motioned Charlie inside the house, "I'm Joyce Garrett. We haven't seen Lilly in a long time."

Charlie found herself sitting on a comfortable brown loveseat in a lovely light blue living room. The windows looked out on to a tidy backyard. More of the same beautiful flower gardens lined the fence around the back.

The fireplace in the room had a mantel full of family pictures. More pictures were housed among the books that lined the shelves to each side of the fireplace. A version of Lilly was in each one of them. There were pictures of Lilly as a baby, as a toddler, a few with her and her dog, as well as a teenager Lilly standing next to horses. What Charlie couldn't find were any pictures of Lilly as a jockey or even past her teenage years.

Robert Garrett was sitting across from Charlie in a well-worn recliner. He hadn't spoken a word to Charlie, and they waited in silence until Joyce walked back into the room from the kitchen carrying three bottles of water. She handed one to Charlie and then sat in a chair pulled up close to the recliner and grabbed for her husband's hand.

"Tell us," Joyce said.

Charlie didn't know where to start. She had not been prepared for what she had walked into here on Winner Avenue as she looked at the visibly stricken parents of Lilly Garrett.

"Joyce, Robert, I'm here today to try to find out about Lilly as a girl. You see, she is very dear to my family and my horse, Storm." Charlie was still trying to comprehend how these two people, who lived in sight of Pimlico, were not aware that their daughter had won America's biggest racing event just last Saturday.

"Ms. Jenkins, we have not seen Lilly since she was 18 years old," Joyce said. Charlie stared at them, her turn to be speechless. Joyce squeezed her husband's hand and he turned his head to look at his wife. A look passed between them.

"Is she okay? She hasn't been hurt, has she?" Joyce leaned forward in her chair, unable to hide her eagerness for news about her only daughter. Charlie's heart broke for the parents sitting across from her. Her hands had turned ice cold and shook a little as she put the top back on the bottle of water and decided to give these parents as much as she could.

"No, she's not hurt. I'll start at the beginning of when I met Lilly. It was towards the end of last year. I needed to find a jockey to ride my horse..." Charlie proceeded to tell Lilly's parents how Charlie had met Lilly at Laurel racetrack and convinced her to give her horse a chance. She told them about Lilly's special talent of connecting with problem horses and how she had helped Storm learn to love to run, culminating in their exciting Derby win last Saturday.

"Lilly has become a special part of my family. My daughter adores her, as does my son, and my horse runs only for her. After the Derby, Lilly told me she had fulfilled her obligation of riding Storm, that her part was done, and she would not ride Storm in the Preakness. Nothing I said could convince her otherwise. She has gone back to playing horse whisperer at Laurel, effectively turning her back on all of us," Charlie summarized, her sadness and frustration coming through in her final comments.

Robert and Joyce sat quietly, listening to Charlie. Joyce looked at her husband and he nodded his head, his eyes showing the pain of not knowing about his daughter and her accomplishments.

"Ms. Jenkins...Charlie, I know you may find it hard to believe that we weren't aware of Lilly winning the Derby. We stopped following horse racing many years ago. It was too painful to read about Elizabeth when we knew she wanted nothing to do with us." Joyce's voice trembled, but she continued. "When Elizabeth was a teenager she went to work at Pimlico for a trainer whose name I cannot recall."

"Tom Malone," Charlie filled in.

"Yes, that was his name. Elizabeth loved being around the horses each and every day. We allowed her to work there as long as her grades at school were straight A's. Elizabeth was our only child and we wanted the best for her."

Charlie could almost feel this mother's need to tell her story that she had kept inside for over 15 years.

"I didn't realize how much she had fallen in love with that way of life.

She had continued doing well at school, but Elizabeth had started to become more and more withdrawn and only talking about the horses and…" Joyce paused to take a breath, "and becoming a jockey." Charlie noticed it was hard for her to get the words out.

"Our children's passions are sometimes very hard to understand," Charlie said, smiling slightly. Joyce returned the look tentatively before continuing.

"We had big plans for our daughter, Ms. Jenkins," she said, squeezing her husband's hand. "We used to sit around the dining room table talking about the doctor or lawyer she would become. You see, Robert and I never had a chance to be whatever we wanted to be. Elizabeth had the world in front of her. She had a lot of friends and was an excellent student and she was a beautiful person inside and out. She could have been anything she set her mind on."

Charlie listened as this compassionate mother spilled her soul to her about the daughter they had lost.

"Elizabeth had been spending all her free time at the track. Between that and school, I never saw her anymore. She had that boyfriend, I think Buck was his name, and if she wasn't at the track, she was usually with him. She was growing up and I couldn't control her path anymore. She came home one night and told Robert and me she wanted to become a jockey. A jockey, really? I was shocked. We had all these plans. It wasn't just Robert and I forcing her down a path, Elizabeth had been a part of all our conversations and now she was changing her mind.

"I couldn't believe it and I lost it. We had a huge argument and Elizabeth moved out that night, with no looking back. Packed up a few things and then that boyfriend came and picked her up. I tried to reach out to her, but it seemed the world she had entered closed in around her. She wouldn't take my calls. I tried her friends from school, but they were a close-knit group. The only thing I could get out of them was that Elizabeth was still going to school.

"Robert and I had hoped she would change her mind, come to her senses. But she didn't. For the next few years we read everything we could about Elizabeth, the jockey. Robert and I would even go to the track and watch her in races sometimes. We saw how happy she was, and thought maybe we'd been too quick to dismiss her dream; we tried calling her at the track and even tried several times to get through the security gate to see her in person. We left messages for her with the trainer, but we never heard back from her. It got to be too painful to read about her, so we just stopped. We always hoped she would come home, that she would know that we loved her no matter what she decided to do. But the damage had been done, and to a teenager, that damage can last a lifetime."

Joyce sat there spent, her shoulders heaving as she took a deep breath and fought back her emotions. Robert kept his eyes focused on the picture of a bright-eyed beautiful blond teenager that sat in the center of their mantle.

Charlie reached for Joyce's hand. "Joyce, I want to let you know that Lilly, your Elizabeth, has grown into a loving, compassionate adult. She obviously takes after both of you. I can't tell you why she allowed the rift between the two of you go on for so long. I have a teenager of my own right now, and I can tell you there are many times I imagine he would like to walk out the door and not come back."

Robert and Joyce smiled at her weakly.

"I can promise you that I will do what I can to bring you and Lilly back together. I know how it feels to lose family, and if I can mend this, I will. She and I have formed a good relationship and I think she looks up to me a bit. Maybe why she won't ride my horse for me has something to do with why she has never come home to you," Charlie said softly, her mind already processing all she had learned today.

"Thank you." It was the first time she heard Robert speak, but there was no doubt in her mind that they were the two most sincere words spoken that afternoon. Charlie felt her throat close slightly and the tears well up in her eyes.

"I have taken up way too much of your time today. I am so thankful you took the time to talk to me. It would be my honor to have you over to Pimlico to watch my horse run, with or without Lilly riding him. Would you consider coming?" Charlie asked.

Joyce looked over at Robert, and shook her head slightly. "I don't think so, but thank you. The memories are too painful. If you are fortunate enough to have Elizabeth ride your horse, then we wouldn't want to distract her. She obviously has become quite accomplished. We only wish we could be a small part of her life. But we won't be forced upon her. She needs to make that decision. If the timing is right, please let her know we love her and miss her terribly."

Robert stood up and walked toward the front door. "Thank you for coming, Ms. Jenkins. Good luck next Saturday."

Charlie shook his hand with both of hers, trying to shake away the sadness that emanated from his body.

New Jockey

Charlie's visit to Lilly's parents had given her more information, but also raised more questions. Where did Lilly go after her argument with her parents and why did she never return? She had continued to ride, obviously, but she had stayed away from Pimlico for the most part.

Charlie and Ryan were sitting in their customary spot on a couple of Adirondack chairs outside the barn overlooking the paddock. Skylar's pony Hershey was enjoying himself in the late afternoon spring sun. Unlike most horses that enjoyed being part of a herd, he was perfectly content to be by himself, basking in the love of his little girl. Skylar was also propped up in her customary spot, leaning against the big oak tree in the center of the field, her nose in a book. Hershey wouldn't stray very far and was making a circle eating the grass within a ten-foot circumference around the tree.

Ryan was adamant they needed to give a new jockey a few days with Storm, so they needed to make a final call. Buck was the only suitable replacement for Lilly. There was little chance he would leave his position as jockey on Duke, Storm's number one competition, but still Charlie had to try.

She'd dialed the number. All she had to do was push the call button. It was Saturday evening and her day had been taken up finding all she could about Lilly's past. She was tired.

"It just seems so final," she said. Ryan was staring intently at his mother.

"I know. Lilly said she's not coming back though, and Jenny can't ride Storm in the race, so unless we want to forfeit…" He looked pointedly at the phone in Charlie's hand.

"Ugh! Okay, I'm just gonna do it." Charlie pushed the button and raised the phone to her ear. It rang twice, and then a voice sounded through the speaker.

"Hello?"

"Yes, hi. Um, is this Buck Wheeler?" Charlie suddenly found herself unprepared for the conversation she had called to have.

"Yes, can I ask who's calling?" His tone was polite, if not wary.

"My name is Charlie Jenkins, I'm—"

"You're the owner of Genuine Storm," he said, clearly surprised.

"That's right. I'm…well, I'm calling because our jockey has decided not to continue on with us, but she was kind enough to leave us a list of names of other jockeys who might be interested. You were at the top of the list, so I thought maybe I could convince you to at least meet me and talk about the possibility of you riding my horse in the Preakness next weekend."

Charlie waited.

———————————

It was fifteen minutes until she was supposed to be meeting Buck. They had agreed on a small coffee shop halfway between Shamrock and Pimlico, a bit off the beaten path so they wouldn't be noticed. She was still trying to avoid all media until the decision on who was going to ride Storm was finalized.

She walked somberly into the establishment. She had been so confident Lilly would change her mind, having to make this decision seemed like such a betrayal.

"Mrs. Jenkins?" She spun to find out who'd hailed her. It was a man she'd never seen before.

"Can I help you?" she asked, warily. The man motioned to an empty table for them to sit at and smiled. As they each took a seat, the man said, "My name is Paul Ritter, I was Lilly's agent before she stopped racing."

"Oh, okay." Charlie raised an eyebrow, still uncertain what this man's intentions were, and how he knew where she'd be.

"I didn't mean to make you uneasy, Ms. Jenkins. Buck Wheeler and I go way back, and he told me you called him about riding Storm next week." He hailed a waiter and ordered two waters for the table.

"So…you're here to negotiate the terms? Does this mean he accepts the offer?" Charlie asked.

"What? Oh, no, I'm not his agent," Paul said, laughing at the idea.

"Well then forgive me for asking, but exactly what are you doing here? My meeting was with Buck. Why would he tell you about it?" Charlie's annoyance was getting the better of her, and Paul, sensing that it was not a time to test her, folded his hands on the table in front of him and leaned forward.

"Ms. Jenkins, first off, Buck is not going to give up his ride on Duke to ride Storm. He's made a commitment to Duke's owners and he doesn't take that lightly. Buck called me and asked me to meet you in hopes that I could find a solution for you. He knows that Lilly will regret not riding in the Preakness and given that I was Lilly's agent, Buck thought I might be able to help you get through to her."

Charlie was speechless; this was not going as she had planned. She nodded and tried to hide her frustration. She liked being in control and needed to take a few minutes to organize her thoughts.

Looking around, she noticed they were seated in more of a café than a coffee shop. A waitress approached their table. She set down the waters that Paul had asked for, and then all but rolled her eyes when they ordered different drinks and asked for a few more minutes to peruse the menu.

Charlie opened her mouth to speak, but found that no words had come to her yet. Paul was looking at her with a half-smile, waiting for her to speak before he said anything else. They sat in silence for a few minutes until the waitress returned with their lattes. Charlie wrapped her hands around her coffee mug, wishing it was mixed with something a little stronger to help her through the next few minutes. Finally, she couldn't stay quiet any longer.

"Obviously, like I told Buck, I need a jockey," she said, her abruptness startling even herself. She took a deep breath and smiled. "I mean…Lilly is amazing, and the fact that she's not riding for me anymore has been harder on my team that I care to let on, but circumstances being what they are, and the Preakness being only a week away, I'm in rather a bind."

"Ms. Jenkins—" Paul started.

"Oh, you can call me Charlie," she said.

"Okay. Charlie, I am more than aware of your situation. Lilly was my client for years, I know what she's capable of, and I'm telling you, she's the one you want," Paul said. Charlie stared at him for a moment before speaking.

"I'm confused. Why would you tell me that? You're an agent, surely you should be plugging your current clients, rather than someone who left you." She realized after she'd said it how rude it sounded, and she was shocked with her own abrasiveness. Her embarrassment must have shown on her face because he held up a reassuring hand.

"Don't worry, it's a fair question. I take no offense."

"Still, that was rude of me. I'm sorry," Charlie said. Paul took a sip of his coffee and then sighed.

"Lilly…Lilly has a gift, there's no doubt about it. I don't know many jockeys who can retire and then come back to win a title like the Derby. She was meant to ride. And I don't mean just helping with the problem horses like she has been, but really ride, against the best, in races."

"Well, we're on the same page with that one. That doesn't answer my question though." Charlie was starting to sense something more than professional courtesy in the tone and demeanor of her companion.

"I've known Lilly for a long time. I…we were really close when…" he hesitated, trying to find the words, and suddenly a thought struck Charlie.

"You know why she quit," she said. Paul didn't look at her.

"Yeah, I know why she quit, and it killed me not to be able to do anything about it." He swallowed furiously, as though trying to dislodge the words from his throat.

"Hey." Charlie reached out and grabbed his hand. "Lilly is really important to me. I only want to help her." Paul stared at Charlie for what seemed like an eternity. Finally, he sighed, and his shoulders lost their tension. He nodded, took a sip of his water, and then spoke in a voice so low that Charlie had to lean almost all the way across the table in order to hear him.

"Listen, the horse industry is a close-knit community, especially the everyday workers—the grooms, the exercise riders, the hot-walkers—all of us who really need to make ends meet doing what we do. The owners, they come and go, and the trainers may not be very loyal to us, including the jocks who they can supplant minutes before a race is to go off, so we need to find ways to look out for each other. Even though we compete with each other on a daily basis for the rides and the horses, we still look out for our own," he started.

"I've always respected that aspect of the racing community," Charlie said.

Paul nodded. He took a deep breath, steeled himself for what he was about to say, and then said, "The first thing you need to know is that Tom Malone is an angry, cheating bastard."

 # Confrontation

Charlie's mind was reeling.

She didn't know what she'd expected. Obviously, something horrible had happened, but Charlie had never really imagined how horrible it would have to be to stop someone like Lilly from doing what she was born to do.

Now she knew. Paul's hesitation to tell the story had eased the more he'd spoken, and by the end, the words had poured out of him. Charlie could only imagine how hard it had been for him to keep all that to himself for so long, especially given their close relationship. It was clear how much he cared for Lilly, and how much the thought of her pain troubled him.

Charlie was driving aimlessly, unsure where it was she needed to be. She could go to Laurel Park and talk to Lilly, but how would that work? She'd have to say how she knew everything, and then Lilly would probably be mad at Paul. She could go to Shamrock and see Doug and ask his advice, but then she'd have to tell him everything, and maybe Lilly didn't want him to know. She could go find Tom Malone and stab him repeatedly in the leg with a pitchfork…

Or she could just go home. She could start calling the other jockeys on the list Lilly had given her, and hope to God that one of them would agree to race for her. Lilly would be free to make her own decision about whether to tell Charlie about her past, and Charlie would be free to pretend like she was just as ignorant about it as ever.

Could she do that though? Knowing what she now knew, could she still see Lilly and pretend not to know the hurt she was hiding? Her maternal instincts reared defensively. No, she wouldn't be able to look at Lilly and pretend she didn't know. She would have to come clean.

Before she'd finished thinking, her subconscious had started her on her way to Laurel Park. Charlie sighed, wondering how she was going to breach the subject with Lilly.

The barns at Laurel were relatively easy to navigate, and Lilly was even easier to find. It was late afternoon and Charlie found her sitting on a bale of hay quietly murmuring to a horse with its head low over its door. The horse was big, and jet black, and looked similar to the horse that Lilly was on when Charlie first met her. This one seemed to be listening intently to whatever Lilly was saying, its nostrils quivering and ears flicking back and forth.

Lilly looked up when she heard Charlie approaching, and the expression on her face changed from one of ease to one of cautious greeting.

"Charlie, I didn't expect to see you here. Is something wrong?"

"No, nothing's…" Charlie stopped; if she didn't say it outright, she felt as though she would never say it at all. "Actually yes, there is something wrong. I know why you don't want to ride," Charlie said. Lilly's expression was unreadable. When she spoke, her voice was even and calm.

"What do you mean?"

Charlie was, not for the first time, torn between a maternal response and knowing that there was absolutely nothing she could do for the girl in front of her. At the very least, she knew honesty was the best course of action.

"I set up a meeting with Buck today to ask him to ride Storm in the Preakness. When I got to the meeting, Buck wasn't there. A man named Paul Ritter was." Lilly's face drained of color and she sat so still, Charlie could have mistaken her for a statue. She continued, "He had some interesting things to say about Tom Malone."

The change in atmosphere was instant and palpable. Lilly's face stayed blank, but her body tensed, she stood up from the bale of hay, and moved away from Charlie.

"What did he tell you?"

"Lilly, he told me everything. I just want—"

"No, listen, I don't want to talk about it. I have never wanted to talk about it. Paul doesn't know anything. It's none of his business!"

"Lilly, I am so sorry. I never meant to get involved like this. I'm not here to make you relive anything or…I just wanted to let you know that I love you. You are family to me, and I will do anything for you. All you have to do is ask." Lilly broke her stare and looked determinedly away. Charlie waited for a minute before she turned and started to walk back the way she came. She made it five steps before a choked sob reached her ears and stopped her in her tracks.

"He…wasn't supposed to be a bad guy. He's the one who gave me my first shot at being a jockey. He introduced me to Buck. Tom was like family to me. When I had a big argument with my parents, he took me in. Tom was my mentor, my boss…he was like a father to me."

Charlie couldn't say how she'd gotten there, but suddenly she was across the barn, holding Lilly in an embrace so tight that she could almost feel her ribs bruising. They stayed like that for several minutes, with Lilly holding onto Charlie as though letting go would mean certain death.

The Accident

Lilly talked slowly and methodically as the two women sat side by side on the hay bales, describing to Charlie what had transpired between her and Tom so many years ago, the day she walked away from her dream.

Lilly had been making a name for herself and had quite a following, winning races from coast to coast. She had overcome the barrier of women in racing. It had been challenging, but worth every ounce of grit she had in her petite body.

Trainers were requesting her and there were many times she had to decide between which horse to ride in an important race. From Santa Anita Park in California to Gulfsteam in Florida to Saratoga in New York, Lilly had her pick of the best racehorses in the country.

But she always came home to Tom, no matter what track she was at. Especially when he needed her.

Tom would get a problem horse in his barn and her cell phone would ring. She would call her agent and rearrange her rides and fly home to help him. She couldn't let Tom down, not after he helped her get where she was now. If it weren't for him she never would have sat on her first racehorse. If it weren't for him, she never would have stopped riding racehorses.

Lilly had gotten the call so many years ago.

"I need you Elizabeth. Got a fireball in the barn and only you can handle her," he had said over the line.

"Can you give me a few days, Tom? I've got some big rides this weekend that I need to gallop for and I have to get to know the horses," she had said. It was getting exhausting flying or driving back and forth depending on where she was in the country.

At times, it seemed Tom called her on a whim. Lilly would arrive at his barn only to find that the horse he was complaining about wasn't such a problem. She would spend a few days helping him out, galloping and riding races as he needed. But in reality, he could have found another exercise rider or jockey to help him out. Lilly had recommended a few over the years, but he would say no and was only happy when she came home.

"Can't do, little lady," as he still liked to call her, "please just come for a day and I'll have you back for the weekend races," he pleaded.

Lilly paused with her hand on her cell phone. "Of course, Tom, I'll plan on being there tomorrow afternoon."

"Excellent!" Tom replied, relief that she would come back evident in his voice.

When she arrived, Lilly sat in her rental car, her head leaning back against the headrest. She knew she had to get out and start the day, finding out what problem Tom had, but she needed a few minutes of quiet reflection.

The morning mist was starting to lift. Lilly opened the car window and took a deep breath through her nose.

With her eyes closed, a small smile crept across her face. She loved the smell of the barns, the backstretch of the racetrack. She could hear the muffled sound of horses pulling themselves up from their beds of straw, nickering to the grooms as they prepared the first meal of the day.

Lilly missed the simplicity of those days. The days as a teenager when her only responsibility was to make sure the horse she was in charge of was well cared for. She would groom them until their coats shone in the early morning sun as they jogged onto the track. She would wait patiently until they returned after the workout. She loved the act of bathing a horse, soaping them up and hosing them down. Watching all the day's dirt from the track wash off and returning them to their original state of cleanliness.

Lilly sighed at the thought. She wouldn't trade places with anyone in the world right now. She loved being a jockey. It was just that life wasn't so simple anymore. There were horses to ride and races to win. Not many people realized the hard work it took to be a jockey, let alone a successful one.

Lilly thought about all the horses she rode each day, many of which she had no idea about, yet each owner had expectations that their horse could win the race. The pressure of being on the favorite and not winning was overwhelming. As much as winning gave her an adrenaline rush, winning was also a relief when it was expected. Her favorite races were those she won on a long shot, the horse that no one expected to win, except its owners.

Her cell buzzed. Lilly opened her eyes and glanced at the text.

"Hurry back, I'm busy lining up rides for next week and you have a full slate tomorrow afternoon. P." Paul would work his fingers to the bone to ensure Lilly had the right horses to ride. They made a great team.

Lilly closed her eyes again, a part of her wishing she could go back in time to the easy days of yesteryear. Back when all she had to worry about was getting good grades and meeting Macy at the mall for some shopping time. Did she regret the path her life had taken?

Not one bit. Oh, she definitely would have changed how things turned out the night she fought with her parents and felt like she could never go back. Her mom had said things, she had said things. Things she thought at the time were unforgivable. She had been so naïve. Rushing out the door and moving out. Then getting in too deep with Buck.

Buck.

He was the biggest regret she had. She had shut him out for his own good, she had thought at the time. Who knows how things would have turned out if she had made a different decision so many years ago. But she hadn't wanted to ruin his dream, or hers, she selfishly thought.

She was who she was and where she was due to the decisions she had made. She couldn't change things now.

Lilly pushed open the door of her car and got out. She grabbed her helmet and protective vest from the backseat, and walked down the barns in search of Tom's set of stalls.

"Hey Lilly! Glad to see you haven't forgotten about lil' old us," came a call. Lilly waved to Gus.

"Good to see you, Gus," she said as she walked up to him. Gus stood up from the chair that he had been leaning on against the barn. Lilly held out her hand in greeting, knowing this was the easiest way to avoid getting a hug in return.

Gus took her hand, questioningly, but said, "What brings you to Pimlico?"

"Tom. He called with some big issue with a horse that 'only I' can address," she said candidly. She had had a great relationship with Gus, and she had looked up to him when she started out as one of his hot walkers. It was the job that Tom first gave her after she had stumbled her way into the backstretch of Pimlico. He had introduced her to Gus and that was that.

She was responsible for taking each racehorse after they worked on the track and walking them around to cool them off after exerting themselves. Gus had taught her much of what she knew about handling horses and had promoted her to be one of his grooms, then cheered her on when Tom promoted her to exercise rider.

"Speaking of Tom. This isn't his barn. Why are you way over here?" Lilly asked.

"I'm not workin' for him no more," Gus replied.

"What? Gus, why? You were together for so long. What happened?" Lilly questioned him.

"He's different, Lilly. Word is getting around. He was taking too many chances and I just didn't agree with his way anymore. You be careful, girl. You hear me?" Gus said earnestly.

"Really? That doesn't sound like the Tom that I know," Lilly replied.

"I can't put my finger on anything specific and I never found anything. I just knew I needed to move on. Sometimes it is what is best for everyone," Gus told her.

"I'm sorry to hear that, Gus. But I can't do the same. I appreciate your words and will keep an eye out for anything that I am not happy with. You like your new boss?" Lilly asked.

"He's a good one. Has just a small group, and it's only me. But that is fine by me, as I am gettin' older and don't have the patience to mind all the young whipper-snappers who think they know more than me." Gus smiled at her. "You take care, Lilly."

"I will, Gus. Thanks," Lilly said. This time Gus caught her in one of his big bear hugs as she turned to leave. Lilly stood silently, and then softly patted his back.

Lilly hurried off, the conversation with Gus weighing on her mind. She had to be quick and get with Tom and his problem horse. Paul was expecting her back by the afternoon tomorrow.

Lilly walked the familiar rows of stalls.

She had to steady herself as the memories came flooding back, memories of when she was just starting out and loving the feel of a racehorse, and loving Buck.

Her thoughts turned to her parents and her home just down the street. Lilly knew they still lived there. But she couldn't bring herself to stop in. They would never forgive her.

Lilly swung her leg over Lady's back and jumped to the ground. She couldn't put her finger on it, but Lady was not acting right.

"What do you think?" Tom asked Lilly.

"I'm not sure," Lilly said, her mind deep in thought. "It's like she's afraid to run. She's certainly not a fireball like you claimed over the phone, Tom. She barely wanted to gallop."

"Well, she better want to run. I have her set to run in the sixth this afternoon," Tom said.

"What?" Lilly gasped.

"Yep. I figured since I had you in town, I would maximize your expertise. She runs in a seven-furlough race," Tom said confidently.

"I'm not riding her, Tom. You know I don't ride horses if I am not 100 percent confident in their ability to run. She doesn't want to go for some reason, and I can't figure that out in just one ride," Lilly said defiantly.

Tom stepped closer to Lilly. "She will run today, and you will be on her."

Lilly took a step back. Why was he pressuring her? Things had gotten more intense the last several times Lilly had been back to help Tom. She always came knowing he had helped her so much when she had started out, but this demand seemed a bit much. The conversation with Gus came flooding back.

"But Tom, she won't win. Why race her if she has no chance?" Lilly asked.

"Her owner wants her to race and damn it, I am going to do whatever it takes to get her in a race. If I don't race her, he is pulling her out of my training," Tom finished, looking a bit wild-eyed. "You need to help me," he finished.

Lilly stood in front of Tom, her mind racing with indecision. Her instinct told her Lady shouldn't run this afternoon, but she felt she owed it to Tom to try to help him. She took a deep breath, knowing her next comment would not be perceived well. "Tom, Lady cannot run and I can't support you in this decision."

Tom's eyes reflected the darkness of a desperate man. He leaned in close to Lilly's face. She could smell the stench of old cigar on his breath.

"You will ride her, Elizabeth. You will ride her because I helped you when no one else would. You will ride her because if you don't, I will tell Buck the secret you don't want him to know."

Lilly's face went white. What did he know? Was he just threatening her, or did he really know what Lilly had kept to herself for so many years? She couldn't chance calling his bluff.

She put her hand up. "All right, Tom. I don't know what you think you know about me, but I will help you. This will be the last time that I ride for you. I think you are taking a big chance on a nice horse. She doesn't deserve to be pushed into something she's not ready for. I am going against every fiber of my being, and this will be the last time."

Tom smiled eerily at her. "Let's not jump to conclusions just yet, *Elizabeth*."

Lilly sat atop Lady in the starting gate. The filly didn't feel settled. It wasn't that she was hot-headed, but something else entirely, like she couldn't focus on the race at hand.

"Come on girl, let's just get through this race together. I'll give a call to your owners and let them know they should move you from Tom's training." That was the right thing to do.

The bell rang and the gates opened. Lilly sat quietly as Lady found her stride. She didn't push her, she wanted only to get Lady around the track to the finish line safely. Something was just not right with the mare. Why had Tom said she was fireball on the phone, yet this morning Lady didn't even toss a head? Thoughts ran through Lilly's mind as she guided Lady around the track. They were sitting mid-pack. Luckily the pace wasn't very fast, so Lilly didn't need to push Lady and her slow pace would go unnoticed by most people. But Tom would know. He had watched her ride so often that he knew when she was working hard and when she wasn't. Why had he needed her to ride this horse? Was he trying to prove his control over her with his veiled threat? What had he done to this lovely mare to turn her from the fireball he proclaimed on the phone to this lethargic mess?

Suddenly, Lady veered to the right. Lilly had been so distracted by her thoughts that she was a second too late to avoid the collision. Another horse had been racing close up at Lady's flank and Lady moved right into its path. The horse behind them clipped Lady's heels, causing her to stumble. Lilly tried to right both of them, but the force of the impact was too much. Lilly lost her balance and fell hard onto the track right into the path of the horses racing up behind them.

Instinct took over and Lilly rolled into a ball, folding her arms to her chest and pulling her knees up as tight as she could. She knew she couldn't do anything else except pray that her helmet protected her head and the injuries wouldn't be too bad. The sound of hooves pounding around her was deafening. She closed her eyes and held her breath and waited for it to be over.

As Lilly lay on the track, she tried to assess the damage. There was some pain in her shoulder, but it was manageable. She could feel her legs, she could move her arms, and her helmet had protected her from any serious head injury. She sighed with relief. The accident would never have happened if she hadn't agreed to ride Lady, then been distracted by her thoughts. She'd put the horse in danger, herself in danger, and the other horses and jockeys in danger. She hated herself for making that mistake. She hated Tom for forcing it on her.

When the ambulance arrived, Lilly was still curled up in a ball, afraid to move. The paramedics slowly straightened her legs. As they rolled her on to her back, she grimaced in pain.

"My shoulder, it's my shoulder," she grunted.

"Collar bone, more like it," the paramedic said. "Keep her right arm stable. Bring the board!" They gently slid on a neck brace as a precaution. "Just be still while we lift you on to the board. It may hurt a bit, but we will keep your arm as stable as we can."

"Thanks, but I'm fine," Lilly said, trying to move away from the hands trying to stabilize her. The pain in Lilly's right shoulder radiated down her entire arm. The adrenaline from the race and the fall was wearing off and she felt beaten up, like she had been run over by a steam engine.

"I guess that means you don't have any serious neck injuries," said the second paramedic, smiling slightly at the effort Lilly was exerting. Both men were strong and tall, and Lilly quickly realized that she would never be able to overpower them. She stopped fighting, but they barely seemed to notice the difference.

"You are very lucky," the other paramedic said to her. "The other riders did everything in their power to avoid you as you fell. Your shoulder is probably either the result of the fall or a hoof that nicked off your shoulder as the horse behind jumped over you. Your instincts were spot on; otherwise, your injuries could have been much worse. There is a reason you all wear the protective vests, but it's a shame they can't cover your entire body."

The paramedic gently removed Lilly's helmet, which was covered in dirt. He showed it to the other paramedic and then to Lilly.

"Cracked in two places. These are life-savers." Lilly closed her eyes, pushing the thoughts of the fall out of her mind. Wasn't that what Buck told her jockeys do? Jockeys don't like to think or talk about the falls or injuries they endure to ride. Lilly had to start using his advice right now or she may never get on another horse. The fall was frightening, yes, but she made it through. It would take a few months to recover, but she vowed to ride again.

"We'll be at the hospital in no time, they'll take good care of you." Lilly tried to smile at the paramedic's reassuring tone, but as the doors closed on the ambulance, tears filled her eyes.

Lilly sat patiently through the doctor's visit. She focused all of her anger and pain toward Tom. Gus had warned her about him. She'd ignored her own instincts. Even the horse had sensed that something was wrong with the situation, and Lilly had let Tom bully her into doing what he wanted, rather than what was right. Lilly was seething.

Tom hadn't tried to come see her at the hospital. Her collar bone had been broken in two places, and she had a hairline fracture in her humerus, the upper bone in her right arm. It would be a while before she could ride again. She would be in a brace for several months to ensure everything healed properly.

After she left the hospital, Lilly went back to the track. She went straight to Tom's office and kicked on the door. She heard a sound like glass breaking and then a grunt that she chose to mean 'come in.' When she entered the room, she saw Tom at his desk, disheveled and holding a tumbler of amber liquid that Lilly assumed was whiskey.

"Lilly? Your arm…what—"

"You're a bastard, Tom Malone. I told you I didn't want to ride that horse. I *told* you she wasn't right. I don't know what happened to you, but you are not the man I knew, and I'm done helping you. Do you hear me? I'm DONE!" She took a step forward and felt something break under her foot. She looked down and saw glass littering the floor. A broken bottle lay only a few feet away. From what was left of the label, Lilly could tell that she'd been right about what was in Tom's glass.

Tom's chair scraped across the floor, drawing Lilly's attention. There was something in his eyes that made her scared. She backed away from him.

"I gave you everything. I gave you your start, you ungrateful brat. I took you in. The only reason you're even riding today is because of me. You should be thanking me. You should be worshiping the ground I walk on!" He closed the distance between them. Lilly turned to leave the room, but Tom was faster. He reached past her and slammed the door.

"Get away from me!" Lilly yelled. Tom grabbed her by the arm. Lilly cried out in pain. With her other arm in a sling, she was virtually helpless.

"You lost me a client today," Tom snarled. He was so close to her face that she couldn't see him clearly.

"Let me go!" Lilly struggled helplessly against the drunken man. She could smell the alcohol on his clothes and she guessed that the glass on his desk hadn't been his first of the day. He used his grip on her arm to push her against the door.

"You cost me money." His words were slurred. She could feel his breath on her face. His grip on her arm tightened and brought her off of the door slightly, only to slam her against it again. Her broken shoulder made contact with the wood and she screamed in agony. He slapped her face.

"Shut up!" He slapped her again. Lilly closed her eyes. She didn't want to know what was going to happen next. She didn't want to be there. She let her mind travel. She was vaguely aware of more pain coursing through her. She could hear someone screaming, but it didn't sound like her.

She was back on the outside of the fence; it was one of those days when her dad had walked with her to see the horses work out in the morning. They talked about school and her friends. He'd woken her up early to go buy some bulbs for her mother's garden.

They'd gotten coffee together, and then he'd taken her to their favorite spot by the track. She remembered seeing the most beautiful bay, running around the track. Her father had talked about how graceful the horse was, and how brave and strong the riders were. She'd always loved horses, but that was the day she'd decided to pursue her dream of becoming a jockey.

Suddenly, there was another voice in the room. The pain eased. There was yelling. Someone grabbed her and she tensed. She felt tears falling from her eyes, and couldn't tell when they'd started. Whoever had her now was supporting her weight. She felt herself being lifted and carried out of the room. She heard boots scraping against the floor.

She tried her best to focus on the hands holding her. They were callused and warm. The smell of the person was welcoming and familiar.

"Did you—oh my god! Bring her up here, Gus. Set her down!" Lilly recognized that voice, but it didn't belong here.

"Paul?"

"Lilly, what happened?" The callused hands lowered her onto a bed and laid her down. She heard a kettle whistling, she felt something cold on her forehead, and then she drifted off, back to the golden day with her dad as they stood outside the world she'd given him up to live in.

A New Way of Life

When she woke up, she saw that she was in her old room. For a moment, Lilly felt at peace. Then the events of the day came back to her and she panicked. She sat bolt upright, which made her gasp as pain wracked her body.

"Easy there. Lilly, don't move too much." Paul appeared at her side, which startled her. He helped ease her up. He handed her a glass of water and pulled up a chair so that he was facing her.

"What are you doing here?" Lilly asked. Her voice was weak, and it hurt when she talked. Paul rolled his eyes at her.

"Well, when my number one client has an accident, I make it a point to help in any way I can." He smiled at her. She attempted to smile back, but the pain was immense.

"You shouldn't have come, it wasn't a big deal at all. Barely hurt my shoulder. I'll be riding in no time." Lilly made to stand up, but Paul held up a hand and she sat back down. She was grateful. Her chest hurt immensely. She closed her eyes and tried to find a part of her body that didn't hurt. She failed.

"Lilly…what happened?" Paul's voice was quiet, but there was anger in his tone. She opened her eyes and saw him looking at her. His eyes were searching. She sighed, and grimaced in pain.

There was no denying anything. There was no way around the truth of what had happened to her. She related every detail, just as she remembered it. Paul listened quietly. She went through the morning, everything Tom had said to her, how she'd gone to confront him. She went through everything except the threat about Buck. She rushed through it at parts in order to get to the thing she really wanted to talk about.

"How bad is it?" she asked. He hesitated and her heart sank. Paul was always straight with her. If he wasn't saying anything right now, it must be worse than she thought. She shook her head in disbelief.

"Lilly, I think you should press charges," Paul said.

"I can't. I can't risk it." She felt the tears fill her eyes again and she tried to swallow them back down.

"What do you mean? Lilly, he deserves to be in jail! He deserves—" Lilly stood abruptly. Paul could tell it caused her a lot of pain, but her face was set, and her voice was steady.

"You're right. He does. But I can't. He said he would tell Buck, and I can't risk it."

"Tell Buck what?" Lilly shook her head. Paul didn't press the issue.

"Tom did a lot for me when I was starting out. I'm not pressing charges."

"Lilly, that's ridiculous! He assaulted you! You'll be lucky if you ride again for the rest of this year!"

"Paul! I'll be fine! I'll take some time off. I'll go back to helping out troubled horses. I'll…I don't know what I'll do. I can't think about it right now."

"You have to think about it right now. If you're going to press charges—"

"I'M NOT! Paul, you don't get it! There's more than just my career at stake here, and I'm not willing to let him take anything else from me! Respect that!"

Paul was quiet for a minute. He could see that the words were costing her a lot, and he could tell that she wasn't going to change her mind any time soon.

"Okay. Just tell me what you need right now," he said.

Not long after, she collected her car from the track and headed back out to California. She needed to get as far away from Tom as she could. She needed to heal, as well as find out what her next move would be. She spent a few weeks waiting for some sort of backlash to come, but it seemed that the race was so small no one really covered it, and anyone who'd heard about it just assumed that all of her injuries were from the fall. Lilly spent weeks worrying that Tom actually did know her secret, and she waited with baited breath for him to spill the beans. Nothing ever came of it, and she finally went back to the east coast.

It was Tom's fault that Lilly wasn't yet racing again. He had put her in a situation she couldn't say no to, and had threatened her. And then he'd beaten her. She couldn't stomach the thought of seeing him again, but he was a big part of the racing world, and if she really wanted her career back, then she might have to face him. She was afraid, and there was no place for fear on the racetrack.

But she was determined to ride. As her arm and shoulder healed, Lilly spent hours working with horses that were also being rehabbed. Paul was kind enough to introduce her to any trainer he came across who had horses that were injured. They and Lilly healed together.

Lilly fine-tuned her abilities to relate to them and find out what made them tick. Horses under her care healed more quickly, rumor had it. Hot-headed horses were more manageable and sour ones turned energetic in her presence. Trainers started searching Lilly out. When she was ready to get back in the saddle, she had a long list of clients who wanted her services to help with troubled horses.

It was extremely gratifying to work with horses that needed help, and Lilly found herself being called upon to travel to different tracks. Before heading to any track, she would find out if Tom was stabling any horses there. She avoided him at all costs. If she was at a certain track and she caught wind he would be bringing in a horse, she abruptly packed up her things and moved on to the next track.

Lilly settled at Laurel racetrack, knowing that since it was a smaller operation with not a lot of high-profile races, Tom would be less likely to bring any horses there.

She settled into a routine. She loved what she was doing. She missed racing, but she was enjoying her daily life. She ate chocolate sometimes, without worrying that she'd have to sweat it out to make weight. She took days off without worrying what huge, career changing horse she'd missed out on. Laurel was good for her.

After a while, she reached out to Doug again. He'd heard about the accident from Paul. She told him she was fine, that she just needed a break. She apologized for not contacting him. He, of course, welcomed her back with open arms. She'd been close with Molly and Doug both, and it felt so rejuvenating to be around them again. Lilly worked at Shamrock Hill Farm as often as she could. It was home. It was safe. She got used to working, not racing, and it seemed like fate. She made Laurel her base of operations, and she became enmeshed in her routine.

It was there that her worlds started to collide. When she met Charlie and Genuine Storm.

PART THREE

 # Early Morning Mist

The early morning mist floated over the track as Lilly on Storm and Jenny on Sarge walked up the ramp to the track. They turned left to head clockwise along the outside rail. The dirt had yet to be disturbed, the tractor furrows still fresh from being dragged moments earlier.

Lilly wanted to get Storm on the track early to avoid the later morning craziness with the other Preakness contenders' workouts. It was Thursday morning, and they had just brought Storm to Pimlico from Doug's farm the previous afternoon. Storm was jigging along, nipping at Sarge. Sarge's ears were back and he tossed his head at the youngster and his impatience.

"He certainly enjoyed his time at the farm," Jenny commented, sitting lightly in the saddle on Sarge's back.

"Well, it's back to work for him now," Lilly replied, her attention on Storm. She could feel his motion, the rhythmic pattern of his four legs. She could tell from her saddle if he took a misstep or if he was favoring one leg over another. All seemed okay.

Lilly took in a deep breath. Only the night before she had agreed to ride Storm in the Preakness. That Charlie; she certainly had a way about her. She had been convincing on her own, but with Doug by her side, she was invincible.

After her break down at Laurel with Charlie, Lilly had driven out to Shamrock in the morning to see Storm off in the van that would take him over to Pimlico. While Jenny, Ben, and Cappie drove out to the track, Doug, Charlie, and Lilly had sat in the office with Molly, Doug's sister, talking through Lilly's anxiety with riding in the Preakness and potentially running into Tom Malone again. She told them all about him finding her at Storm's stall after the Derby win and the fear his presence evoked. It was a relief to get all her emotions out on the table, surrounded by the people who had become family to her.

Occasionally, Lilly caught Molly's gaze but she shook her head slightly, and a silent understanding passed between the two women: Charlie had been told enough for now.

It was during their conversation that Lilly could feel the tension she had been harboring for years slip away. There was nothing she could have done to change the outcome. It wasn't her fault. It was time, after all these years, to move past it all.

Almost without realizing it, Lilly spoke the phrase that Charlie had most wanted to hear. "Okay, I will ride," tumbled out of her mouth. She instantly regretted it, but Charlie's reaction calmed her fears once again. Rather than just accepting Lilly at her word, she'd pushed back. She'd made sure it was something Lilly wanted to do, rather than something she was feeling forced into. She'd once again made Lilly feel as though her role in their lives was more than that of just the jockey.

And it was knowing that Charlie thought more of her as a friend than as a jockey that led Lilly back to the track where she now found herself sitting on Storm two days before the Preakness.

Lilly let the breath out that she had been holding. The two horses continued through the backstretch, stretching their legs and warming up their muscles. Storm wasn't going to do a fast workout, but Hunter wanted Lilly to get him used to the track and surroundings.

Hunter. Lilly wasn't sure what to make of Doug's trainer from Florida. He certainly knew what he was doing and had done a great job with

Storm in the last week getting him used to other riders. Yet Lilly didn't like the way Hunter looked at Charlie or the easy mannerisms he had with her when Doug wasn't around.

"This has been such a great time, hasn't it, Lilly?" Jenny's voice broke into Lilly's thoughts. Jenny had been chattering away about how much fun she had had at the Derby and in the days after.

"Sure," Lilly replied. She felt bad for her brevity, but there were still some nerves she needed to work out, and niceties were the last thing on her mind. They trotted past the corporate tents that had been set up in the infield and came around the turn, approaching the clubhouse and grandstand on their left and continuing to stay along the outside of the track to avoid the horses breezing along the inside rail, running counter-clockwise.

As the two horses moved around the track, Lilly and Jenny had more and more company as horses began their morning workouts.

The warning horn suddenly sounded. Storm's ears pricked forward to the sound he had never heard.

The morning mist was still thick around them, other horses around them just a thick outline as they slowed to a walk and then stood still.

"Loose horse on the track!" bellowed a voice over the siren. The warning was on a loop, and rang loud and clear, making Storm squirm and Lilly mildly nervous. Lilly and Jenny brought their horses to a stop to wait for the outriders to wrangle up the loose horse.

"Can you see the horse?" Jenny asked anxiously. Lilly and Jenny were craning their necks to try to see where the loose horse might be.

"Not yet, but the outriders will get it," Lilly replied. A loose horse on a racetrack was not something to take lightly. "Don't move, all right? The fog is too thick, it's dangerous enough riding around out here without a horse on the loose. Just stay still." Lilly tried to make her voice as calm as possible, to make it seem as though it was just another practice scenario.

"Where are the outriders?" Jenny asked; she seemed to be more annoyed than scared at the interruption.

"I'm sure they are on top of it," Lilly said softly. "Outriders are basically track police. They're responsible for ensuring the safety of all horse racing participants, both human and equine. They open and close the track, catch loose horses, help riders, talk to racing officials, and call ambulances if there's a problem. They're great at their jobs and an integral part of the running of the racetrack."

The audio system was still on. "Loose horse on the track!" It wouldn't stop until the horse was caught, so they had to stay put. Storm began to fidget and sweat with apprehension. The horses knew something was amiss.

"Shhh, quiet, big guy," Lilly murmured to Storm as she patted his neck. Sarge stood at attention, ears flicking back and forth, listening for what he could not see.

Storm's anxiety finally got the best of him and he pulled his head sharply, causing the rein to slip from where Jenny was holding it tightly to Sarge's neck. Lilly had been prepared for Storm's outburst and stuck calmly on his back as he took off down the track into the mist.

"Crap," yelled Jenny. "Come on, Sarge, we need to go get him!"

Lilly chanced a glance behind her to see Jenny urging Sarge to give chase. She held up her hand in an effort to stop Jenny from following them. She could handle Storm, and the last thing she needed was for Jenny to get hurt. Unwillingly, Lilly turned her attention back to Storm, hoping Jenny had seen her gesture and heeded her directive.

She hadn't. Sarge responded to Jenny's twitch of the reins with a surge that belied his age. Jenny could make out Storm's hind end and his tail streaming out behind him. Lilly was balled up on his back, not wanting to get him more worked up, but using her voice and hands to try to calm him. A scared horse is never a good thing.

Jenny could see that Lilly was having a hard time calming Storm down. He wasn't running out of control, he just wasn't willing to come back off his gallop. With the mist, it was hard to see exactly where all the other horses were and what was happening with the loose horse and the outriders trying to catch him. Through the wind whipping by her ears, Jenny could still hear the warning siren and accompanying voice—they still hadn't caught their culprit.

Jenny and Sarge ran past an outrider holding on to another nervous Thoroughbred, its jockey already on the ground having decided to dismount for safety.

"Stop!" the outrider yelled to Jenny, but she knew she couldn't do that. She had to help Lilly get Storm under control.

"Let's go catch him, Sarge." Suddenly, the mist cleared. Sarge's keen eyes caught a quick moving object ahead of them and with a burst of speed he hadn't exhibited since he was three years old, Sarge surged ahead and veered into the path of the loose horse who'd been heading straight for Storm.

———————————

Jenny kept her eyes shut. Her fingers could feel the soft dirt and she dug into it to help absorb the pain that was emanating from her right leg. She couldn't move it, but she could feel it, which was a good thing. It meant she hadn't broken her neck or back.

"Jenny!" Someone was calling her name. There were voices all around her. It took her a moment to think beyond the pain in her leg. She could feel a hand brushing through her hair, and someone gasping in air: crying. What had happened? She could hear sirens—ambulances—one for her and one for Sarge.

Sarge. He had saved Storm. Instantly, Jenny lifted her head to look around her and realized why she couldn't move her leg. Sarge's neck and head had come to rest across her lower body. His eyes were open and he was breathing heavily. His pain was obvious as the air shuddered in and out of his nostrils.

"Oh boy, you'll be okay." Jenny lifted a shaky hand and ran it down his forelock. His eye turned up to her. He didn't try to get up. Jenny felt a hand on her shoulder, urging her to lie back down. Lilly came into her line of vision.

"Stay put, both of you. Don't move, okay?" Lilly's voice was thick with emotion. She choked out another breath, and Jenny saw the tears streaming down her face. Lilly was still stroking Jenny's hair while she spoke. Jenny wanted to ask about Storm, wanted to ask if Sarge would be okay, but the pain in her leg had begun to increase, and she closed her eyes against it.

"Lilly! Jenny!" Jenny recognized the voice immediately, and she felt better knowing that Charlie was near, because that meant her Uncle Doug was close. She risked opening her eyes enough to see if she was right, and was rewarded with his face hanging over hers, the worried crease between his eyes deeper than she'd ever seen it.

"Uncle Doug, fancy seeing you here." She managed a small smirk and saw the worry lines ease on his face.

"Well, someone has to clean up your mess." Doug's voice shook, and Jenny could see that he clenched his hands to keep them from shaking. Suddenly, Doug moved sharply sideways, and Charlie stood above Jenny, the same worry creasing her face.

"Jenny, are you okay? Do you remember what happened? How many fingers am I holding up?" Charlie hadn't meant it to be funny, but Jenny breathed out a laugh.

"I'm fine, I promise," Jenny said, unable to keep the strain out of her voice at the surge of pain from her leg. There was no more comforting hand running through her hair, and she wondered where Lilly had gone.

"What happened?" Charlie asked again, less frantically this time. She had moved to kneel in the soft dirt next to Sarge's head. Jenny could see her running her hands over Sarge's neck. Jenny risked raising her head and noticed that Sarge's legs didn't move. The only thing that did move were those deep brown eyes blinking at her.

She swallowed a sob, the tears starting to run down her cheeks—not related to her own pain, but for Sarge.

"He saved Storm," Jenny choked out, laying back down and covering her face. "That loose horse was running right for him as the fog started to lift and Sarge just burst in front of him and took the impact."

"She's right, Charlie," Lilly added. Jenny turned her head to see Lilly walking up to them, leading the medic. Her face was bright with recently shed tears, but her eyes were now dry, her breathing even, and her voice under control.

"I was focused on calming Storm. I looked over just as Sarge careened past us." Lilly knelt and one hand rested lightly on Sarge's neck, the other went to Charlie's shoulder. "He knew what he was doing, Charlie," she said softly.

"We need to get Sarge off Jenny," Doug said. He could have been addressing anyone in the crowd surrounding the scene, but no one moved.

Charlie couldn't move. Her best friend was just lying there and she couldn't help him. "Why won't he try to get up?" she cried, feeling the hysterics overtaking her emotions. Jenny tried harder than ever to keep the tears from falling.

"His neck is broken, Charlie," Doug said. He could see from the angle of his neck, as well as the stillness of the rest of Sarge's body.

The paramedics began bracing Jenny's neck as the track vet examined Sarge, black bag by her side. She looked up at Doug and nodded.

"We need to get this young lady into the ambulance now, before she goes into shock," the paramedic urgently said to the group.

"Please, just lift his neck so you can slide Jenny's leg out from under it," Charlie implored. She felt exceedingly bad for Jenny, but she couldn't just let them toss Sarge aside like a 1,200 pound rag doll.

Doug seemed to share her hesitancy, and motioned to some of the outriders standing close by. The vet grabbed a syringe from his bag.

"Wait! What are you doing?" Charlie screamed hysterically.

Doug knelt close and said softly, "Charlie, we need to move Jenny out from under Sarge's neck and we can't have him trashing his head about and causing more injuries to Jenny. The vet is going to give him a sedative first." As he spoke, the vet inserted the syringe directly into Sarge's blood vessel where it could take effect immediately. Within a few minutes, four sets of hands moved under Sarge's head and neck and lifted it gently while the paramedics moved Jenny onto the back board.

Jenny grimaced from the pain but refused to scream out. How could she possibly draw attention to herself while Sarge just lay there on the track? She looked down from the gurney and at the scene unfolding before her.

Lilly walked quietly over to Doug and whispered to him, "I will go with Jenny in the ambulance, you stay here with Charlie." A knowing look passed between them. Doug nodded. His face grew somber as he watched Lilly jump into the back of the ambulance. The doors pulled closed behind her and it drove away.

The track vet stood quietly holding a second syringe filled with pink liquid. He waited for Charlie to move away from her horse. Doug knelt beside Charlie and pulled her close. It was all too clear, to everyone present, what the only course of action could be.

"Come on, Charlie," Doug said. He tried to get her to stand up with him. Sarge was already showing his own signs of shock as his eyes had become teary and dilated and his breathing had quickened.

"I can't leave him!" Charlie yelled, pushing away Doug's hands. "Do what you need to, but I am not leaving his side." She stroked his face, whispering into his ears that everything was going to be alright and how much she loved him.

Doug gave up his attempt to remove her. He kneeled next to both of them with one arm around Lilly's shoulders and his other hand resting on Sarge's shoulder. He nodded to the vet.

Sarge looked up at Charlie as the vet inserted his long needle into his jugular vein, and then Charlie's best friend closed his eyes for the last time, a long steady breath leaving his body. There was no more pain. Not for Sarge, at least.

 # The Aftermath

Charlie needed the security of her own home around her. They'd left the track and the media frenzy behind them, but Charlie still couldn't hear her own thoughts over her grief.

Every reporter had flocked to their barn, but the questions were not about the Kentucky Derby winner and his preparations. They were about the euthanizing of Charlie's beloved Sarge, Storm's sidekick.

The reporters tried to be understanding, but they also wanted the story. No one could really understand what had truly happened. They couldn't understand that in five minutes, Charlie's family had been shattered, yet again, in the most irreparable way. Sarge was dead, Jenny was in surgery to repair her broken leg, and Lilly was going to have to deal with another emotional upheaval after just overcoming her past.

Ben had cooled out Storm, hosed him off, and made sure he was fed and watered. Then he'd retreated to the tack stall, taking Skylar with him. Cappie had gone with Sarge's body. Charlie had screamed instructions that they were not to cremate him, but that he would be buried back at the farm. Cappie had offered to make sure all went smoothly.

Ryan stayed close to his mom, offering his support. Her face was white, but she stood tall in front of the line of reporters.

"Ms. Jenkins, do you blame the outriders for what happened?"

"Why did Storm and Sarge continue to gallop after the alarm for an all stop?"

"Where's Lilly?"

"Charlie, who will pony Storm on Saturday?"

Charlie took a deep, shaky breath. She heard herself talking, but couldn't feel her mouth making the words.

"With all the mist, no one saw what happened. From what I've been told by both Lilly and Jenny, Storm got anxious and got away from them. Jenny was attempting to recover Storm when Sarge pushed his way into the on-coming path of the runaway horse."

"Ms. Jenkins, do you blame either of them for the death of your horse?" Charlie turned toward the questioner, her body drained of emotion.

"Absolutely not. Horses have minds of their own. As much as we would like to think we have control over them, there are times when their natural instincts kick in. It's what makes them special and gives them the drive to race and compete.

"Accidents happen: jockeys fall off, horses get away from their handlers, and sometimes horses and jockeys gets hurt. It's the nature of our sport. It's the risk that each rider takes every time they put a foot in the iron. They take their life in their hands on the back of a 1,200 pound animal."

"What about Storm?" A camera flash momentarily pulled Charlie back to reality.

"I am thankful to say that Lilly and Storm were unharmed, and that Jenny is being taken care of by the best doctors at Johns Hopkins Hospital."

"How do you feel about Sarge's death?" The question shocked Charlie. It was a moment before she could answer, and when she did, her voice shook with the effort of keeping her grief in check.

"I am shocked and saddened by the loss of life today. Sarge, for his part, was doing what he has been doing for the last six months—protecting Storm. He was making sure no harm came to his brother. He was my best friend and helped me through some of the toughest times in my life." The tears Charlie had been holding back slowly fell.

"Ms. Jenkins—"

"Please give all of us a little space over the next day so we can come to terms with the loss of one of our team members. We will be closing off media access for the next 24 hours. Thank you."

With that Charlie turned, walked into Storm's stall, and asked Ryan to shut the door behind her.

Tour of Pimlico

"Come on, Skylar, let's go for a walk." Ben held out his hand to lift Skylar to her feet. He needed to distract her from the sadness of losing Sarge. She was only nine years old, and losing Sarge was like losing her puppy.

"Where are we going?" Skylar asked.

"Have you ever been to Pimlico racetrack before?"

"No," Skylar replied, walking sluggishly next to him along the stalls toward the track and the grandstand that loomed over their heads. Ben held the door for Skylar to enter.

"Well, there's a lot to see here at Old Hilltop," Ben said.

"Old Hilltop?" Skylar asked, looking up at him as they walked through the lower level of the grandstand.

"Yep," he said and winked at her.

They walked by closed food stands and banks of empty teller windows where people would place their bets later in the day. Although the day's races weren't until much later this afternoon, the place was abuzz with activities. Workers were cleaning all areas of the building, as well as preparing all the shops and eateries for the crowds that would descend over the next two days.

"Everyone is getting ready for the big day," Skylar commented as they continued their walk.

"Not just Saturday, Skylar, but tomorrow is Black-Eyed Susan Day. Similar to Kentucky Oaks day, the day before the Derby, tomorrow has become as big of a day to Pimlico as Preakness Day."

"Why do they call it Old Hilltop?" Skylar asked as they walked.

"Well, Pimlico here is the second oldest racetrack in America, behind Saratoga in New York. It opened its doors for its first race in 1870 and the greatest racehorses over the centuries have raced here, including Man o' War, Seabiscuit, Citation, and Secretariat," Ben told her. They walked out the double doors and onto the asphalt apron of the grandstand.

"They call it Old Hilltop because in the center of the infield in front of us was a small rise that used to be a favorite gathering place for the crowds to watch their favorites compete. Families would come from all around and set up fancy spreads and enjoy the day."

"What happened to the hill?" Skylar asked.

"Well, some higher-ups decided to remove the hill because they claimed it was blocking the view of the backstretch from this side of the track. It was also a problem for the crews filming the entire race from start to finish."

"Well, that stinks. It would be fun to watch Storm race around the track from on top of a hill!" Skylar smiled.

"Yes, it would be. But you are going to be up there," Ben said, pointing at the owners' boxes rising high behind them, "representing the owners of Genuine Storm, Kentucky Derby winner!" Ben high-fived Skylar and spun her around. Skylar giggled and then grew somber again.

"Sarge won't be here to help Storm get to the gate. You know, be his side pony during the post parade." Skylar eyes welled with tears.

Ben had to think quickly to keep his own tears at bay. "Hey, how about we jump in the trailer and go grab Hershey? Storm would love to have a familiar face next to him in the barn. Obviously, Hershey can't be his side pony, but he can be with him right up until he goes to the paddock."

Skylar threw her arms around Ben. "Yes! Let's go get Hershey." Skylar let out a shaky sigh.

They walked hand in hand back the way they'd come, through the grandstand towards the Preakness barns. Skylar walked a little lighter, like a heavy weight had been lifted from her shoulders just thinking about getting her pony.

"Hey, Ben, what's that stand over there?" Skylar asked. They were passing a table different from the standard food offerings. The yellow banner above the table read "Alex's Lemonade Stand."

"Well, that is a very special lemonade stand," Ben replied. He guided Skylar over to the table. It was covered in a bright blue tablecloth with several yellow coolers on it.

"Check out this poster, Skylar." Ben pointed at a large poster with a bay Thoroughbred horse along with an image of a little girl.

"Afleet Alex," read Skylar. "Who was he? And who is this little girl?"

Ben knelt down next to Skylar and pointed at the horse. "Afleet Alex won the 2005 Preakness, but," he pointed at the little girl in the poster, "this Alex is the real story. She was his guardian angel."

"Guardian angel?" Skylar asked.

"Yep. Alex, the girl, had been very sick. At the age of 4, she told her parents she wanted to open a lemonade stand to raise money to fight the disease she had. She had cancer and she wanted to help others who had it, too. Many people took notice and starting opening up their own lemonade stands to contribute to her cause. Over the next four years, Alex raised hundreds of thousands of dollars, with a goal of reaching $1 million dollars.

"The owners of the horse Alex had read about Alex's Lemonade Stand and had been donating money anonymously to help her reach her goal. Sadly, in the summer of 2004, at the age of eight, Alex passed away."

Skylar squeezed Ben's hand. "That is so sad!"

"It sure is. The owners of Afleet Alex wanted to help raise awareness of Alex's Lemonade Stand. They called Alex's parents and asked if they could let it be known publicly that they were donating a portion of their horse's winnings to their cause. Afleet Alex was a pretty big deal and was going to be running in the Derby, as well as the Preakness and Belmont. Churchill

Downs agreed to having an Alex's Lemonade Stand set up during the Derby, as did Pimlico and Belmont during the running of the Preakness and Belmont Stakes that year.

"In the Derby, Afleet Alex finished third, but it was in the Preakness that he solidified his greatness, as well as brought notoriety to Alex's Lemonade Stand." Ben took a breath.

"How?" Skylar asked quietly, listening to the story intently while running her hand along the blue tablecloth.

"Well, the horses were coming around the far turn and entering the homestretch in the Preakness. Just as Afleet Alex tried to make his move around the outside of another horse, the horse veered out into his path. Alex stumbled badly and went down to his knees and his jockey had to hold on for dear life. Miraculously, Afleet Alex regained his footing and his jockey stayed on. They proceeded to regain momentum and raced past all the other horses to win by over four lengths!" Ben finished.

"Alex was up in heaven looking out for them, wasn't she?" Skylar asked.

"I believe so. In my experience, 10 out of 10 such collisions would have caused the horse and jockey to fall and all the others behind them would have been in trouble," Ben told her. "But on that day, with that horse, and with the support of many millions behind Alex's Lemonade Stand, everyone made it home safely."

Skylar stood looking at the lemonade stand in front of her. Ben visibly watched as Skylar's shoulders began to relax and she reached for his hand. "I would like to come visit the stand tomorrow and donate some money in memory of Sarge."

"I think that is a great idea," Ben replied, squeezing her hand. "Now, let's go get Hershey. It'll keep you busy tomorrow, having him around. Everyone's gonna want to meet another Jenkins horse." Ben led them down the stairs and out the door, wondering to himself what tomorrow would bring.

Overcoming Grief

Doug found Charlie in Sarge's stall.

She was sitting in the corner next to a pile of hay that would never be eaten. Her eyes were closed, but he could see the tears running down her cheeks. He stood there, debating his best course of action. Doug had had to make the tough decision to either check on his niece in the hospital or stay with Charlie. He'd gone to check on Jenny. Once his sister and her husband had arrived, he waited around until Jenny made it safely out of surgery, and then he drove to Charlie's. Ryan had already texted him that they had left Pimlico.

It seemed like an eon had passed since that morning. It was late afternoon at the farm, and the last rays of sunlight flickered into Sarge's stall and across Charlie's face. Doug waited quietly, not wanting to intrude on her thoughts.

"You can come in," Charlie said, her eyes closed.

Doug took two large steps across the stall and slid down the wall next to Charlie. She leaned into him and he gathered her into his arms. Charlie grabbed onto his shirt and the sobs that suddenly wracked her body were absorbed by Doug. He held her close until she shuddered out one last sob. Her breathing became steady.

"I don't think I can go back," Charlie stuttered as she wiped a hand across her eyes and looked up at Doug. Doug pushed a wisp of hair out of her face.

"Everything will remind me of Sarge and I won't be able to stop crying. A part of me doesn't care anymore about all of this! I just want to bring Storm home, and go back to my quiet life."

"That won't bring Sarge back," Doug quietly said. Charlie sat and just stared at the wall, her hand picking up a pile of hay and squeezing it hard in her fist.

"Sarge got in front of that horse to save Storm. Jenny said as much," Doug commented.

"Oh my god, how is she? How is Jenny?" Charlie jolted; having been lost in her own grief, she hadn't bothered to follow up on Jenny.

"She is going to be fine. She came out of surgery and the doctor said her leg was only broken in two places. It could have been much worse. He put some pins in to stabilize the healing. She's tough. She'll be back to riding in no time," Doug assured her.

"How is Lilly? Have you talked to her?" Charlie asked.

"She's fine," Doug hesitated, "however, she was very quick to leave the hospital once Jenny got out of surgery and she found out she was going to be fine. I thought she was going back to the track to meet up with you."

"No, I haven't seen her or heard from her," Charlie replied. She turned to Doug worriedly. "Where did she go?"

The last thing Charlie needed was something else to worry about, but at the same time, she thought maybe one more thing to take her mind off of Sarge was exactly what she needed.

Doug ran his hand up and down Charlie's arm and smiled soothingly. "I don't know," Doug said slowly, his mind churning. "It's just that Lilly tends to disappear. She's pretty good at it too. When things get tough, she retreats. And today was pretty tough."

Doug knew he needed to take charge with Charlie in such a state. Her limp body still rested against his, and he knew her mind was elsewhere. Losing a horse is difficult in any circumstance, but given Sarge's importance to Charlie and Storm, getting through the next two days was going to be more than just a minor challenge.

Doug's mind worked quickly and he glanced at his watch.

"Come on," he said. Doug rose to his feet and pulled Charlie with him. Charlie's bloodshot eyes looked at him coolly. "I am not going anywhere."

"Yes, you are," he said firmly. He knew he needed to get her mind distracted quickly. Charlie had told him enough of her dark days after Peter died. He couldn't let her sink close to that level of depression again. The best course of action was to get busy. If she let the sadness overtake her again, she would hide in her bed and never make it back to Pimlico.

"You have another horse that relies on you, as well as several people. Cappie and Ben, Ryan and Skylar. They need you to be strong." Doug moved slowly toward the stall door.

"I don't want to always be the strong one. It's exhausting! Just when everything was going great, things go to hell in a hand basket," she cried softly.

"Yes, but the rule of life is that you are either coming out of a problem or heading towards a problem, right? It's how you handle each curve of the road that makes you stronger. Isn't that what you told me? Everything happens for a reason, Charlie. You believe in that. Sarge's death was not in vain. You may not know the reason or purpose behind what happened today, but you will, at some point, be able to look back and say 'that is why.'" Doug rubbed his thumb along her hand.

His cell phone buzzed. Without taking his eyes off of Charlie, he reached in his back pocket and put the phone to his ear.

"Hey," he said, and then listened for a moment. "Okay, let me know if you find anything out. Any time tonight, no matter the time. I'm with Charlie, but we will be back at the track tomorrow." He squeezed her hand tightly. "Thanks for the help," he finished and hung up.

Charlie's curiosity broke through her fog. "Who was that?" she asked, shamelessly wiping her nose on her sleeve.

"Buck," he said.

"Buck? What is he doing calling you?" she asked.

"He's looking for Lilly, I told him to keep me updated," Doug said flatly, though Charlie could see that his face was creased with worry. Lilly had become a big part of their team, but Doug had known her long before that, and they were close. She was tight with Jenny, too. Doug was sure she was taking the accident hard and blaming herself for every little thing that had gone wrong. Jenny, Charlie, and Lilly, the women in Doug's life, were not having a good day, and Doug was struggling to find any way he could to make it better.

 # The Woodlawn Vase

Doug and Charlie walked out of the barn, his arm around her waist. She steered them out to the paddock and spent several minutes with her arms around Hershey's neck, tears running into his mane. Doug decided it would be best to let her be for a few minutes.

Hershey could sense something was wrong and didn't move a muscle. He didn't even fight to continue eating grass. He stood patiently, looking over at Doug with his deep brown eyes, like he already knew Sarge would not be coming home.

Slowly, Charlie removed her arms from around Hershey's neck and kissed him on the nose. "You'll be joining us tomorrow on the big stage, so Skylar informed me today. Tomorrow Ben and Skylar will put you on the trailer and take you to the track to help with Storm. It's just the two of you now. Make Sarge proud."

She walked back over to Doug by the gate.

"Okay, I'm ready. At least as ready as I can be," she said.

Doug wrapped her in his arms and gave her a kiss. Her lips were wet and she tasted like salt from her tears. He didn't want the moment to end. She melted into him and the kiss deepened. She grabbed at him with all her sadness and she needed an outlet; she couldn't contain it anymore.

Doug backed her slowly into the barn and slid the big door closed behind them. His other plans would have to wait.

She pulled him into Sarge's stall, and stood motionless, staring at the pile of hay. He let her be for a moment, and then gently touched her shoulder. She turned to him, yet again fighting to keep her tears from falling.

"I'm so glad I have you," Charlie said. She smiled weakly and a few tears rolled down to her lips. Doug brushed them away. He cupped her face and brushed her hair behind her ears. She closed her eyes and leaned into him. He kissed her lightly, barely brushing his lips against hers.

He wasn't surprised when she deepened the kiss. He knew she was looking for an outlet for her tumultuous feelings, and he was more than prepared to be that for her. She was angry, he could feel it in the way she kissed him. She was sad, he could taste the salt from her tears on her face. She was tired of being the one in charge, he could feel it in the way she yielded to him.

They stayed in the barn together for a long time, just enjoying the peace in the shelter. All the troubles of the day seemed farther away from where they sat, in their little haven of peace.

"I just realized that I haven't told you yet how sorry I am that Sarge is gone," Doug said, hugging her close to himself, and willing her to stay whole and safe in his embrace.

"I…don't think anyone has. The reporters just wanted to know what happened, and who I would blame, and the kids were just in shock I think. No one seemed to realize that I just lost…I mean, he was my…"

"He was your best friend. I know. I'm so, so sorry."

"He was getting old, and I knew that it wouldn't be long before I had to…I just thought I'd have a little more time! That I'd get to be there to nurse him and help him, like he deserved."

"Charlie, you did. You were there for him when it really mattered. You were with him at the end."

"What am I going to do without him? Who am I gonna talk to about everything that's on my mind?" Charlie was falling back into hysterics.

"If I say 'me' does that make me sound selfish? I love you, Charlie. I could never replace Sarge, obviously, but I can be your best friend."

"You are already pretty high on the list..." Charlie said quietly.

Doug smiled at her, "Really? How high?"

"Top five, at least. Maybe top three," she said, coyly. "There are some challenges you'll have to get through, in order to reach the number one spot: clean stalls, empty water buckets, that kind of thing."

"I would do anything for you," Doug said, staring down at her with almost heartbreaking affection in his eyes.

"You would?"

"Yes. I want you to be happy." He lifted the hand he had been holding and kissed it. Then he moved to her mouth. She smiled against his lips and he pulled away to look at her.

"I love you too, Doug." He kissed her again, and by the time they came up for air, it was nearly dark in the world beyond the barn.

———————

Ryan was on the computer and Skylar was curled up on the couch wrapped in a blanket, hugging her stuffed animal horse, Starlight, when Doug and Charlie entered the house.

"Come on you two, we have a little field trip to go on," Doug announced. Neither of them looked away from their screens. Doug easily slapped shut the top of Ryan's laptop, grabbed the remote from off the table and powered off the TV.

"What happened today was a tragedy. I am not going to try to tell you otherwise, but in this business, unfortunately, horses die. We do our best to protect them, but sometimes things go wrong. We can mourn, but we also have to remember that we have others who need us to carry on. Storm needs our help. We cannot all just fall apart on him. Now, get up and let's get out of here."

———————

Doug made some calls while they made their way back into Baltimore. Charlie sat in the front seat gazing out the side window, not really paying attention to any of them. Ryan had his hand locked around his phone, texting Jenny. Skylar had drifted off to sleep. She was still wrapped in her blanket, holding tightly to Starlight, her stuffed horse.

"Jenny is asking about Lilly. What should I tell her?" Ryan asked from the dark of the back seat.

"Just tell her that she is fine. Her job is to get better and not worry about everyone else," Doug threw over his shoulder.

"How is she feeling?" Charlie asked.

"She said she doesn't feel anything right now. The cast goes all the way up to her hip."

"I can't imagine how scared she must have been when it all happened," Charlie said, imagining briefly what her reaction would have been had she found herself trapped under a horse.

"I wouldn't worry about it too much, Mom, she's already mapping out a plan to start riding again. Crazy. How can she possibly think about getting back on a horse after this?"

"That's what riders and jockeys do, Ryan," Doug replied. "It is in their blood and they wouldn't want to be doing anything else. You should hear the stories I've got about some of the injuries that my jockeys have endured, only to get right back in the saddle. They don't like to talk about it much, because it reminds them of the danger they constantly put themselves in, but I don't know a single one who would trade the rush of riding a galloping horse for a less dangerous job."

Charlie didn't want to talk about it anymore. "Where are you taking us?"

"You'll see, we are almost there," Doug said, glancing over at Charlie. She had recovered the color in her face. He liked to think his distraction in the barn played a part in that.

Doug turned the SUV into a parking lot and drove past a sign that read "Baltimore Museum of Art."

"An art museum? Why are we at an art museum?" Ryan asked.

"You'll see," Doug said. "Come on, Skylar, time to wake up."

The four of them got out of the SUV. The parking lot was empty except for one other car. The museum had closed at 5, and it was now well after 8. Doug led them around to a side door and hit a doorbell button.

They waited, Skylar rubbing the sleep from her eyes, still holding onto Starlight. "What are we doing here, Mr. Doug?" Just then the door opened.

"Well, hello!" A tall, impeccably dressed young man greeted them from the doorway. He held out his hand to Doug.

"Hi James, thank you so much for accommodating us."

"No problem. Anything for the owner of the Kentucky Derby winner." He held out his hand to Charlie. "James Monroe, at your service." Charlie returned his handshake and smiled, caught up in his vibrant personality.

"And hello to you both," he said, shaking Ryan's and Skylar's hands. "I see you brought a friend as well," he added, referring to Skylar's death grip hold on Starlight.

Skylar looked down at her stuffed animal. "Our horse Sarge died this morning," she said in a whisper.

James knelt next to Skylar. "It is hard to lose someone you love, isn't it?" Skylar's tear-filled eyes turned up to his, and she nodded her head.

"What I do know is that when an animal we love dies, it is reunited with all the animals we have ever had in the past. Are there any other pets you have owned that have passed away?" he asked Skylar. It was a very serious conversation for a nine-year-old girl, and Skylar took his question very seriously.

"Y-y-yes. We had a cat named Sparky. He was orange and loved to sleep on my head." Charlie smiled at her brave daughter, dealing with another death in her young life. "He died of old age. He was 15 years old and we had him from when he was a kitten. Sparky was the first pet my parents had picked out together." Skylar looked over at Charlie.

"Well, isn't it great that Sparky now has a friend that he can play with up in heaven. I am sure Sarge is up there telling him all about you and the treats you gave him. They are spending time in green pastures and Sparky is rolling in the golden hay in his stall."

Skylar looked over James' shoulder at her mom, and then asked hesitantly, "Do you think my dad is with them?"

James didn't miss a beat. "I am sure he is, Skylar. It's quite possible that your dad was looking for a friend and a horse to ride, so he needed your horse to come hang out with him."

Skylar laughed a little. "Oh, my daddy didn't ride, but he loved watching my mom on Sarge. He said he wanted to learn, but I think he was scared."

"Maybe so, now he has Sarge up there with him to keep him company and fill him in on everything that you all have been doing," James said. This seemed to make Skylar feel better. Her shoulders that had been tensed into her neck relaxed a little.

Charlie let out the breath she had been holding. She, too, felt a little better thinking that Sarge and Peter were together. James stood up from where he had been kneeling next to Skylar.

"James worked for me years ago at the farm, until he realized his passion for art outweighed his passion for horses. He used to spend days in the trophy room studying the details of the pieces," Doug commented, throwing his arm around James' shoulder.

"I wouldn't be where I am today if it wasn't for Doug. He encouraged me to go to college to get my degree in art history. I loved working around the horses—they are each a work of art in and of themselves—but my calling was to be around the beautiful pieces of art we have here at the museum. Come with me, there's one very special piece we keep here at the museum that I think you will be particularly interested in." James grabbed Skylar's hand and walked them into the museum.

Charlie had always loved museums, and this one was no different. The lights were dim, but they could still see all the different pieces hanging on the walls and sitting under their protective glass casings. Their footsteps echoed on the tile floor, and it made them sound like a bigger group than they actually were.

James led them through several rooms and down a long hallway, all the while talking easily with Skylar. Charlie could see her daughter soaking in the art around her, and she smiled. More than anything, she wanted her children to be happy, despite all the tragedy they'd faced.

"Have you guessed where we're going yet?" Doug asked, pulling Charlie out of her reverie. Charlie shook her head, a slight smile playing at her lips. Doug tilted his head toward the doorway and Charlie looked up at the name of the room they were about to enter. She froze momentarily. Doug kept moving forward and with his hand entwined with hers, pulled her into the Woodward room.

There may have been other things on the walls or on stands, but Charlie didn't see them. Her eyes were drawn to one item, the one Doug had been right in assuming she would want to see: The Woodlawn Vase.

In 1860, Tiffany and Company spent $1,500 to create a gorgeous trophy that, almost 60 years later, would become the official trophy of The Preakness in 1917. After decades of giving the trophy to winners of the race, it was relegated to the museum in 1953, and decided that winners would instead get a replica of the stunning piece in order to preserve the original.

Charlie was so mesmerized by the beauty in front of her that when James started talking, it gave her a start.

"You'll be getting a trophy like this if you win that big race in a few days," he said to Skylar. Her daughter's eyes widened, and Charlie could see the sliver reflected in the blue of her iris.

"It's bigger than I thought it would be," Ryan said. James looked at him with a smile, and Ryan walked closer to the case. "I mean…it's three feet tall, I know that, but…man it's big!" Ryan's voice was awed.

"It probably weighs 100 pounds," Skylar said, moving forward to stand next to her brother.

"No, just 30, but that's still too heavy for you," Ryan said, not taking his eyes off the sterling masterpiece in front of him.

"That is not too heavy for me," Skylar said. Charlie laughed.

"The only ones who will be holding this trophy are the National Guard, when they bring it to the track on race day. They have to wear special gloves so they don't get finger print smudges on it," James said.

"That's a good idea, it looks so pretty without smudges," Skylar said.

"Tell them how much it is worth in today's dollars, James," Doug piped in.

"About four million dollars, which is why we have some extra security around it." Skylar gasped at the number and Ryan let out a whistle.

"That's Lexington, right? The horse on top?" Ryan pointed up to the model of the silver horse that sat at the top of the trophy. Skylar took a step back and craned her neck to see it properly."

"Who's Lexington?" she asked Ryan.

"A horse," he said, circling around to the other side of the case. Skylar glared after him and opened her mouth to retort, but James stepped in just in time.

"Lexington is the father of the horse that the race was named after. I guess they thought it was appropriate to use him on the trophy as a symbol: the father of Preakness," he made a sweep of his hand that encompassed the whole trophy, and Skylar looked once again at the silver giant in front of her.

James turned to Ryan, "Do you know about the Civil War, young man?"

"Of course," Ryan replied, "why do you ask?"

"This trophy was so special that it was hidden and buried during the Civil War so that it couldn't be melted down for gun shot for the Confederate soldiers," James said proudly, giving them their history lesson.

Skylar and Ryan continued asking questions, but Charlie tuned them out and turned to Doug.

"This is incredible," she said, squeezing his hand.

"I know it doesn't make anything okay, but I thought it might bring a little light to the day," he told her. She kissed him quickly and then put her head on his shoulder and watched as her children absorbed all the knowledge they could about the trophy they hoped would be theirs in just a few days.

The Hospital

Lilly peered through the small window in the hospital door. She could just make out the long cast on Jenny's leg. Her hands trembled a bit and she pressed them to her thighs. Her petite frame was hidden by a baggy pair of jeans and long t-shirt. She had a baseball cap on her head, with her long blond hair in a ponytail out the back. The aviator sunglasses she wore hid her blood shot eyes.

She debated what to do next. The whole situation was her fault; she shouldn't have agreed to ride Storm yesterday, she should have stayed strong. Here she was again, at the center of another train wreck. She clenched her fists as she added Sarge and Jenny to the growing list of things eating at her conscience. All the horrible memories she had locked away were flooding back now.

Lilly opened the door slightly so she could see into the hospital room. Jenny had her eyes closed and was breathing deeply. Her mom sat next to the bed, also resting, her hand wrapped in Jenny's to ensure she would be awakened the minute Jenny stirred.

Lilly loved their family. How could she have let any harm come to them? A tear slid out from under her glasses. She was so lost in thought that she didn't hear someone approach from behind her. A hand rested on her shoulder and Lilly tensed.

"Why don't you come over here, Lilly," a familiar voice said. With a look of surprise on her face, Lilly turned and looked into the face of a long-lost friend: Macy Godwin.

Stunned, Lilly allowed herself to be steered back into the hallway by the strong, sure hand of the woman she hadn't seen in many years. There was a small waiting area near Jenny's room. Macy led Lilly to a seat and then sat down next to her, her body angled towards the petit blonde.

"I didn't know you worked here," Lilly said after a silence that lasted several seconds. She couldn't bring herself to look at the woman she'd lost touch with. It wasn't an awkward encounter; Lilly saw that Macy was sitting easily, her back against the seat and her hands in her lap. Lilly checked her posture and tried to get rid of the tension in her own legs and back.

"That's not surprising," Macy said. Lilly looked into the eyes of the friend she'd left behind all those years ago and saw hurt lurking in the depths.

"Yeah, I guess not. Do you like it?" Lilly asked. She remembered how Macy's older sister Angela had gone to work at the hospital, but didn't know that Macy had followed her into the same profession.

"I do. I never thought I would do the same thing as the rest of my family and become a doctor, but it turns out I love it! Remember when I thought I wanted to go to California and be an actress?" Macy said, with a laugh. She smiled brightly at Lilly, and the latter finally felt the last bit of tension leave her.

"I'm really, really happy for you," Lilly said.

"What about you? I saw you win the Derby, you must be over the moon." Macy put a hand on Lilly's knee in congratulations. Lilly attempted a smile, but the tears that had been falling throughout the day filled her eyes again. She tried to pull her lower lids out to avoid the tears spilling over, but there were too many and no hope of keeping them at bay this time.

"It's been a rough few weeks, actually. I don't know what I'm doing anymore, Mace." Lilly let herself crumble completely in the arms of her long lost friend in the chair next to her. Macy didn't miss a beat; she gathered Lilly in her arms and spoke comforting words over her. Macy knew everything; she'd been there when Lilly had started working with Tom, she'd seen Lilly with Buck, she'd comforted Lilly after she'd left her parents' house, she'd helped her when Lilly hit her breaking point and stopped racing.

Macy was the only one who truly knew how deep the pain went for Lilly. The catharsis Lilly felt at crying and talking with her was like nothing she'd experienced from anyone else, except Buck before they'd split up.

Her tears rolled down her cheeks for what felt like hours, but Macy sat with her, patiently listening to the trials of the last few weeks, the horror of the last day, and how hurt and lost Lilly felt. When Lilly had finally calmed down enough, Macy looked at her and said the last thing Lilly thought she would ever hear her say.

"You're gonna need to move on, Lil."

Taken aback, Lilly moved away from Macy. She could feel her expression change from anguish to one of shock. Macy didn't wait for Lilly to speak, but continued with her own train of thought.

"You're killing yourself with all this guilt, when none of it belongs on your shoulders. I've known you, Lilly, through good times and bad times, and the things that keep you stuck have always been the things that you have no control over," Macy said, keeping her voice low and kind. Lilly shook her head, but Macy gripped her shoulder.

"What happened today was not your fault. You didn't put Jenny on that horse, and you didn't make her chase after you. What happened with Tom was not your fault. You didn't ask for it, you didn't invite it, and he doesn't deserve any more of your life than he's already gotten." Macy listed off some of the biggest pits of Lilly's life, but there was one glaring absence.

"What about my parents? What about Buck?" Lilly asked. Her throat closed a little when she said his name, but there were no tears left for her to cry.

"Lilly...you were eighteen. You did the best you could, and no one can fault you for that," Macy said.

"I loved him, Macy. I loved him, and I left him, with no explanation!" Lilly's breath was coming in short gasps. Macy made her put her head between her legs in order to calm down. Lilly thought briefly that it might come in handy to have a doctor around for every day ailments like panic attacks.

"I'll say it again; you did what you had to do. You owed it to yourself and to him to see where your careers could take you. But Lilly, it's not too late to try to fix things with him. Or with your parents." Macy's hand on her back was soothing. Lilly's mind stuck on what her friend had said. Macy was right, it wasn't too late. There was still time for her to make some things right.

Lilly sat straight up in her chair, her mind suddenly clear of everything except what she could do to erase some of the guilt she'd been carrying around for the better part of sixteen years.

"It's not too late," Lilly said. Macy smiled at her friend with so much love that Lilly's heart almost broke under the weight of the friendship she'd neglected. "Macy, I regret this too. You know, that we didn't stay close. You and Angela were my rocks for so long, and I didn't do my part in keeping up with either of you. I'm sorry." Lilly gripped Macy's hand in her own and hoped that she could feel all the sincerity Lilly was putting into her words.

"Look at you, already taking my advice," she squeezed Lilly's hand back, and then pulled the small blonde girl into a tight hug. "You know what to do, Lil. You always have." Macy broke away, and Lilly's train of thought was suddenly interrupted by the flash of a diamond on Macy's finger as she moved some hair behind her ear.

"What? What is that? When did that happen?" Lilly asked, grabbing at the hand sporting the impressive ring. Macy laughed and opened her mouth to answer, when a beeping sound took her attention away. Macy grabbed her pager from her belt and read the message on it, then stood quickly.

"I have to go take care of this. We'll talk later, okay?" Macy backed out of the room and blew Lilly a kiss to show that she meant to continue the conversation. Lilly smiled her first truly genuine smile in what felt like years. She took a deep breath and readied herself for what she knew she needed to do next.

She walked slowly back to Jenny's room. Molly started awake when Lilly touched her shoulder, but Jenny didn't move. The two women went out into the hallway. Lilly looked up at the woman that she admired with all her heart—the woman who was a huge part of the story that Lilly had kept hidden for so long.

Buck and Lilly

Buck stood quietly behind Lilly, trying to figure out the best way to approach her.

It had been years since they had talked. Sure, he had run into her at the Derby, but she was so closed off that he didn't want to ruin her big win. And then, an hour earlier, she'd called him and asked him to meet her here.

He wiped his hands on his jeans. It was now or never. Doug had reached out to him after the accident and Lilly's disappearance. Buck respected Doug, and what he knew of the Jenkins family was all good. He had to do what he could for them to try to convince Lilly to ride tomorrow, but he was also intent on getting some of the answers he'd been denied for so long. Time was not on their side. The Preakness was tomorrow. She couldn't avoid him any longer.

The sun was setting in the distance and its rays reflected off of Lilly's blond ponytail. Buck walked up behind her.

"Did you watch him work this morning?" he asked her.

Lilly's back straightened at the sound of his voice. She didn't turn around. Buck leaned on the railing next to Lilly, the same spot they had leaned on years ago, when Lilly was just starting out. They had spent hours talking about their dreams and goals leaning on this fence. That is until she abruptly disappeared.

He knew she had come back into racing a few years later. He had followed her rise to success, reading the details of every race she rode. But he never called her. If she didn't want to talk to him, then he wasn't going to pressure her. Buck was busy with his own rides and building a steady client base. It did cross his mind that Lilly was never riding at the same track as he was. It wasn't until a few years ago that he found out why.

———————————

Buck was galloping horses one morning at Gulfsteam in Florida. He jumped down and handed his horse to a groom when he spotted his old friend Paul Ritter chatting with one of the trainers a few yards away.

Paul had just turned to walk off when Buck called out, "Making any living in the agent world these days?"

Paul turned around and smiled at his friend. "Certainly not tearing up the tracks like you, buddy!" He slapped Buck's back.

"Business is good though, I can't complain. Will Hackney is riding well and it hasn't been hard for me to find him rides. When my jockey is successful, it makes my job easier," Paul said.

"Maybe you are the one finding him the right horses?" Buck replied earnestly.

"Could be, could be. But that is what makes a solid relationship, trusting each other to do our jobs. I'm still looking to find a second jockey to represent, but haven't come upon one that I wanted to work with since Lilly stopped riding." Paul stopped short and looked at Buck.

Buck held up his hand. "No worries, bud, I knew you were representing her. I figured since she hadn't been interested in reaching out to me, she certainly wouldn't want you to talk to me about her. I'm just surprised our paths never crossed. We were both pretty high on the jockey rankings, I would have thought we definitely would have ridden in the big races against each other."

Paul looked at his friend, a bit of sadness in his eyes. The air was quiet between the two of them for a few seconds, and in that time Paul decided to break his promise to Lilly. "Hey man, I'm sorry, but she wouldn't let me put her on any horse racing in a race that you would be riding in."

Buck felt both anger and sadness. He hoped one day he could make amends for whatever he'd done to hurt the woman he loved.

With Lilly now standing next to him, and actually talking to him, he was going to do everything in his power to find the answers he'd sought for so long.

Lilly stood still next to Buck, not moving a muscle. Her breathing slowed and she closed her eyes to meditate for a few seconds and calm her racing heart. It had taken all she had to ride in the Derby knowing she would see Buck in person. She had kept her comments to a minimum, or else she might have lost it then. She'd never wanted to have to face Buck after the pain she'd put him through, and seeing him without warning had made her heart shoot up into her throat.

It was time now to stop hiding from the past. She was ready to face everything she'd been running from, and she was beyond thankful that Buck had agreed to meet her now, after everything she'd done to avoid him. She grabbed at the railing in front of her tightly. "Hello, Buck."

Buck looked at Lilly, trying not to scare her off, torn between wanting to ring the answers out of her or wrap his arms around her. He did neither, and just stood there.

"It's been a while since it's been just the two of us," he said. Lily's hands began to shake on the railing. He placed one of his on top to try to quell the shaking. Her hands were stone cold. At that moment, his hand on hers, everything that Doug had asked him to do flew out of his mind. He'd wanted for so long to be able to touch Lilly again—to hug her and kiss her and talk to her like they'd used to. He was determined now to stay with her until he got the answers he wanted.

Buck said softly, "You can tell me, you know."

Lilly turned her face to look at him, and Buck was shocked by the sadness he saw there. He caved in and pulled her close. Lilly collapsed into his arms. Like a child, she grabbed at him while her body shook with the uncontrollable sobs that had plagued her throughout the day.

Buck slid both of them to the ground. He held her for a long time. In the distance, he could hear the soft nickers of the horses getting their last meals of the day. Finally, Lilly's breathing slowed and she relaxed against him.

After a while, Lilly lifted her head. She pushed herself out of Buck's lap, but continued to keep contact with his side. She held his hand in hers, alternating between squeezing it and relaxing. Buck didn't say a word while Lilly tried to figure out the words she knew would wreck his life.

But she had to tell him. She couldn't keep this secret any longer. It was unfair to Buck and it was eating her alive.

Lilly took a long shaky breath.

"I know you heard about the accident. It really made me realize a lot of things," she said. "To start with, I can't run away anymore. Charlie has done too much for me not to give her my all with Storm, so you don't have to convince me to ride," she continued.

Buck didn't interrupt. He watched her struggle to find the words to talk to him. Lilly's jean-covered knee bobbed up and down against the ground as she hesitated.

"A few days ago, I finally opened up about why I'd stopped riding races a few years back. The short story is Tom Malone is a bastard. I can tell you more about that later, but that's not why I called you here," she said.

"I figured it was something like that. Paul refused to work with Tom after you left. I'm sorry, Lilly," Buck said. He'd tensed a little, but his voice was still calm and Lilly pushed on.

"Don't be. I did a lot of good, helping the horses before they stepped onto the track. I love the work and I didn't have the time for it when I was a jockey. You know what it's like, you just get five minutes with the best of them and then you are on to the next ride. I get to spend time with each and every one of my horses and truly get to know them and what will help them race better or if they should even race at all." Buck started to interrupt and then closed his mouth.

"Don't get me wrong, I missed the adrenaline rush of racing and winning, but I found a greater calling for the benefit of the horse, and I get great satisfaction out of seeing a horse I've worked with win a race. I know I played a hand in their success. The trainers know it to, so I'm not at a loss for work," Lilly continued.

"I'm glad you're happy," Buck said during Lilly's pause. She smiled at him briefly, but she couldn't hold it. The truth was coming, and she was beyond scared about what his reaction would be.

"When I talked to Charlie the other night, I told her what she needed to know, but not everything." Lilly looked at her hand intertwined with Buck's. "She knew it, but didn't press me, which is why I love her. I felt a weight had been lifted off my shoulders and we talked about how to deal with Tom if he showed up. With Charlie's support I felt I was ready to get back on Storm and finish working him for the Preakness and get ready for the race." Lilly stopped again.

"But yesterday's accident made my heart stop." Lilly wasn't sure she could go on. She was about to tell a secret that no one in the world knew except four others, and it would significantly impact the man sitting next to her. She closed her eyes. "Yesterday's accident wasn't only scary for me as a jockey, but also because...it caused our daughter to wind up in the hospital."

Without stopping, Lilly launched into telling Buck the story of their past that he had been anxiously waiting to hear.

Unexpected News

Lilly had cried all morning. Actually, she'd cried herself to sleep the night before, and woken up with the tears still streaming.

It was one of the days that she'd set up with Doug to come and learn more about his operations, and also see if she could help him with the behavioral problems a few of his horses were having.

Since Buck had introduced her to Doug and Molly, Lilly had gone out to his farm several times. She'd come to love the atmosphere, as well as the people. However, that day she'd wanted more than anything to call and cancel, but had decided that if anything could help her calm down, being around the horses at Shamrock Hill Farm could.

She drove down the long, tree-lined driveway, trying desperately to stop the tears before she stopped the car.

"Come on, Lilly, get it together," she said out loud, slamming her hand on the steering wheel.

Lilly had just managed to get her tears under control when she stopped the truck. Molly was waiting by the door of the office, a smile on her face. Her exuberance faltered when she saw Lilly's tear-stained face. Molly raced up to the car as Lilly stepped down.

"Hey, what's on the docket for the day?" Lilly asked, trying to hide the tremor in her voice. Molly wasn't fooled and she immediately wrapped Lilly in her arms. Lilly's precarious hold on her emotions was broken, and the tears fell freely again.

Without fully understanding how, Lilly ended up in the office with a cup of hot tea in her hands and Molly sitting beside her, rubbing her back and waiting patiently for any explanation Lilly would offer her. After several minutes, Lilly looked up at Molly and said the two words she'd been holding in since the night before, afraid to say them out loud.

"I'm pregnant," she sobbed. Molly's face betrayed her surprise, but she quickly got her features back under control and pulled Lilly back into her motherly embrace.

"Buck—" Molly began, but Lilly cut her off.

"He doesn't know, and I…Molly I don't think I can tell him! He's worked so hard to get where he is, I don't want him to have to worry about this," Lilly sobbed. She started rambling. "We didn't mean for this to happen! We were careful and used protection; we are not even twenty years old! Having babies is for older people. I'm so mad and sad and…oh, Molly, what am I going to do?"

"Oh, Lilly, babies change everything, but the changes don't have to be bad," Molly said. Lilly thought about her son, Sam, who was such a joy to Molly.

"I know that, but we're not ready for this. I know I'm definitely not ready! I'm not old enough to have a baby, I want to be a jockey! I'm barely supporting myself right now, I don't have the money for a baby!" Lilly cried out.

"What about your parents? Would they help?" Molly asked.

"I don't know. I haven't talked to them since I moved out," Lilly told her.

"Well…have you considered…" Molly let the sentence trail off, but they both new what she'd meant.

"I considered it for about three seconds. I just…I don't think I could go through with that, you know?" It was a decision she'd never thought she would have to make. Of all the options ahead of her, abortion seemed the most final, and it was something she just couldn't bring herself to do.

"Okay, well if you're sure you're going to have the baby, and you're also sure that you can't raise it on your own, then your only two options are to tell Buck and figure things out, or look into giving your baby up for adoption." Molly's voice was still low and soothing, but at her words, an icy feeling enveloped Lilly and the deluge of tears began anew. Her stomach tightened at all the overwhelming thoughts running through her head. She closed her eyes to try and push them away, while at the same time knowing she had to deal with her situation.

"Buck has worked so hard to get where he is," Lilly repeated. "I can't take that from him. All we have talked about are the dreams we have of becoming famous jockeys—not anything to do with having a baby! I know him though, he would want to make sure the baby was well cared for and he would most definitely quit riding to find a job that was more consistent and not as dangerous." Lilly's anguish showed on her face, and Molly did all she could to stop her own tears from falling.

"Then adoption?" A pit formed in Lilly's stomach at Molly's words. "Steve and I have been looking into it, given I can't have any more of my own children after Sam was born. I could give you some of the pamphlets we have, maybe set you up with an agency."

"What if the family that gets her doesn't love her?" Lilly whispered after several seconds. She looked down at her belly and put her hands over the nonexistent bump. It was still early, but she thought she could tell what it would be. The thought made her heart skip a beat. A little girl. Lilly looked up to see a small smile on Molly's face.

"That is the first unselfish thing you've said since you got here," Molly said. Lilly was taken aback. She wanted to argue that looking out for Buck wasn't selfish, but Molly saw the fight in her eyes and continued.

"The hard truth is, it's not about you or Buck anymore, Lilly. This baby may not have been planned, but it deserves love all the same. What you need to be deciding now is what will be best for...her." Molly put her hand over Lilly's, on the latter's stomach.

"You're right. My baby deserves a good mom. Someone who will look after her and love her and give her all the things she needs," Lilly looked back down at her stomach.

"And if that can't be you—"

"It should be you," Lilly blurted out. She hadn't meant to say it. It wasn't even something she'd considered; but now that the words had been spoken, there was nothing in the world that made more sense to her. She looked at Molly, at the shock on her face. She grasped Molly's hands and turned to face her, staring into her eyes and trying to put all the sincerity of her heart into the words she was speaking.

"Lilly, that's a big decision," Molly said, caution the dominant tone in her voice.

"Molly, I want you to have my baby. You're the most loving, caring person I know. I see how happy and loved Sam is, and I want that for my... you would be a perfect mom for my little..." She couldn't get the words out. Molly's arms were around her. Both women were sobbing, knowing they had an uncertain future ahead and would be forever linked through the little life that grew in Lilly's belly.

———————————

Lilly met with the agent that Molly and Steve were using to broker their adoption. She answered some questions, signed some papers, and then cried the whole way back to the barn at Pimlico.

After her breakdown with Molly, Lilly had spent several days at the farm in order to work through the details. Molly also wanted to make sure that Lilly's decision was not made in spur of the moment fashion and she was truly comfortable with Molly and Steve adopting her baby.

Lilly was indeed relieved with the solution they had arrived at, that someone who she had come to love would be getting this gift from her, a gift they too had been desperate for. Frequently, her mantra of "Everything happens for a reason" popped into her head.

She spent the few days in quiet reflection and meditation; she sat in the fields with her favorite babies at the farm, asking them what they thought of her decision. Doug had found her whispering to them on her last day on the farm before she was to return to Pimlico to pack up her stuff.

"You are a strong woman, Lilly," he said to her, leaning on the top rail of the paddock fence. Lilly turned her head to look at him. Molly's one request was that Doug know the truth.

"No, I am not, Doug, I am selfish and a wimp and a liar," she said back to him. Not telling Buck was the hardest thing for her to wrap her mind around.

"You need to find a way to come to terms with your decision. You have your whole life ahead of you and you can't let this eat at you. It is not healthy," he said strongly. Lilly let out a sigh.

Doug continued, "Sometimes the hardest decisions are the best decisions. Your comments about being too young and not being ready are very real. You are very fortunate to have Molly and Steve here for you and the baby. Many kids your age either choose abortion or don't have a clue as to where their baby winds up."

"See, I am being selfish, not appreciating Molly as much as I should." She trembled. Doug climbed over the fence separating them and came to sit with Lilly. The babies she had been talking to scattered a short distance away, but not far enough that they couldn't still check out what these two people were doing in their pasture.

"You see that chestnut foal over there, the one with the big blaze and three white stockings?" Doug asked.

"Yeah," Lilly replied.

"Check out the mares over there; do you see anything different about any of them?"

Lilly looked at the four mares, three bays and one the color of sand. "Well, that Palomino doesn't look like a Thoroughbred."

"She's not, she's a nurse mare. The chestnut foal's momma died a few days after giving birth, complications from colic that we couldn't save her from. We had to find him an adopted momma to raise him and provide his care and nutrients." The two of them watched as the chestnut colt nuzzled up to the Palomino. She softly touched his nose and pushed him toward her belly to nurse. They watched as he twitched his tail while getting his fill of milk.

"See, she loves him just as much as his real momma would have. Just like Molly and Steve are going to love your baby," Doug said. "And the great part is that you are making the best decision for your baby, while also getting the opportunity to watch he or she grow up and be a part of his or her life."

They had all decided it would be best that the baby not know who Lilly really was. Sometime in the future, they would address how and when to tell him or her the truth, when he or she could understand the decision Lilly had made without judging, if that would be even possible.

Lilly leaned her head on Doug's shoulder. "What happens to the nurse mare's foal?"

"Generally, the foal nurses for several days after being born to make sure it gets the critical nutrients in the colostrum, and then it is hand-raised by the owners of the mare. The farm we use does a great job of finding future homes for their foals. Having quality nurse mare farms is critical to the industry."

"Why is that? This is the first I have heard of such a thing," Lilly commented. She was feeling a bigger attachment to the little chestnut.

"Unfortunately, for several reasons, such as a mare dying in childbirth or shortly thereafter, like this one. A friend of mine has a very well-bred mare, one with Native Dancer in her pedigree, and she is meaner than a snake after she has a foal. She is fine for about 24-hours, and then turns savage, attacking her foals. They have to be very watchful for those first few days in order for the foal to nurse to get its colostrum and they have a nurse mare ready to go. The purpose of the nurse mare is not so the mare can go get re-bred, like many people like to portray as the ugly side of the business. We all hope for happy and healthy mares and foals."

Lilly felt better having Doug distract her from her own situation, but she knew she would need to deal with the hardest part in just a few days. She stood up and gave Doug a big hug. "Thank you."

Doug squeezed her back, "We all support you, Lilly. We are all family now."

Moving On

She still hadn't told Buck, and every step she took towards a finalized adoption put one more nail in the coffin that was the end of their relationship.

She'd thought in the beginning that she would be able to hide it from him and still be with him. Then she'd realized there was no chance of that, but thought maybe if he knew about the adoption, he would stay with her.

The more she thought about it, the more she realized that she couldn't stay with him. She wouldn't make him feel guilty, or drag him into this situation where the path had already been chosen.

Now that everything was decided and finalized, it was time for her to end things with him, and that was going to be the hardest part for her.

She had decided the best course of action for everyone was to just leave, disappear for a while until everything was over. It would only be for nine months, she rationalized. She wouldn't lose too much time out of the saddle. Hopefully Tom wouldn't be too angry with her, and would take her back when the time was right.

She packed up her small little apartment above the stalls at Pimlico and left a note on the bed that read, "Thanks for everything Tom. I need to take a leave of absence for a while. I hope to see you soon." He would be mad, she knew. He had come to rely on her for almost everything, but she also didn't want him trying to find her. She didn't want to leave too much information.

She walked down the shed row, touching the noses of each of the Thoroughbreds she had come to know so well. She stopped at Hank's half door. He was lying down in the thick straw, his eyes closed, and she could hear him snoring. Smiling, Lilly opened the door. She quietly sat down next to his neck and leaned into his strong body. Curling up into a ball, she closed her eyes, breathed deeply in the horse-y smells that surrounded her. It was in this moment that Lilly finally understood and accepted the decision she had made.

A soft noise brought Lilly out of her slumber. She had fallen asleep leaning against Hank.

"Ready to go?" a voice quietly said to her. Lilly opened her eyes and saw Macy standing in the open half door. Macy, her best friend, the only other person in the world who knew about the baby.

Everyone had thought it best if Lilly distanced herself from the area for a few months, and having Lilly around Shamrock would raise suspicion about where Molly's adopted baby came from.

And she couldn't lie to Buck. He was the one she'd either have to come clean with, or leave completely in the dark. He'd been away at races a lot, so she'd only talked to him on the phone. I was easier that way, to keep him in the dark.

Lilly got up from her nap, gave Hank a big hug and kiss on the nose. "I'll be back, big guy, don't win too much without me."

She grabbed her bag and walked over to Macy's car. "Thanks, Macy."

Macy smiled at her, gave Lilly a big hug. "It will be all right, let's get out of here."

Lilly walked around the back of the car and went to grab the handle of the door when a big arm came up behind her and pulled her close.

"Where do you think you're going?" Buck whispered in her ear.

Lilly hadn't expected Buck to be around for a few more days. He was riding in California, which is why she picked today; with him all the way across the country she felt it would be easier on them both. Lilly stiffened.

She hadn't expected the sudden sense of drowning that overcame her when she heard his voice. Lilly turned in his arms to face him, steeling herself over what she had to do.

"I've missed you. I got in just an hour ago and wanted to surprise you." Buck nuzzled at her ear and smiled down at her, and she could feel her knees buckle. "Hi Macy," he called through the open window. Macy waved and returned her attention back to her cell phone, pretending to go through her Facebook page and knowing the next few minutes were going to be toxic.

Lilly moved out of Buck's grasp and leaned against the car for support. "Well, actually, we kinda need to talk." His face registered his concern, but he smiled and nodded anyway.

"What's up?"

"Um…god, I don't want to do this, but…" she said aloud. She could feel her eyes watering.

"Lilly, what's wrong?" Buck put his hands on her shoulders. She knew she should tell him not to, but his touch was so comforting that she couldn't make him stop. She wanted to savor his closeness for as long as she could.

"Buck…I can't see you anymore," she said as she raked her finger nails against the side of the car door to give her strength. He took a step back, as if the words had physically punched him.

"What?"

"This isn't what I want. You're distracting me and I need to focus on my dream. It's been fun and you have taught me a lot. It's time I moved on. I'm leaving Pimlico." She stood there stoically, feeling her world crumble around her. Watching Buck's emotions cross his face was almost too much to bear. She could see the wrinkles in his nose and his eyes narrowed as he registered what she was saying.

"You're breaking up with me?" his voice was quivering with shock.

"Yes," Lilly said, looking down at the ground. She couldn't meet his gaze without breaking down.

"But I love you. I love you, Lilly. Whatever it is, I can fix it. Don't do this," he pleaded. He grabbed her hands in his and she made a meek attempt to pull them away, but his grip was strong.

"You can't," she was having a hard time breathing and squeezed her eyes shut to fight back the tears. She had to be strong or he wouldn't believe her. She could feel her heart breaking in her chest. The pain of it was overwhelming, but she couldn't stop now.

"Just tell me what's wrong, I'll fix it. I'll do better!" Buck's eyes were watering now. She'd never seen him cry before. The pieces of her heart shattered even further.

Lilly braced herself. "Buck, I don't love you anymore."

Buck stood still in front of her, his hands gripping her waist tightly. Lilly was glad he couldn't feel the effects of the pregnancy yet. "Lilly, that's not true. I know it's not. I know we haven't seen each other much, with me riding up and down the east coast and needing to go out west, but I will change. I won't travel, I will stay right by your side. I promise to—"

His words reinforced her decision. She knew he would give up his life for her and she couldn't bear that responsibility. She knew later in life he would resent her and their baby.

"Goodbye," she said. She moved his hands from her waist, and pushed him away. She grabbed at the door handle of the car as the tears burst through the dam she had been able hold up, and it took everything in her not to turn back and look at him. She slammed the door and Macy pulled away from Buck as he stood there in shocked silence. Lilly kept her head averted so he wouldn't be able to tell how big the lie was she had just told him.

PART FOUR

The Paddock

Charlie followed Genuine Storm as the starters for the Preakness Stakes walked from the stabling area to the paddock. She held Skylar's hand tightly as she stomped in the puddles that the downpours had caused. Doug walked close by her side, shielding her as much as he could from the reporters who were interviewing each of the owners and trainers.

Hunter walked up ahead and took the bulk of the interview in order to provide Charlie a buffer from getting asked any uncomfortable questions, especially about Sarge and his untimely death. Charlie appreciated all that Hunter had done with Storm over the last week while she dealt with the death of her best friend and worried about whether Lilly would ride Storm. She was still surprised every time she ran into Hunter at Doug's farm about how small the world was and the realization that her life had come full circle back to someone she had known so many years ago.

She let out the air she had been holding and continued her search of the crowds around them. Charlie had studied pictures and was intent on making sure that Tom Malone was nowhere in the vicinity of her and her extended family.

Lilly stood at the front of the line of jockeys waiting to descend the steps that would take them to the paddock area, where they would receive their last-minute instructions from their trainers and be hoisted into the saddles for the running of the second jewel of the Triple Crown.

Buck hadn't said much to her while they were getting ready. They had agreed to keep their distance today, given what was at stake, but Lilly felt like a weight that she had been carrying for over 15 years had finally been lifted.

"It's post time gentlemen, and lady," the man in front of them said as he opened the door. The wind blew the door open, and Lilly could feel the dampness from the rain that had been falling all day. They all braced themselves against the weather as they marched out the door.

The rain had let up a bit from the monsoon it had been just an hour ago. Lilly prayed it would stay that way, but the forecast wasn't hopeful. The jockeys walked down the stairs and toward the platform that had been put down so they could cross over the track to access the traditional paddock area specifically set up for the Preakness Stakes.

All of the horses were being saddled in Pimlico's unique inside paddock area, located beneath the big old grandstand in order to stay out of the rain as much as possible.

The Preakness is limited to 14 starters. Pimlico doesn't use an auxiliary gate, like the Derby; therefore, the races are limited to the number allowed in the starting gate. The inside paddock area consists of 14 saddle stalls back to back with a full-length window along one side for the people in the clubhouse area to observe the horses. The other side of the area is open to the general public from the grandstand area, but it could fit few more than 100 people in that area. The crowds were gathered all around, watching the horses as they left the inside paddock to meet their jockeys in the Preakness paddock in the inside of the track.

Lilly knew there would be no postponing or canceling the Preakness. Races were only impacted by severe cold or lightning. The rain that had been falling in a steady deluge since dawn was not nearly enough to stop the race. The track had been sealed by the tractors to try to get as much rain as possible to flow off the dirt, but there was only so much they could do. It was going to be a soggy mess once the horses dug their hooves into it.

As Lilly walked down the stairs from the jockey room towards the crowd below, she reflected on the morning. They had been up early, all of them—Doug, Charlie, Skylar, Ryan, Ben, and Cappie—to kick off the second leg of the Triple Crown. Jenny would watch from home with her leg in its full-length cast. She had tried to persuade everyone to allow her to come, but Molly had put her foot down. Plus, wheeling her around in a wheelchair in the rain would have been impossible. They had dropped Ryan off at her house that morning. He was adamant that someone be with her during the big race, given all she had been through.

Lilly owed so much to Jenny, her daughter. And to Sarge. Lilly blinked away tears. She definitely wouldn't be there if it hadn't been for Sarge and Jenny putting their lives on the line to save her and Storm.

And to Buck. If it wasn't for him, she wouldn't have returned to the track late last night to let Charlie know she would ride.

Buck and Lilly hadn't known how to move forward with telling Jenny the truth, but she had called Molly early this morning to let her know how her conversation with Buck had gone. When she had approached Molly in the hospital, she was actually relieved that Lilly had finally come to terms with the decisions she had made so long ago and was supportive, as they had always talked about how this day would come. They decided they would get together after the race and figure things out.

Lilly took in a long breath and slowly let it out. She continued to lead the line of jockeys making their way toward paddock where her ride awaited her.

As she was about to step out onto the track, a hand reached out and grabbed her arm. Lilly turned her head to stare at the one man she had dreaded seeing since he showed up two weeks ago at the Derby.

"Elizabeth." He pulled at her. Lilly yanked her arm out of his grasp. How did he get this close to the track? Buck had said Tom had been banned from coming to racetracks years ago due to all the violations he had from drugging his horses. A ball cap was pulled close over his eyes and half his face was covered by the rain slicker he wore. He reached out to grab her again, desperation in his eyes. Lilly froze, feeling like the little girl she had been when she had met him. How had he become such a lost soul?

She could feel the world closing in as commotion broke out around her. The one thing she registered was Buck pushing past the other jockeys to reach her. He stood in front of Lilly, reached back, and landed a punch across Tom Malone's face, knocking him to the ground.

"Don't ever come near her again, you bastard," Buck said to him through clenched teeth. His fist was pulled back in order to land another blow should Tom come at them. But Tom's bravado shriveled up. Lilly noted he was but a shell of the larger-than-life figure she remembered. Two policemen pulled Tom up by his armpits and marched him through the surrounding crowd.

Buck turned to Lilly. "You okay?" She nodded slowly.

"You okay, Lilly? You okay?" came from all the jockeys surrounding them. An arm went around her shoulders. "We got your back, Lil." These were her friends, the people she had grown up with and had found her dream with. And she had missed them.

Lilly broke into a smile. "Yes, thank you, I'm fine. Now let's go out there so I can kick your butts in this race!"

They all laughed, and then returned to business. Getting in her place to continue their march across the track, Buck grabbed Lilly's hand as he made his way back into line. She squeezed it back.

Charlie looked at Lilly as she approached through the rain that had started to fall again, relieved to see her jockey. A small part of her thought Lilly would be a no-show. Then watching what had transpired across the track and the commotion caused by Tom, she wouldn't have been surprised if Lilly had turned around and marched back up the stairs into the jockey room.

"What a jerk," Lilly called over to Charlie as she approached them, a smile on her face. Charlie relaxed, knowing Lilly had finally overcome her demons.

Charlie turned her focus across the paddock where Buck was getting last minute instructions from Royal Duke's trainer. He was all business, but she saw him glance Lilly's way. Charlie caught Lilly return his look and give a small smile. A confident smile. Charlie knew that Buck played a big part in getting Lilly to ride today, but she wondered what else was going on behind the scenes.

"All set?" Doug asked Lilly.

"Ready as I'll ever be," Lilly joked. Skylar slowly grabbed at Lilly's hand.

"Please be safe out there, Miss Lilly. It doesn't matter if Storm doesn't win, I just want him and you to make it around safely on that muddy track."

"Storm will take care of me," Lilly replied. "He's practiced in the rain and even raced on a muddy track. Remember his trip in the Lexington Stakes? Hadn't rained as much as this, but he handled the muddy track fine."

"Do you have enough sets of goggles?" Ben asked Lilly.

"I am sure I will go through them all, as Storm likes to come from behind," Lilly said.

"Why do you need so many?" Skylar asked.

Lilly tilted her helmet toward Skylar. "Can you count how many I have?"

Skylar counted through the number of goggles stacked one on top of the other on Lilly's helmet.

"Ten," she said, "you have ten sets of goggles on your head! And why are they covered with Saran Wrap?!"

"The Saran Wrap keeps them dry until right before the race starts. I will pull it off before I enter the starting gate. As for why so many goggles, if I wind up behind horses at the break, the mud will get kicked up into my face. As the goggles get dirty, they are harder to see through, so then I just pull the top one off and it drops to my neck, with the clean pairs below."

"But if you come out in front, you won't get the mud in your face, right?" Skylar asked.

"That's true, but no matter what your game plan may be going in, you never know what truly is going to happen until those gates open," Lilly replied.

"So good luck getting to the front first!" Skylar exclaimed.

"Well, either way, no matter where we are, I will help make sure Storm is safe running in this muck." Lilly smiled at Skylar, and Skylar hugged her tightly. Charlie noted she was getting a bit more comfortable with the hugs that Skylar liked to shower on her.

"Riders up!" came the call.

"Alrighty, that's us, big guy." Lilly bent her leg for Doug to launch her into the saddle. She smiled at Doug and Charlie as Ben led them out of the paddock area and onto the track.

Cappie reached for the leather strap Ben handed up to him that was looped through Storm's bridle.

"Who is this big fella you are riding?" Lilly asked him.

Cappie nodded his head. "One of the best. A sorry replacement for Sarge, but he will do. "

Storm jigged next to his new side pony, unsure of what to make of the big appaloosa walking next to him. "Well, he certainly is a pretty one," Lilly commented, winking at Cappie.

They two worked their way along the grandstand as the words to "Maryland, My Maryland," the official song of the Preakness Stakes, rang out from the crowd.

The Preakness

The rain steadily fell in front of Lilly and Storm as they looked through the rails of the starting gate in front of them. Being the first to load in the number one hole meant they had to wait for the other thirteen contenders to load up.

Storm's ears were flicking back and forth between the track ahead of them and the noise behind. One of the horses, BigOldOak, was causing a raucous loading, and the wait was almost unbearable. His name fit him, as he stood over 17 hands, and the handlers were having a hard time getting him into the gate. Usually they would grab hands and arms behind the horse's rump, but with the rain, they kept losing their grip.

Lilly didn't chance a glance to her right. Two horses away were Buck and Royal Duke. Lilly knew he wouldn't make it easy on them, no matter what their relationship. Once on the track, they were both all business. She did, however, send up a prayer that Buck would be safe, that they would all be safe, while looking at the muddy track ahead of them.

The white inside rail gleamed to their left.

When Charlie had pulled the number one post, the entire team had spent time strategizing on how to get Storm to race along the rail when he broke out of the gate. No one had come up with a good answer, not even Hunter.

Lilly hadn't participated in the discussions, but she knew she would have her hands full. The minute the gates opened, Storm would pull to the right. Anything to get away from that inside rail. It was the one leftover demon from his time before Charlie claimed him. The scar on his chest was the physical sign that would fade as he got whiter, but the emotional scar was much deeper. He would not race along the rail.

Fortunately, or unfortunately, they had not had to race from the number one position in any of their prior races. Lilly truly didn't know how he would break from the gate. Their training had gotten them as close as the third hole for Storm to break straight. Any closer than that and Storm would break into a sweat, tossing his head anxiously, and when the gate would open, he would veer to the right.

She could taste the dangerous position she was in. She tried to swallow, but couldn't. Her hands were slick, not from the rain, but from sweat. Crazy as it was, she needed to distract Storm to allow the others to break before he got out of the gate. That would allow Granite Man and Duke on his other side to get a jump ahead before Storm came out of the gate and veered into them.

Lilly reached deep into Storm's mane and set her boots hard against the stirrups. It would take all of her strength to keep Storm from running into Granite Man when they broke. She shortened her left rein, but made sure to take all the slack out of her right rein as well. If she pulled too hard on the left rein, it may cause Storm to come out crooked and he might hit the gate with his back right hip. She had to think of all possible scenarios in the blink of any eye.

She couldn't hear or see when they got BigOldOak into the gate, but a second of quiet overcame the participants in the gate as they collectively anticipated the bell.

The bell rang and the announcer's voice rang out, "And they're off for the 140th running of the Preakness Stakes!"

If he had meant it or not, Storm had perfectly timed the bell and got a jump on the other competitors right as the gates opened. This was fortunate, as his first inclination in his first stride out of the gate was to veer right to avoid the big white monster to his left. His anticipation saved him from crashing into Granite Man, as he came out ahead of the rest of the field.

Now what, Lilly thought, because for the first time in Storm's career, he was in the lead. No playing tag today.

Storm's ears were forward and he seemed to be curious about what to do. The crowds in the grandstand had squeezed under the overhangs and were cheering on Storm. He had grown accustomed to the attention and the cheers from the crowd and he seemed to respond to their urging.

The rest of the horses sprang upon them as they all cleared the gate. Royal Duke had taken up on the rail, the space Storm had vacated. Granite Man was to their right and Lilly was pretty sure his jockey was not happy about Storm cutting in front of them at the start. His horse was the speed in the race, expected to be the pacesetter, and he'd been planning to take the lead. Things were not panning out like any one had speculated.

None of the jockeys, including Lilly, had planned for Genuine Storm to be in the lead at the start. Now everyone had to change their game plan. The horse expected to come from the back of the pack, the closer, was now in the lead.

Lilly threw her hands at Storm. "Come on, big guy, things change. Instead of your game of tag, we are now playing a game of keep away." Lilly worked her entire body to encourage him along.

———————————

"Oh my god!" Charlie said under her breath as the horses broke out of the starting gate. She instinctively squeezed Doug's hand, her nails biting into his flesh. Doug grabbed her hand in both of his.

"He'll be fine," he said confidently as they watched Storm take the lead. Doug silently prayed he was right. Lilly could work miracles sometimes, and he hoped this was one of those times. It was very hard to take back a horse out of the lead and expect him to turn it on again in the late running of the race. It was like asking a sprinter to run two races back to back.

"Mom, he knows what to do, I just know it!" Skylar hugged her mom's side. "He used to love when Sarge chased him around the field and he would try to keep out of his nips. Maybe he'll just keep ahead of them."

"I hope so, Sweetie Pie," Charlie replied, a bit teary-eyed at the mention of Sarge, but focusing on Storm and Lilly, trying to figure out what they would do. The good thing so far was that Storm hadn't "stopped," he hadn't just decided that this just wouldn't do with him in front. And she was thankful that his quick move to the outside hadn't injured another horse. The other jockey could claim a foul when the race was over, but she couldn't think about that now.

Lilly continued to urge Storm on with her entire being, her hands, her legs, and her voice. He was running smoothly and she decided to take a small hold on him to see if she could conserve some energy for the home-stretch run. Storm would have none of it. With Granite Man on their outside and Duke on the rail, he had risen to the challenge. Neither jockey was letting up on their charge to try to take the lead.

They would run themselves into the ground. At the pace they just finished the first quarter, 22.37 seconds, there would be no fuel left in the tank when the stretch runners came at them.

Lilly glanced quickly at Buck on Duke. His face was drawn, his lips in a thin line. He had taken up on Duke as well, but his horse didn't seem to be responding either. It was as if the two horses didn't realize there were riders on their backs and had reverted to the age-old instinct of running for the love of running and rising up to the challenge of a competitor. It wasn't the jockeys deciding the course of action for this race, but the horses themselves.

Ryan spoke up as they watched the race unfold in front of them on Jenny's big TV screen. "It's Affirmed and Alydar all over again."

"Who?" Jenny asked without taking her eyes off the horses who'd entered the back stretch.

"Affirmed and Alydar battled in each of the Triple Crown races in 1978, with Affirmed finishing first and Alydar finishing second in all three. It was a big rivalry," Ryan explained as he watched Storm and Duke push at each over on the far side of the Pimlico oval. "They were just a nose apart at the finish line in the Belmont, pushing each other for most of the race to finish with one of the fastest running times ever."

They watched as the horses ran as one into the far turn, neither Storm nor Duke wanting to relinquish the lead.

"They are going to run themselves into the ground," Ryan said under his breath.

Jenny grabbed at his hand and he squeezed it back, not taking any attention off the battle taking place a world away at the track. Ryan would have liked to be there in person, but there was no way he was going to let Jenny be alone today.

———————————

Lilly grabbed at her goggles and yanked one down. Given they were the front runners, she hadn't needed to change them out, but the water, combined with her sweat, was making them blurry.

"Oh goodness, Storm, what are you doing?" she said quietly, sitting as still as possible. There wasn't much she could do but try to ease his burden. The blistering pace Storm and Duke were setting would come back to haunt them in about another half mile, during the last eighth of the race. Her internal timer had just checked off 46 for the half mile, on a muddy track. Crazy fast.

Storm and Duke had left Granite Man behind. The pacesetter couldn't even keep up with the pace these two hellions were setting. Lilly looked under her shoulder at the field behind, there was no one close. Not yet.

The rain continued to pelt Storm and Lilly. Heading down the backstretch, they were racing right into the rain, and the pellets stung Lilly's cheeks. Storm's ears, normally forward, were pinned against his head to avoid the rain drops. His beautifully dappled grey coat shined black from the wetness.

His breathing wasn't labored yet; the last weeks' conditioning was paying off.

———————————

The muddy track continued to grab at both horses' legs as they slogged their way into the final turn. Lilly listened for signs of beleaguered breathing from Storm, but he was racing in fine form. She silently thanked Jenny for all the hill exercises she had done with Storm back at Shamrock.

Normally, on a muddy track, the rain rolls to the inside of the track and is the deepest dirt to run in. The jockeys liked to keep their horse a lane or two away from the rail. Buck and Lilly knew differently. Their experience of racing at Pimlico was on full display now as both jockeys positioned their horses to take advantage of the tight turns that Pimlico was known for, with Buck on Duke against the rail and Lilly on Storm just to the outside of them. As they rounded the turn, the wind and the rain were now at their backs. Storm's ears shifted forward at the same time Buck asked Duke to raise his game with an attempt to pass Storm.

Storm would have none of it. At the first sign of Duke trying to overtake him, Storm matched him stride for stride. Storm wasn't pulling away, but he wasn't losing any ground either. Lilly wondered if the early days of racing in the fields as babies was helping drive him on. Storm was racing head to head with one of his first pasture mates. Lilly firmly believed that horses had a strong memory, and she wouldn't be surprised if he was living out one of his early memories of foals establishing seniority in the field while protected by their mommas.

However, they weren't in a peaceful field frolicking in the sunshine. They were in the second leg of the Triple Crown, on a very muddy track. She needed Storm to move past his old friend. Duke was running just as easily as Storm, and Buck was a savvy jockey, so Lilly knew it wasn't going to be an easy task to get to the wire first. Buck would pull out every stop to move past Lilly, regardless of their relationship.

———————————

They came out of the turn with the expansive homestretch ahead of them. The crowd, caught up in the excitement of the dueling horses, moved out from under the cover of the grandstand to cheer them on.

Lilly was clicking off in her head one of the fastest times she could ever remember for the mile. They were in the last eighth of the race. *Now or never, Storm,* she thought. She kept her focus on Storm, and with a slight nudge on his neck with her right hand so Buck couldn't detect it, Lilly asked Storm to move into the next gear she knew he possessed.

Storm flicked an ear and flattened out, jumping ahead by a nose. Buck glanced over at them with a bit of surprise. He had thought he had Storm beat. Lilly kept her head straight and tucked herself lower on Storm's back, urging him on.

Buck pumped at Duke, switched his whip to his left hand, and Duke rose to the challenge. Duke came up on Storm again. Storm eye-balled Duke, dug deep into the muddy track, and raced on.

Heads bobbing together, the two horses raced down the homestretch to the cheering of thousands, and crossed the finish line.

No one could definitely say who'd won.

"Did he win? Did he get his nose in front?" Charlie looked at everyone around her.

"He totally did, Mom," Skylar said, with the confidence of her young years.

They all wanted to believe their horse had taken the second leg of the crown. The TV cameras were all around them, as well as on Duke's owners.

They'd all have to wait for the "photo finish" sign shining bright on the tote board to change to an announcement about the winner of the race.

Charlie looked at the board. She watched as the words she'd hoped to avoid lit up: "Inquiry." One of the jockeys had claimed foul.

The Inquiry

It was as though the air was being slowly let out of a balloon. The noise of the crowd was subdued but not silenced. Doug's hand on Charlie's back seemed to her to be the only thing keeping her attached to the world.

"Did he cross first?" She was in a daze. There was a 50 percent chance that her horse had won the Preakness Stakes.

"Even if he did, there's a chance…" Doug didn't finish the thought. Skylar was looking up at him, her eyebrows furrowed, her expression daring him to think the worst. He smiled at her passion.

There was a collective gasp throughout the stadium as the announcer's voice settled over the spectators.

"Ladies and gentleman, after reviewing the photo of the finish line, officials have found that the first horse to cross the finish line was…GENUINE STORM!" The roar from the crowd was so loud that it drowned out the rest of the announcement. Skylar was jumping up and down. Charlie's phone was buzzing non-stop in her pocket. Doug was laughing.

As if to bring everyone back to reality, the word "Inquiry" flashed several times up on the board.

Charlie stood still, staring at the word lit up on the tote board. She had to hold her emotions in check.

"Mom, Storm won! Why aren't we celebrating?" Skylar asked innocently. Charlie looked down at the exuberant face of her daughter.

"We have to wait and see, dear. You see that word lit up on the tote board? The word 'inquiry' means that the stewards are reviewing the race to see if there was anything Storm did to hurt another horse's chance to win. Sometimes, a jockey makes a claim that their horse was cut off by another. In this case, I would venture to guess that they are reviewing the start of the race when Storm veered over to the right as he broke from the gate."

"But Lilly had him clear of that other horse. I saw him break first," Skylar said adamantly, indignant that anyone would accuse her hero, Lilly, of not playing fair or purposely running into another horse.

"Well, we will see what the stewards decide. It doesn't take long," Charlie said, squeezing her hand.

Charlie felt the buzzing in her pocket and thought maybe looking at her phone would make the waiting less excruciating. There were so many notifications on the screen that she wondered briefly how so many people had gotten her phone number.

Rather than read through them, she looked specifically for a message from Ryan. There were eight. She smiled as she read through them. He'd texted her about the break right when it had happened. There were three texts about Storm's pace, two about Duke running him into the ground, one worrying that he hadn't got his nose in front, and the last one read, "Don't worry. He ran clear."

She warmed at her son's confidence and knowing she needed the support. *No matter the result, they won,* she thought as she reflected on Lilly and all that she had gone through the past two weeks. Charlie turned to look at the couple standing a few rows behind them.

Lilly's parents were huddled close, Robert's arm around his wife's shoulders, and Joyce was squeezing her rosary between her hands, tears streaming down her face. Charlie thought about all the years they had missed out on and prayed that Lilly would understand the reasons behind Charlie convincing them to come to the race with her.

––––––––––––––––––

As they eased their heavily breathing Thoroughbreds, Buck yelled out to Lilly, "Another great ride, but I'll get you in the Belmont!" She smiled over at him.

"That is, unless you chicken out again," he quipped.

"Not on your life," she called back.

"Watch out, Buck! If she's back for good, she might knock you off the top." Another jockey had caught up to them to congratulate Lilly. Lilly smiled but said nothing as Buck joked back with the newcomer. Lilly's feelings were threatening to envelop her, but she managed to thank the man before he rode off.

Buck's face turned serious, "You have to head to the winner's circle now, missy." Lilly knew they were far from okay, that Buck must be feeling all sorts of things about her, and the fact that she'd just beaten him for a second time would not be helping his pride right now. She was scared for them, but she knew she'd finally done the right thing.

She smiled at him as he turned Duke away and headed for the stables. Lilly slowed Storm and eased him into a bouncy trot as Donna Brothers approached with her microphone.

Cappie got to her first and steered her a bit away. "Inquiry on the board, Lilly," he said quickly, knowing she hadn't had a chance to look over at the tote yet. Lilly glanced over at the tote board looming in the infield.

"Crap."

"Yeah, the break from the gate seems to be the culprit," Cappie said. Donna rode up alongside Storm.

"Another great ride, Lilly. Unfortunately we will need to see what the inquiry is all about. What do you think happened?"

"Well Storm broke a bit to the right as he left the gate, but I don't think it was bad enough to impede the horse there. We had a big jump coming out of the gate and there was no contact," she replied confidently.

"I've also heard that the jockey of Granite Man would have filed an objection if the stewards weren't looking into it," Donna said, turning the microphone on Lilly.

"Like I said, Donna, we had a big jump coming out of the gate and I'm confident that there was no contact between Storm and his horse," Lilly said.

"What about you and Buck sticking to the rail coming around the far turn? The inside rail is known to be the hardest to run through on a muddy track," Donna said.

"Well, me and Buck, we have a lot of experience on this track. This is where I started riding, and we've ridden a lot of races here. We know how the rain settles here. We also know that Pimlico's turns are tighter than most tracks. The pace the horses were running out was blistering and we needed to find the shortest way home. So Buck taking the rail was a smart move on his part. I'm just lucky Storm's nose got home in front," Lilly replied.

"Good luck to you both! It would be great to have the Preakness win along with the Derby," Donna said. "I guess we will all have to wait and see, back to you Jack." Donna signed off and turned the TV broadcast back to the announcers.

"Good luck, Lilly," Donna said.

"Thanks." Lilly started to trot off, but pulled up. She waited until Donna caught up with her.

"More to say, Lilly?" she asked.

"Not publicly," Lilly replied. "I just wanted you to know that I read a book many years ago all about you and your mom and the other female jockeys that had helped pave the way to ride. The book helped me through some tough times. I am so honored to be able to continue your legacies."

Donna smiled. "You bear the torch well, Lilly. You will have us all riding with you in the Belmont."

"Thanks," Lilly said as she and Storm trotted off towards the crowd that was gathering near the winner's circle.

Cappie turned Storm over to Ben, who was waiting, and Lilly jumped from his back. "Stewards want to talk to you, Lilly," the nearby race official called to her. She nodded her head, grabbed her saddle, and went to stand on the scale to clear her weight assignment. Her valet was standing close by and she handed off her saddle as she walked to the phone that was a direct line to the stewards.

Charlie, Skylar, and Doug pushed through the crowd as the television cameramen swarmed around them. It seemed like an eternity before they could make it down to the track level. Charlie could see Lilly talking on the phone to the stewards. She couldn't stop her hands from shaking, so she clasped them tightly to her chest while they waited. The media was all around them and they collectively held their breath, waiting for the tote board to change its order of finish for the Preakness from unofficial to official. Charlie could do nothing but stare at the dreaded lit up word, wishing it to burn out.

She saw Lilly hang up the phone and glance her way. Charlie hoped that was a small smile she saw on her face as she turned and grabbed her saddle back from her valet.

Suddenly, a wave of cheering engulfed them and Charlie looked to the board to see the word "Official" and the number one listed in first place. Her knees buckled, and Doug had to hold her up,

"Come on Preakness winner, let's go get our picture taken." Doug's voice could barely contain the tremor of a laugh, and Charlie was sure she'd never seen a bigger smile on his face. Skylar pulled at Charlie's hand.

"Mom, look!" She was pointing at the jockey and horse weather vane atop the replica of the Old Clubhouse copula. A painter, standing atop a crane, had been waiting patiently for the results to become official. As the tote board declared the winner, he applied the first strokes of blue to the jockey.

"A tradition started in 1909," Doug told them. "Each year, the jockey's silks get repainted with the colors of the silks worn by the Preakness winner."

"Even with the three yellow bands around the arm, and the white ribbon on the sleeves?" Skylar asked.

"Yep, exactly like the shirt and cap Lilly is wearing over there in the winner's circle." Doug picked up Skylar, grabbed Charlie's hand, and all three of them walked over to their horse, who had just won the second leg of the Triple Crown.

Back at the Barn

Lilly walked slowly down the row of stalls, her emotions raw from the last few hours, a smile playing on her lips as she thought about the last few strides Storm had taken to overcome Duke at the finish. *Gosh, what heart,* she thought to herself. Storm had taught her so much over the last few months. She would use Storm's courage to get through the next several days, as they would be turning points in her life, as well as the lives of many others.

She stopped at Storm's stall and patted his big grey head as he munched happily on the hay hanging in the bag just outside his stall. Her ears picked up the conversation happening around the end of the barn. Lilly couldn't see who was talking, but she recognized Charlie's voice at once.

"Doug, this is Joyce and Robert Garrett. Joyce and Robert, this is Doug Walker. He's a big part of our winning team and I believe he has known Lilly for quite some time."

Lilly's hand froze on Storm's nose. Her parents had been on her mind all morning; they were next on her list of people to apologize to, but she hadn't expected to see them so soon. Her stomach turned to lead as she listened to the other familiar voice now speaking.

"Nice to meet both of you," Doug said, holding out his hand to both

Robert and Joyce. "Your daughter has been a godsend to me and my horses over the years."

Joyce smiled sadly as Robert said, "We appreciate you being a part of her life. Obviously, her dream has come true and she has turned into quite a celebrity." Lilly took a deep breath and gave Storm one last pat.

"Give me strength, boy." She squared her shoulders and walked around the corner of the barn. Charlie saw her first, and Lilly noticed a definite hint of fear in her expression. Lilly did her best to smile and reassure Charlie that she wasn't mad or upset. Seeing her parents was the right thing to do, and if it had to be now, then so be it

"Hello Mom, Dad." Her parents turned around. Her mother gasped. Her father put an arm around his wife as if to hold her up, but as Lilly looked closer, she saw his knees shaking and thought maybe it was more for his support. They all stood looking at each other, not sure what to do next. Lilly glanced over at Charlie, hoping for some help. Charlie smiled and grabbed Doug's hand.

"Come on, dear, we have some reporters to go talk to." Doug looked at Charlie and followed her lead. Charlie shook both Robert's and Joyce's hands.

"Thank you so much for coming out today. I hope you enjoyed the race," Charlie said. She turned and gave Lilly a big hug and whispered, "Don't hate me. I love you too much to not have you close the loop on your past." Lilly closed her eyes and gave Charlie a big hug back.

"Thank you. For everything." Doug winked at her and then he left with Charlie. Lilly and her parents were finally alone after long years apart, and it was time to get to know each other again.

Calm Waters

Charlie looked out the window of her kitchen. Jenny and Ryan were sitting in what Charlie had dubbed her "customary Friday evening chairs," the big Adirondacks overlooking the paddock. Storm and Hershey were happily grazing in the paddock.

It was still shocking to Charlie to look in the paddock and not see three horses grazing, but she knew Sarge was looking down and keeping an eye on Storm. She could feel his presence in the barn and knew it would always be that way. One day there may be another horse to ride, but for right now she knew her attention was needed elsewhere and for other people.

Jenny had been over to visit Ryan a lot since her accident, and most of the days she hadn't made the drive, Ryan had gone to Shamrock to see her. Charlie made a mental note to have a discussion with Jenny's mother about the boundaries they were going to set. As far as the kids actually dating, Charlie was on board. Jenny was a wonderful, driven girl, and Charlie was pretty sure she'd gotten Ryan to stop being so moody.

"Only a few weeks until the next one," a voice came from behind her. Doug stood leaning against the door jamb.

Charlie turned. "Crazy, right?"

"Ready to take on the Belmont, The Test of Champions?" he asked her.

"I think that is a better question for the guy eating grass out there," she replied.

"Well, you are on the road to potentially having the first Triple Crown winner in over thirty years. Pretty awesome," Doug said as he crossed the room and looped his arms around Charlie's waist.

"Pretty awesome," she said pushing him slightly, but not wanting him to let her go.

"Sarge?" he asked, looking out the window behind Charlie.

"It's just weird, not seeing him out there. He's been out there as long as I can remember," she said.

"I know. It's not fair. I'm so sorry," Doug replied. Charlie was quiet for a moment.

"I saw Buck and Lilly talking after the race. What do you think is going on there?"

"Oh, I have no idea. He's been around the farm this past week a bunch. Lilly seems happier," Doug said. He was looking out at Ryan and Jenny. His eyes narrowed as a particularly loud giggle floated his way. Charlie smiled.

"Are you just here to spy on your niece?"

"Well, it's definitely one of the reasons," Doug said, still staring out the window.

"Ryan is a good kid!" Charlie said pointedly.

"Ryan is a great kid, but he's also a teenage boy. You know who else was a teenage boy? Me. I know what they think," he said with concern for his niece.

"Overprotective much?" Charlie laughed. Doug looked down at her, a serious look on his face.

"I think you're underestimating the danger here."

"I think you're forgetting what it was like to fall in love for the first time," Charlie put her hand on his chest, just over his heart. He was still for a moment, and then he put his hand over hers.

"Are you turning sentimental on me, Ms. Jenkins?" Doug teased.

"Not on your life," Charlie laughed.

Doug grew serious again. "What do you think about changing your last name?"

"My last name? What do you mean?" Charlie said, thinking his comment was still in jest.

"Like, changing it to Mrs. Walker?" Doug asked. There was no hint of a smile on his face, or laugh in his voice. He even had his eyebrow cocked in the same way he did when considering something very intensely. Charlie grew still in his arms.

"Are you asking me to marry you, Doug?"

"Listen, this isn't coming out all romantic and such, but I love you, Charlie, and I want to spend the rest of my life with you. So yes, I am asking you to marry me." Doug smiled down at her.

Charlie stood there dumbfounded. She hadn't expected this. She knew she loved Doug, but getting married again? Her hesitation was just a little too long. Doug dropped his arms and moved away from Charlie.

"I guess not the question you were expecting," he said dejectedly.

"Doug, wait. No…it's just that…" she stammered, not sure what to say.

"No, it's okay Charlie. Let's just forget I said anything." He backed away toward the door. "We have a potential Triple Crown winner to train. I'll see you in a couple days at the farm." Doug quickly opened the back door and closed it quietly behind him.

Making Up

There was a long list of reasons that they shouldn't be seen together, not the least of which was the fact that they were riding rival horses. Buck and Lilly were meeting despite all that. Shamrock was the safest place because of all the work Doug had for riders. There was an empty stall at the end of the barn, and Buck and Lilly had started meeting there to talk.

It was a nice little ritual that they'd developed. One of them would bring lunch, the other drinks (mostly water), and they'd have a little picnic. There was a haybale that was perfect for a table.

Sometimes they talked about the things that had happened since they'd last seen each other. Sometimes they talked about the time they'd spent together as kids. They reminisced about how naïve they were and how new everything was for them. A lot, it turned out, could happen in fifteen years.

Buck avoided asking too many questions, Lilly noticed. She thought he might be afraid that questions would drive her away again. She felt guilty about that. She tried to make up for it by doing most of the talking. If he did ask a question, she made sure to answer it truthfully and without pause. She reminded herself constantly that he deserved to know everything.

She arrived at the stall before Buck that day. She'd talked to Molly about their meetings and mentioned Buck's hesitance to ask her questions. Molly's advice had been simple: "Tell him everything you think he wants to know."

That was easy for her to say. Lilly had avoided telling everyone what was going on for over a decade. It was second nature now, for her to keep secrets.

Lilly's thoughts were interrupted by the sound of the stall door creaking open. She turned and faced Buck. The smile that lit her face was involuntary, and the smile that lit his face made her legs feel weak. She loved being around him again. She'd forgotten how free she could feel. Buck was the only person on the planet who could make her heart beat as if she'd just won a race.

"Have you been here long?" he asked.

"No, not too long," she said. His eyes narrowed as if he didn't quite believe her, but a smile tugged at his mouth. She helped him set up the meal and then sat opposite him at their makeshift table.

"You really look like you're wanting to say something…" Buck said after a few minutes of polite conversation.

"Well I do. I just…don't," Lilly answered. She sighed and closed her eyes. Buck let out a breath that she took to be a laugh.

"You don't have to say anything until you're ready," he told her. She opened her eyes and looked straight at him. He showed no sign of impatience. She was furious.

"That's ridiculous! You should be angry with me! You should be screaming and yelling at me right now, and instead, you're telling me to take my time and blah blah blah!" she yelled. Buck's expression didn't change. Lilly threw up her hands in frustration.

"Buck, I kept something from you that could have changed your whole life. I took something from you when I left. You shouldn't have to wait for me to be ready." She couldn't stop the tremor in her voice or the tears that filled her eyes. Buck still hadn't moved or changed expression. Lilly decided that she wasn't going to say anything else until he'd asked her to.

"I am angry, Lilly. I am hurt, and I am sad, and I am beyond mad that you kept my daughter from me. The fact that you made those decisions without me kills me. It causes me physical pain when I think about all the time we could have had together if you hadn't lied to me back then." His voice was calm and even. She wished he'd screamed. It would have been a lot easier to handle. Still, she sat across from him and said nothing.

"I spent years thinking I'd done something wrong. I thought you'd met someone else. I thought you'd stopped loving me. I didn't win a race for six months after you dumped me. I almost lost my entire career! Why wouldn't you tell me you were pregnant?" His voice was pleading. She saw that there were tears in his eyes as well, threatening to spill over. She hung her head in shame.

"You almost lost your career because I dumped you. You definitely would have lost it if I'd told you I was going to have a baby," she said.

"You don't know that." He was losing his temper now.

"Really? What would you have done? If I had told you about it back then, what would you have done about it?"

"I would have married you. I would have done the right thing by you and that baby," he answered without any hesitation, and it broke Lilly's heart all over again.

"Exactly." Her tears began to fall. He opened his mouth to retort, but there was nothing he could say. He knew as well as she did that if they'd gotten married and kept the baby, neither of them would have been able to race anymore. They were young and new to the sport. It would have been one or the other: family or career.

"You did everything alone," Buck said. There was awe in his voice.

"I had Molly. And Doug. Plus, it was hard being sad about the baby when I spent all my time crying about you," she joked. He made a noise that sounded like half sob, half laugh, and then took a sip of his drink.

"So after you'd given her up, after you'd started riding again, why did you tell Paul not to book us at any of the same tracks? If you loved me…"

"I was afraid that I would tell you. I was afraid that we would pick up where we left off and the guilt would eat me alive and I would tell you and you would hate me." Lilly knew that she would never have been able to ride another horse if Buck hated her. She'd avoided it at all costs. She'd pushed him away and hurt herself, rather than risking him hurting her.

"I could never hate you, Lil." Buck reached across the plates and grabbed Lilly's hand. They sat holding hands for several seconds. They could each feel themselves beginning to heal from all the hurt that the past had pushed on them.

"Can…you tell me about her?" Buck's voice was soft. Lilly understood his hesitation completely. Was it better to know nothing and stay detached, or learn whatever he could and risk getting too attached to something he could never have?

"Well, you've seen her, so you know she's gorgeous. Jenny's an amazing rider. She's smart, Buck. She's more mature than I was at her age. She can be fiery though, and she definitely has a temper," Lilly said. Buck laughed and squeezed her hand, urging her to continue.

"She likes to read. I've caught her on more than one occasion reading to the horses. She's tough. She loves deeply. She is kind and she has a great sense of humor," Lilly told him.

"I think…I think you made a good choice, Lil. Molly is an amazing mom, and Jenny is lucky to have her. And it's good that you've been around, too. I'm glad you know her so well," Buck said.

"I didn't want to be. I thought it would be too hard. It was, for a while. Molly insisted though. She wore me down. I really don't know where she finds all her strength," Lilly said. Lilly had always admired Molly for the way she handled hardships.

"Do you think she'll ever know? Jenny, I mean," Buck asked. His voice was quiet, and Lilly almost didn't know if he was asking her, or just thinking aloud. She decided to answer, regardless.

"If she does, it will be because Molly and Steve have decided that it's best for Jenny. I will never tell another soul." Buck looked into her eyes. She could tell that he felt the same way. Their role in Jenny's life, whatever it was destined to be, was not as her parents. It was not up to either of them to deliver any life-altering information.

Lilly and Buck sat quietly for a few more minutes. Eventually, the talk turned to lighter subjects. They laughed together and ate together. Neither of them noticed the figure that stood up from the stool by the stall door and walked silently from the barn.

Epilogue

Doug tossed and turned in his bed. After several hours of being unable to sleep, he got up and sat in the armchair in the corner of his room. He pulled his iPad into his lap, attempting to distract his brain by reviewing the day's races and the horses that had run under the Shamrock Hill colors. He slammed the cover on the iPad.

What had he been thinking?

He had brought up the marriage idea spur of the moment three days ago and things hadn't been the same between him and Charlie since.

Doug closed his eyes. He was always so meticulous, planning all aspects of his life, but that evening just seemed liked the perfect moment. Storm had just won the Preakness, and Charlie had looked so lovely in the sunlight that had streamed through the window.

Of course she wasn't interested in marrying him, he sighed. She had already married the love of her life. He would never be able to compete with Peter's ghost. But boy, he wanted to try; he loved her so much.

He loved her passion, as well as her tenacity. She was compassionate and an awesome, caring mom. She had worked her butt off helping Lilly come to terms with her past, something none of them had been able to do.

He was pretty sure Ryan and Skylar liked him too.

Doug leaned his head back against the chair. The air was still and all was quiet in the early morning hour. He drew a deep breath through his nose.

Doug's eyes flew open. He drew in several quick breaths through his nose, sniffing the air.

Was that smoke?

He jumped out of the chair and ran to the window. He grabbed at the string and ran the blinds up.

His eyes grew wide with fear.

Flames were rising out of the roof of one of the barns, down the hill from his house.

The barn that Charlie had just settled Storm into earlier this afternoon was on fire!

Doug grabbed his cell phone, hitting 911 while he thrust his leg into his jeans.

"Yes, this is Doug Walker, Shamrock Hill Farm, we have a fire here in the main barn. Send everything you've got."

His heart sank as he ran the length of the house and out the door. He didn't take the time to get his truck, but ran down the steep hill that would take him to the barn that was ablaze in front of him.

As he ran, he hit the direct dial button to call Charlie, knowing she would never forgive him if anything happened to Genuine Storm.

To be continued in...

The Height of the Storm

The third book in the *Triple Crown Trilogy*.

Author's Note

During the running of the 2015 Preakness, my husband and I came across Alex's Lemonade Stand inside the grandstand. We soon learned that Alex's Lemonade Stand was founded by Alexandra Scott, who raised money for pediatric cancer while bravely fighting it herself until her untimely death at the age of eight.

We also had the wonderful opportunity to meet the owner of racehorse Afleet Alex, Chuck Zacney, and his son, Alex. Thanks to the partnership between the foundation and Afleet Alex's ownership group, Alex's Lemonade Stands can be found at many racetracks and portions of Afleet Alex's earnings have been donated to the foundation.

If you'd like more information on this wonderful foundation, I encourage you to visit www.alexslemonade.org.